LIKE
A
MOTHER

Also available by Mina Hardy

We Knew All Along
After All I've Done

LIKE A MOTHER

A THRILLER

MINA HARDY

CROOKED
LANE

NEW YORK

Copyright © 2024 by Megan Hart

Published in the United States by Crooked Lane Books, an imprint of The Quick Brown Fox & Company LLC.

Crooked Lane Books and its logo are trademarks of The Quick Brown Fox & Company LLC.

Library of Congress Catalog-in-Publication data available upon request.

ISBN (hardcover): 978-1-63910-623-3
ISBN (ebook): 978-1-63910-624-0

Cover design by Nicole Lecht

Printed in the United States.

www.crookedlanebooks.com

Crooked Lane Books
34 West 27th St., 10th Floor
New York, NY 10001

First Edition: February 2024

10 9 8 7 6 5 4 3 2 1

To my children
the ones whose mother I am,
and the one I'm like a mother to

C H A P T E R

1

S ADNESS AND GRIEF are not the same.
Compared to grief, sadness is as shallow as a puddle. Grief is an ocean, fathomless. Grief is insurmountable. Sadness fades, but grief goes on and on.

"Excuse me, but I need some fresh air," Sarah Granatt said to the kind-faced woman whose name she did not know and could not be bothered to learn. A coworker of Adam's, she thought. It didn't matter.

Ignoring the woman's murmur of concern, Sarah walked steadily but double speed out of the crowded kitchen, where she'd been trying to get a glass of cold water. Through the dining room, past the table groaning with platters and trays of food she had not provided and had not been able to eat. Through the living room and the line of low chairs the funeral home had set up. Past the shrouded mirrors and the front door, unlocked and open to allow those paying their respects to enter without knocking.

By the time she got to the top of the stairs, she didn't think she'd make it to the bathroom in time. She lurched through the overwhelming mess of her bedroom and into the small en suite. The cool tiles pressed into her knees as she folded onto them. Bile surged upward in her throat, acrid and foul, and she spat into the toilet bowl, helpless to do anything but wait for the sickness to overtake her. She heaved, stomach muscles aching, but nothing more came up. The nausea remained, relentless and brutal.

Minutes ticked past until at last Sarah pushed herself to her feet. She splashed her face with tepid water from the dripping faucet Adam had promised he would fix. He never had. He never would.

She found no anger, no matter how hard she searched for it. Only this vast and depthless mourning doing its best to drown her, but although Sarah wished she could let herself succumb to the pull and simply sink, down and down, she had to fight it. She had Ellie to think about, and there was also this baby inside her, the one she and Adam had tried so hard to create. The last piece of him she would ever have. She could not bury herself next to her husband, even if that was the only place she wanted to be.

Emerging from the bathroom, she didn't expect to be greeted with a glass of chilled ginger ale and a small plate of saltine crackers, but she gratefully took them both and gave Ava Morgan a small smile.

"Oh, Sarah, are you okay? Maybe you should lie down." Ava's deep-brown eyes shone with empathy as she watched Sarah ease herself onto the edge of the unmade bed. She kept a few steps' distance, one arm folded across the front of her classic black dress. Her other hand toyed with her jade pendant necklace.

Sarah didn't want to lie down, didn't want to close her eyes, did not, especially, want to sleep. If she slept, she would dream, and if she dreamed, she would wake up, and when she did, Adam would still be dead, but, terribly, she would have had some brief moments in which she wasn't aware of that loss. Better to stay awake than lose him all over again. So instead, she squared her shoulders and took a cautious sip of ginger ale. It stayed in her stomach, but fresh nausea burbled and she set the glass on her nightstand, next to the plate of crackers she could not force herself to look at, much less nibble.

She settled both feet firmly on the floor. It had worked in college for the spins after a night of too much drinking, and in the times when her mind tried to separate itself from her body and float away. Maybe it would help now too. "Where's Ellie?"

"Graham's reading her a story." Brackets carved the corners of Ava's mouth. "What can I do to help you? You've had a lot of stress. You look . . ."

"I know how I look." Hollow cheeks, dark-circled eyes. Like a grieving widow.

"Why don't you take a little rest up here, where it's quiet," Ava urged. "You don't need to worry about anything going on downstairs. Ellie's fine with Graham. I can tell people you're sleeping if they ask."

"We're sitting shiva. You're not supposed to ask things like that."

Ava took a step closer. "Well, if they do, I'll take care of it. Do you want to . . . talk?"

Nobody was supposed to ask things like that either.

Graham Morgan and Adam had been friends since college and business partners for almost as long as that, but he and Ava had been married for only about a year and a half. Sarah and Ava had formed a friendship, but they'd never become as close as their husbands had been. Still, Ava had helped with childcare, rides to and from the hospital, dropping off groceries when Sarah'd been run ragged and didn't have time to shop. Ava had always been kind, but she'd never really known Adam when he was healthy. *Her* husband was hale and hearty. She couldn't begin to know what Sarah was going through.

"At least try to rest a little bit. Eat something," Ava urged when Sarah stayed silent. "I hear it helps with morning sickness . . . ?"

Her voice trailed off into the question. Instinctively, Sarah placed both palms on her stomach, still rounded from being pregnant with just-turned-three-year-old Ellie. She was twenty weeks along, but the morning sickness had been more like all-day nausea. She'd barely gained even ten pounds. She and Adam hadn't told anyone yet.

At least Sarah hadn't.

"I need to check on Ellie," Sarah said.

Ava tucked a strand of her sleek auburn bob behind one ear. "You need to take care of yourself."

"I'm fine. I appreciate your concern."

This was a lie, but Sarah sold it as best she could. In the past year of Adam's illness and decline, she'd learned how many people wanted to help . . . and how often that help came with expectations. Of gratitude, obviously, but also their right to a certain entitlement. They wanted to be able to pat themselves on the back.

Ava's frown deepened, but her tone became more soothing. "I told you, she's with Graham. You know how she loves Graham."

"She loves me too. I'm her mother. I should be with her." Sarah stood, her legs still a little unsteady. For a moment, it seemed as though Ava was going to physically step in her way to keep her from getting to the door, but Sarah pushed past her.

"Sarah!" Ava's voice turned her before she could get to the doorway. "Wait. Before you go downstairs, I wanted to talk to you about something private."

The doorbell rang. Sarah stiffened. Nobody should be ringing the bell right now, and nobody should be asking her to talk about anything, private or otherwise. No ringing bells, no forced conversations—you were supposed to give the mourners space and time for their grief, not infringe on it. Her fingernails dug into the meat of her palm. People, she thought grimly, did not understand the etiquette of sitting shiva.

"This isn't the time, Ava."

Sarah cringed at another jangle of the doorbell. Her teeth felt bared, her eyes open too wide to help her hold back tears. Her palms stung. She willed herself not to rush downstairs to scream at whoever was ringing and ringing.

"Sarah. Wait," Ava repeated. "This is important."

When it became clear Sarah was still heading for the door, Ava actually did take a few quick steps to get in the way. Sarah's brows rose. So did her gorge. It would serve Ava right if Sarah puked all over her.

"I wanted to make sure you were . . . you know. On board. With the paperwork," Ava said.

"What paperwork?"

"The guardianship paperwork? For Ellie. In case something happens to you." Ava spoke quickly, sharply, her eyes skating over Sarah's face and lower, over her stomach. "Adam asked me and Graham to adopt her."

Blinking rapidly, Sarah moved away from her. "He asked you to do what?"

"He was worried about her. And you, of course," Ava said hastily. When Sarah didn't answer, Ava moved toward her, hands out as though she were soothing a skittish colt. "He wanted to make sure Ellie would be taken care of."

"I'm taking care of her. I'm her mother," Sarah repeated, this time through numb lips.

"Of course, of course. This would just be in the event of . . . well, a tragedy. Or something you couldn't handle. You don't really have anyone else, and they were so close—"

Sarah took another step toward the door. "I can't discuss this with you right now. I'm going downstairs."

This time, Ava spoke more boldly. Her gaze flashed as she blocked Sarah's path. "Please don't disrespect your husband's dying wishes."

The utter gall of those words stopped Sarah as hard as if she'd slammed herself into a wall. The bright-penny taste of copper flooded her mouth as she bit her tongue, trying to sound civil. "If I decide to sign any guardianship paperwork about my child, I'll let you know, all right?"

"We want to adopt your baby," Ava cried in a clipped, ragged voice that shook the same way her hands were shaking, still held out in front of her as though she'd grab Sarah if she had to.

Frozen in place, Sarah let out a soft noise of dismay. At last the anger came, and if she couldn't channel any rage about her husband's death, she sure could find it for this delusional bitch in front of her.

"Get out of my way, and then get out of my house," Sarah said.

Ava didn't move. "I know you don't really want it, Sarah. You *can't* want to raise a baby all on your own, not when you already have a toddler who still needs so much of your attention. I know you thought it was the right thing, trying to get pregnant even though Adam was sick, but—"

"If you do not get out of my way, I will get you out of it," Sarah said in a voice so full of gravel and grit she barely recognized it as her own. "How dare you? How dare you *ever*, but especially right now? What is wrong with you? Are you insane, or just incredibly awful?"

Ava blanched. The glint in her gaze turned steely. "We're only trying to help you. We've been trying so hard for a child—we have so much love in our hearts for a baby. And *you* already have a child—"

"Get out of my way, or I will punch you in the mouth." Sarah's throat worked as she fought against the splash of bile at the back of it. She clapped a hand over her lips. The last and only time she'd ever hit someone was in the self-defense class she'd taken in college.

Ava didn't move. Her voice went from soothing to scolding. "You are in no position to be having another child. You're going to have to get a job, and is that what you want for your baby? To be raised by strangers in a day care?"

Breathing in through her nose and out through her mouth, Sarah stared Ava down. She wanted to feel her knuckles split on the woman's teeth. Her expression contorted into something that must've been horrific, based on the way Ava's gaze sheared away from it. Finally, Ava stepped out of the way.

"Just trying to help," she called after Sarah, who didn't turn.

She needed to find her daughter, make sure she was safe. To bury her face in the mess of dark tangled curls so much like Sarah's own. To hold the small, solid body, to look into the little girl's eyes that were so much like her father's. She needed her daughter, *her* daughter, she thought almost frantically as she scanned the living room for any sight of her. She spotted Graham talking with one of the neighbors, but Ellie wasn't with him.

Her heart wrenched. The room was too full, overflowing with bodies, too much heat. Too much noise. She tried to get to the kitchen but stubbed her toe on one of the folding chairs taking up so much space. Everyone was staring at her. Solemn faces. She couldn't stand it.

For a moment, the world wavered as though she looked at it through a lace curtain. Voices slowed like a record on a player unplugged during the middle of a song. She knew she wasn't moving, but her toes still seemed like her only anchor to the floor while the rest of her drifted up toward the ceiling. If she wasn't careful, she was going to fly away.

The first time Sarah had dissociated from her surroundings had been in elementary school during a classroom discussion about what each student's father did for a living. Her dad had been "gone" only a couple of weeks. She hadn't yet understood that "gone" meant dead, but she'd known something was very wrong at home by the way her mother was acting. When the teacher called on Sarah to share her father's profession, she'd looked at the pencil in her hand and thought both the pencil and her hand belonged to someone else. Words had come out of her in someone else's voice. Nobody else seemed to notice.

The last moments of Adam's life had been that way, his hand in hers, the sound of his breathing getting sharper, desperate and finally, in the end, choking into silence. She'd sat still as stone and loved him into whatever waited for him after he took that final gasp, but she'd done it from a distance. Floating. Watching, but not really there.

In grade school, she'd quickly figured out that not everyone's mother paced the house at night, determined to confront imaginary intruders she fended off with mountains of old magazines. Sarah was in high school when she realized that not everyone sometimes stood outside themselves, watching themselves as though they were viewing a movie. In college, her Intro to Psychology course taught her there were terms for what she experienced—depersonalization and derealization—but Sarah had taught herself how to navigate through it. How to bring herself out of it and back to herself.

Another grind of her nails into her palms centered her, here and now. Through the dining room window, she could see Ellie on the swing set they'd bought for her first birthday, long before she was big enough to play on it by herself. A woman Sarah didn't know was pushing Ellie so high the little girl's curls blew back from her face as she crowed with laughter Sarah could not hear.

She pushed her way out the dining room's sliding glass doors and onto the deck. More people gathered out here, plates of food in hand, chitchatting with each other like this was some kind of party. Sarah moved around them, down the few steps into the too-long grass. The San Gabriel Mountains rose in the distance, so different than the shores of Brigantine, New Jersey, where she'd grown up. She'd lived in California since she was eighteen, but today its beauty didn't move her. Maybe it never would again.

"Underdog, underdog!" the stranger cried in a shrieking, gleeful voice as she gave the swing an enormous push before running beneath it.

Ellie's giggling squeals sounded a lot like screams. Breathing hard, Sarah tried to call out, but she might as well have stuffed her mouth with grass and dirt.

The woman saw her and casually caught the swing with both hands on the chains, slowing and then stopping its rise and fall. Ellie protested, but at the sight of her mother, she waved one small hand. Sarah barked out a warning cry as she watched the little girl start to topple off the narrow rubber seat, but the woman who'd been pushing her held her up as easily as she'd stopped the swing.

Hefting Ellie onto one hip, the stranger smiled with crimson-painted lips as she walked toward Sarah. Her black blouse matched a black skirt and set off her blonde French twist. Diamonds gleamed in her earlobes. She looked familiar, like a celebrity Sarah couldn't place, an actress who'd once been a star but hadn't had a role in a long time. A client of Adam's?

"She's okay, Mommy," the woman said cheerfully. "We were just playing."

Sarah reached for her daughter, who practically leaped into her arms. The force of the sudden weight had Sarah tottering for a moment, but she found her balance and buried her face against Ellie's neck. She squeezed. Tears burned in her eyes and down her cheeks.

"Mama sad," Ellie whispered, her brow creasing. She wiped Sarah's cheeks.

The woman watched them, her grin softening. She tilted her head, looking them both up and down. "Other than the hair, she's his little carbon copy, isn't she? But all that wild hair. That's all yours."

"I'm sorry, who are you?" Sarah shifted Ellie's weight. Her heartbeat was slowing, but she still felt woozy. Untethered. Lost.

"I'm Henry's mother," the woman said.

"Whose mother?"

The woman frowned. "*Henry's* mother."

"I don't know anyone named Henry."

"Of course you do," the woman said. "He was your husband."

2

"MY HUSBAND'S NAME—"

"Was Henry. Adam was his middle name," the stranger added. Two deep grooves crinkled her forehead as Sarah took a few steps away from her. "He must have talked about me."

"He didn't." Sarah's reply was as unyielding as a concrete slab.

The woman's chin lifted, and her lips trembled. "But . . . I'm his *mother*!"

They stared at each other. This stranger had said Ellie was the image of her father, and that was true, but Sarah was stunned to see that the same slope of brow, the same blue eyes she'd so adored in both her husband and her daughter were also present in this interloper's face. She had Adam's pale hair and complexion too. Her heavy foundation covered up any freckles but couldn't shield the high, rosy color flooding into her cheeks. Adam had never been able to keep a secret; those cheeks had always given him away.

Or maybe not.

"I don't understand," the woman said as her hands flapped themselves into birds trying to escape a cage. "I know we had our differences—"

"How did you know to come here today?"

The woman's blank expression was disturbingly, eerily familiar, Adam's face overlaid on hers like a vintage movie special effect. A metamorphosis. Her eyes skated over Sarah's without landing. "I wanted to come to the funeral, but you'd already had it. He's already in the ground. I didn't even get to see him, to say goodbye."

"But I mean . . . *how* did you know?"

She finally met Sarah's gaze, her own sharp and glittering with tears. "If your child was dead, wouldn't you know it?"

"Mama, I hungry." Ellie pressed both her chubby hands onto Sarah's cheeks, again forcing her mother to look at her.

Sarah used her free hand to carefully peel away Ellie's grip from her face. "Okay, let's get you a snack. I'm sorry—"

But she hadn't asked for or been given the woman's name, and so her words stammered to a halt. She wasn't even sure what she meant to say or do. Offer an invitation to come inside? Shout at the stranger to get off her lawn? Neither choice seemed appropriate.

As it turned out, Sarah didn't need to decide, because without another word or a look in her direction, the woman claiming to be her mother-in-law turned on her heel and stalked toward the house. Her shoes left a divot in the grass where she'd spun. She went inside.

"Mamamamamama . . ."

"Yes, ketzeleh, meow meow, meow. Let's get you a snack. How about a nice little kitty treat?"

Ellie giggled and shook her head at the suggestion. Sarah took her to the kitchen. With shaking hands, she sat Ellie on one of the barstools at the island and took a paper plate from the stack on the counter. A little tuna salad, some egg salad, a few apple slices . . . the plate dipped and swayed in her grip. When it hit the floor at her feet, splashing food across the toes of her black flats, Sarah gasped aloud but could not make herself bend to pick it up. If she went to the floor, she wouldn't get up.

"Here, hon. Let me. Bex, can you get the little one something to eat? Sarah, come on upstairs with me."

Sarah looked into the woman's kind blue eyes. Linda Ruttenberg had been the first to welcome them to Temple Beth Or when they'd joined four years ago. She'd always been there to greet them for a Friday night service, or on Sunday mornings when they dropped off Ellie for the preschool program. She'd been a shomeret, one of the people who sit with the dead during the twenty-four hours between death and burial, and she'd also stepped up to arrange the shiva so Sarah didn't have to.

"Ellie," Sarah whispered.

Linda put an arm around Sarah's shoulders. "Bex will take care of her. June's here too. Ellie knows both of them from Kindertime. She'll be okay."

"I shouldn't leave her," Sarah protested under her breath, her cheeks hot, too aware of everyone looking at her. A spring of shame bubbled inside her about the scene she'd made. Her gaze darted around the room and through the doorway, but she didn't see Ava anywhere, or the blonde stranger. Her palms throbbed where her nails had cut into the skin.

Linda smiled. "Whatever you want, honey."

If the older woman had insisted, Sarah would've kept protesting, but in the face of that solid compassion, she broke. Not strong. Not competent. Grateful, though, to be taken upstairs and settled into the bentwood rocking chair Adam had bought at a flea market so she'd have a place to rock their babies. Grateful too for the blanket Linda tucked over her lap and the cardigan she pulled from Sarah's closet to wrap over her shoulders. It was an old one of Adam's, but she didn't care that it was too big as she drew it around her.

Adam, she thought. Or was it Henry?

* * *

"Hi. I'm Adam."

Wide smile, charmingly crooked teeth. Sarah had been instantly wary of him. Too tall, too blond, not as handsome as he thought he was, she'd thought. He had the fresh-scrubbed audacity of someone who'd always been told he was something special and had never been given any reason to believe otherwise.

Before she could move to a new seat, the professor slapped a heavy book down on the podium, sending a rumble throughout the classroom. Adam jumped and gave a little laugh.

"I'd say he scared me out of my wits, but that would mean I had some wits to be scared out of," he said.

And Sarah . . . was . . . smitten.

The class itself turned out to be reasonably interesting—reading the Bible as creative fiction rather than faith-based inspiration had set some of her classmates' heads figuratively on fire. The professor, a shambling, gray-bearded man with wild eyebrows, never once revealed his own religious practices but took great glee in probing into those of his students, trying to get them to think outside the often narrow boxes in which they'd been raised. Adam had been one of those who'd debated with him. Sarah, comfortable and confident in her own beliefs, never felt the need.

Three weeks into the semester, Adam asked Sarah out for coffee after class.

A week after that, he kissed her for the first time under a full moon with a hint of frost in the air.

Five weeks after that day in the classroom, she took him to bed for the first time. After they'd made love, he confessed that she had been his first.

They'd been inseparable ever since. It had never mattered to either one of them that she was a senior while he was a freshman, or that she dreamed of creative pursuits while Adam was focused on the tech world. They'd simply fallen into each other, cream in coffee, sprinkles on a sundae, applesauce on latkes. Sarah and Adam just *went* together.

A perfect match, a perfect little family. At the touch of Linda's hand on her shoulder, Sarah shook away the memories. Perfect like a peach with a rotten spot in the center.

Linda rubbed Sarah's shoulder and pressed a bottle of water into her hand. Sarah cracked the bottle open and dared a sip, hoping her stomach wouldn't revolt. Her hunger rushed to life, and she thought with longing of the platters and trays of food downstairs.

"I'm desperate for a bagel with cream cheese and lox right now."

"I'll text Barry to bring one up. You want everything on it?"

"Everything." Sarah bowed her head to hold back a rush of tears. A sudden terror gripped her. "Can you ask him to check on Ellie?"

"Of course." Linda typed out a quick message on her phone and held it up to show Sarah the reply that came a second or so later. It included a picture of Ellie with Linda's daughters. "She's playing with Bex and June in her room. She's fine."

"I want to make sure Ava isn't anywhere near her. She's got dark-red hair and a black dress with a big green pendant necklace. Or her husband Graham. Tall, dark hair, navy suit?"

Linda's expression scrunched in thought. "I saw them both hustling out the front door while you were in the yard. Not friends of yours, I take it?"

"Graham's Adam's business partner. They've been friends since college. But after what his wife said to me . . ." Sarah swallowed what felt like a handful of razor blades.

"You don't have to talk about it if you don't want to," Linda said.

Sarah took another slow sip of water. A quick rap on the door revealed a solemn-faced Barry, who brought in a paper plate laden with a bagel dressed in all the trimmings. He gave Sarah a small smile and ducked back out without saying anything. Sarah settled the plate on her lap and tucked a stray caper into the gooey cream cheese. She sighed. *Did* she want to talk about it?

"Everyone must think I've lost my mind."

Linda tutted. "Nobody thinks any such thing."

"I *thought* they were friends," Sarah whispered around the lump in her throat. She looked at Linda. "But Ava said they wanted to adopt my baby."

Too late, Sarah remembered that she and Adam hadn't announced the pregnancy yet. Linda's gaze dropped to her belly, then met Sarah's eyes. If the news shocked her, Linda didn't show it.

"Adam must've told them about the baby when he knew he was . . ." Sarah trailed off and bit into the bagel. Cream cheese and salmon flooded her mouth. She chewed and swallowed, chewed and swallowed.

Linda leaned against the dresser. "Why would she think you wanted to give your baby away?"

"Apparently being a widow means I don't want to take care of my children. Or that I'm not capable of it."

"I'm so sorry, honey. I'll have Barry at the door tomorrow evening, if you want. To make sure they don't come in." Linda's expression twisted in distaste. "No wonder you're so upset."

"There was a woman outside. With Ellie. Pushing her on the swings." Sarah choked out the words one at a time like coins clinking into a tzedakah box. She looked up at Linda, who bore a gentle, concerned expression. "She said she was Adam's mother."

Linda went at once to the windows overlooking the back yard and twitched back the curtain. "Is she still there?"

Sarah drew in a slow breath and shook her head. "She came inside, but I didn't see her after that. Maybe she left."

Linda turned back toward Sarah. Frowning, she said, "What do you mean, she *said* she was Adam's mother? Hadn't you ever met her?"

"I couldn't have," Sarah said. "He always told me she was dead."

3

Bᴇ ᴛʜᴇ ᴛɪᴍᴇ Sarah finished her bagel, the shiva hours were over. Barry and Linda, true mensches, both of them, stayed behind to clean up the kitchen and put all the perishables away. Bex and June had read Ellie to sleep with as many stories as she'd asked for. The Ruttenbergs made sure the doors were all locked before they left, and Linda confirmed that Sarah had her phone number programmed into her favorites list.

"If you need anything, you call me. My ringer will be on. Are you sure you don't want me to stay?" Linda's brows knitted with concern.

"I'm okay. Really."

"Try to get some rest. We'll see you tomorrow, late afternoon. We'll make sure nobody comes in that you don't want to be here." Barry gently punched a fist into the opposite palm.

There'd be nothing like sleep for Sarah tonight; she knew that already. She nodded anyway and accepted another hug from Linda and one from Barry too. She shut the door behind them and turned the dead bolt.

In the quiet house, she moved room by room, cataloging all the places where Adam had once taken up space. The couch where they'd snuggled to watch scary movies, their fingers linked as his thumb-stroked the back of her hand. The kitchen where he'd made French toast with sugar and cinnamon and they'd danced to the music

pouring from the speaker connected to his phone. He'd loved pop
music that was popular in his teenage years, when he'd been forbid-
den to listen to it.

She went into the dining room table, where she had lit the Shabbat candles and Adam had sung "Eishet Chayil" to her every week.
A woman of valor, who can find? Her price is above rubies. He'd learned
that song of praise for her. He'd learned everything about their life
for her.

At last she went to the bedroom and the bed in which they'd
made love and babies. His pillow no longer carried the scent of him,
even though she'd refused to wash the sheets since the day he'd gone
into the hospital for the last time. Sarah sat on his side of the bed and
looked at the glass of water on Adam's nightstand. A thin film of dust
covered the water's surface. If she lifted it now and pressed her lips to
the place where his had rested, she wouldn't even be able to taste him.

He was gone.

It would have been easier if she could weep, but instead Sarah sat
with dry eyes and a tight throat, staring at the windows overlooking
the backyard. She hadn't spent a night alone in this bed for years,
and then all at once, she'd been in it by herself forever. Her fingers
stroked the comforter, and she closed her eyes, imagining the rise of
his legs beneath it. His body, firm and athletic, not wasted away from
the cancer that had taken his life. Her eyes shut tighter and tighter
until she gave herself a headache and red swirls infiltrated her vision,
but she didn't want to open them and see the empty place where her
husband had once been.

The faint sound of Ellie's cry pushed Sarah to her feet. She was
down the hall almost without conscious effort, her feet taking her
faster than her mind was able to process the fact that the sound had
come from outside. A cat, probably. Not her daughter, who slept
peacefully, a thumb in her mouth and her favorite stuffed bear tucked
up close to her. Sarah hovered for a moment, debating if a kiss would
wake her. Ellie had always been difficult to get down and almost
impossible to get back to sleep if she was woken.

Deciding she didn't dare risk it for something that would only
comfort herself, Sarah backed slowly and silently out of the room. At
the door, she turned off the light switch operating the small, dim-
bulbed lamp near the window.

A bright flash slashed through the glass, lighting up the room as
quick as a lightning strike. Sarah froze. The past few days had been

warm and bright, with cloudless blue skies. No storms predicted. She waited for the sound of thunder but heard only Ellie's soft snore-whistle.

There. It happened again, not so bright this time but a definite, deliberate sweep of light outside. Sarah went for the windows. Half-way there, her toe connected with a discarded toy, something soft that still managed to make a lot of noise as she kicked it across the room. Ellie let out a whimper, and Sarah froze. From here, she could see through the glass and out to the cul-de-sac.

Had it been a car? The Durwoods to her right had a college-aged son who was home for spring break and sometimes stayed out late. The Forsters to the left both worked early shifts and went to bed early.

Sarah crept to the window and looked down. Their neighbor-hood didn't have streetlights, but the three houses here at the cul-de-sac all had dusk-to-dawn lamps at the ends of their driveways. Hers wasn't lit—someone must've turned off the switch by the door, disa-bling the auto function. Behind her, Ellie turned over in her sleep, murmuring wordlessly.

Nothing was out there. The light must have come from a car turning around in the dead end. It might have been a single freak streak of lightning. Or someone using a flashlight while walking their dog, Sarah told herself as her eyes strained to see into the darkness.

Around her lamppost, the orange lilies waved in a night breeze. Their shadows flickered. From this vantage point, the tall red maple blocked out most of her view. Something shone dimly for a moment. A reflection?

A phone screen.

Not a bright flash this time, and maybe it was just a trick her eyes were playing, but . . . was that a person standing beneath the tree? Pressing against it? Dressed in black so as not to be seen?

Sarah held her breath. Watching. Her heartbeat filled her ears, blocking out Ellie's faint sleep noises. Sarah opened her eyes wide, not wanting to look away for even a second, but no matter how much she tried, she couldn't be sure if she was really seeing something . . . someone . . . or if it was only her imagination.

There was one way for her to be sure. Sarah took the stairs care-fully, hand on the railing, well aware of how easy it would be for her to lose her balance and fall. She'd always been a little klutzy, but pregnancy made her even more so. She stubbed her toe on the newel post at the bottom and hopped, hissing, for a few seconds before she was able to steady herself.

She'd left a light on in the kitchen, but the living room was dark. Sarah went to the living room and looked out the front windows. One, then the other. They offered an even more limited view than she'd had from upstairs.

She flipped up the switch by the door, and the driveway lamp-post came on but went off a few seconds later. Trying to remember how to get it to stay on instead of remaining in the motion activation setting, she turned it off, then on again, in rapid succession. This time, the golden glow spread out over the bottom of the driveway and revealed the end of the driveway and part of the curb.

It did not show anyone lurking beneath her maple tree. Sarah stepped through the front door and tugged Adam's cardigan tighter over her chest. In late March the days were warm but the nights still chilly. She went to the edge of the porch, her toes curling over the rounded concrete ridge. The urge to shout *Hey!* rose inside her, but she clamped her lips shut.

Four houses down the street, a shadow passed in front of the lamp at the end of the driveway. Quick, shapeless, ducking through the small circle of light and into the darkness between the houses, where it disappeared. Another faint cry drifted to Sarah on the breeze, but it was too far away for her to tell where it had come from.

"Hey." The word squeaked out of her. Nobody replied, but someone *had* been there.

She was sure of it.

4

COFFEE.

The rich scent drifted to her nostrils, tempting Sarah to open her eyes. She fought the urge. Her bed, so warm, her pillow so . . . unyielding.

Startled, she sat up, arms flailing. The multicolored afghan that she'd inherited from her mother tangled around her shins. Her neck ached. She'd been asleep on the couch.

A groan scraped her throat as she let her face fall into her hands. There was no coffee, only dreams of it. Adam had always been the one to make it in the morning, filling a carafe and leaving it for her next to one of the dozens of "favorite" mugs she'd collected over the years. That act of love and service had been only one of many during their relationship, but in this moment, it was the only one she yearned for.

"Mammmmaaaaaa!"

Sarah found her voice. "I'm coming!"

Ellie appeared at the top of the stairs. Sarah had managed to get to her feet, the blanket still hooked around one ankle. They'd been working on her using the stairs without help, but Ellie had inherited her mother's lack of balance. Sarah called out a warning for Ellie to stay put, but the little girl was already lifting one foot into space.

There is no swifter runner than a mother pelting toward a child in danger. Sarah kicked aside one of the folding chairs left behind by the funeral home, tripped, and still was able to get herself halfway up the staircase in time to catch Ellie as she tumbled head over heels down the first few steps.

Panting, Sarah clutched the railing with one hand, her daughter with the other. Pulling Ellie onto her lap, Sarah collapsed onto a step. Her breath blew out in a shaky stream, her mind filled with visions of Ellie's small body, twisted and broken, at the bottom of the staircase.

"Shh, shh, ketzeleh. Mama's here. I'm right here." She rocked Ellie, who pressed against her. "Meow, meow, meow."

Ellie snuffled and tipped her little face to look at Sarah. "Meowmeow. Where you were?"

"Mama was downstairs." Sarah twisted to look at the top of the staircase.

The child gate stood wide open. A weight settled in her chest—had she been so freaked out last night that she'd completely forgotten to close it? Shutting that gate had become such second nature she didn't even notice it anymore. She racked her memory but couldn't recall if it had been closed or open yesterday. She shifted Ellie onto her hip and stood. With people up and down, it was completely possible it had been left open, and last night when she came downstairs, maybe she'd simply forgotten to make sure it was shut behind her.

Or . . . someone had been here while she was sleeping.

Someone had left the gate unlocked.

Someone who could have crept up the stairs and into Ellie's room . . .

They come for us at night. They dress up like your dad and try to get me to go away with them.

Her mother's frequent refrain echoed in her mind, but Sarah shook away the intrusive thoughts. Nobody had ever been coming for either one of them. That had always been her mother's paranoid fantasy, one Sarah would not allow herself to fall into. Nobody had been in her house last night. *She* was being paranoid, she told herself as she settled Ellie at the kitchen table and went to the fridge to pull out a carton of orange juice. "You want a bagel or oatmeal?"

"Bagel," Ellie said confidently, and took the sippy cup Sarah handed her. "Wif peanut butter!"

Sarah laughed, shaking her head. "Abomination."

"What abboma-mation is, Mama?"

"It means something wrong. Bagels," Sarah said with mock severity, "should be consumed with a thick schmear of cream cheese, a slab of lox, and oh, more onion and capers than should be legal."

As she spoke, she bent back into the fridge to pull out the plastic package of lox and the small container of sliced onion, capers, and other veggies that Linda had kindly packed up from yesterday's spread.

Sarah's stomach rumbled. "But if you want peanut butter, ketzeleh, then peanut butter you shall have."

Her words caught, snagged like a mermaid in a net. Until they'd come out of her mouth, she hadn't been aware of how often she'd been imitating Adam. Sarah covered her mouth with one hand, eyes closed against the relentless sting of tears. Her other went to her belly and the slightest of bumps there. She had to keep herself together.

Behind her, Ellie hummed and kicked her little feet against the chair legs. "Pea. Nut. Pea. Nut!"

Sarah opened her eyes. She looked for the peanut butter, upside down in the door of the fridge, because that was where and how her husband kept it, no matter how many times she told him peanut butter didn't need to be refrigerated. She could do whatever she wanted with it now, she thought, and another pang of grief dug the pointed tips of its claws into the soft place just below her chin.

The jar wasn't in its usual place, but the entire fridge had been jam-packed with leftovers wrapped up in foil or shoved into storage containers. The jar of peanut butter hid among them. She grabbed a presliced bagel from the bread box and slipped it into the toaster while she assessed the coffeemaker. She knew how to use it, but did she have the strength to force herself through all the steps?

She'd better get used to it, Sarah told herself. She was the only one who'd be doing it from now on. When the bagel popped up, unevenly toasted, she spread it with peanut butter and poured herself a glass of orange juice in place of coffee. The first sip tasted too sour. She emptied the rest down the drain.

After Ellie's breakfast, they usually spent some time at the kitchen table doing coloring pages, small puzzles, learning letters and numbers. Ellie had been going to the synagogue's Kindertime program since she was two, but Adam's illness had delayed her start at regular preschool. She'd be able to start soon, Sarah thought. Now that it was over.

"Where Daddy is?" Ellie asked on cue, as though she sensed her mother's thoughts.

Sarah paused, puzzle piece in hand. "Do you remember I told you that Daddy was very sick? And that he had died?"

How do you explain death to a child, especially the death of her beloved daddy? Sarah had been a few years older than Ellie when her own father died in an accident and she was told only that he'd "gone away." She'd quickly learned not to ask her mother about him and instead waited for him to return. It had been years before she realized that her father hadn't simply *gone away* the way some of her friends' parents had, the ones who'd gotten divorced. Her father was dead and would never come back. She didn't want Ellie to ever have that kind of confusion. Nor was Sarah going to turn into her mother, who was so overcome with her own emotions and mental struggles that she'd been incapable of being a parent even though she'd been the only one Sarah had left.

Ellie nodded and sipped from her cup, then lifted and tilted it side to side, showing Sarah it was empty. "Daddy died."

"That means he's gone. And he can't come back to us, except in our thoughts. But he's always with us in our hearts." Sarah kept her voice as calm as she could. The words felt wrong, but she didn't have any better ones.

The answer seemed to be enough for Ellie, at least for now. She'd probably ask again in a few hours, and Sarah would have to give her the same answer. And then, at some point, would Ellie understand that dead meant forever?

"Do you want to watch your shows while Mama cleans up the fridge?"

Of course Ellie did. A morning of television was a treat. She settled herself on the couch, delightfully demanding her favorite program. Sarah queued up the streaming service—the shows would auto start and keep going for at least an hour before prompting *Are you still watching?*

In the kitchen, Sarah opened the fridge again. The jumble inside it made her twitchy. Tonight was the last night to sit shiva, and she'd been following the custom of not cleaning or leaving the house for the entire six previous days. The shiva candle that had been burning for the entire week was down to its last small bit of liquid wax. After this there'd be another twenty-three days of mourning, but with lifted restrictions.

"I can't stand it another minute," she said aloud. Not being able to find things. Not having everything in its place.

She couldn't wait until tomorrow to clean it out. People would bring more food tonight, and there was simply no room to put any of it. At least some of this could be frozen for future meals, preventing waste, and that was more important than following a religious technicality.

Most people had brought packaged goods from the kosher bakery, and the shul's bereavement committee had delivered a kosher fruit-and-cheese tray along with an array of bagels and cream cheese spreads. Everyone at Temple Beth Or knew the Granatts kept kosher and would've delivered any homemade meals in plastic, throwaway containers marked with the family name or the name of the synagogue so Sarah would know where they'd come from and could trust that anything inside had been prepared in a kosher kitchen. That was the standard at their synagogue, and she'd done it herself many times for others.

So where had this tall deli container come from? Sarah pulled it out of the refrigerator and cautiously lifted the lid. A whiff of something fishy. She sighed, frowned, and looked closer into the pinkish glop. "Shrimp salad."

Ava had probably brought it, Sarah thought uncharitably, irritated. Graham and Ava had been to their house for Shabbat dinner and last year's Passover seder. Graham, at least, ought to have known that shellfish wasn't kosher.

It didn't matter who'd brought it. The entire contents of the container went straight into the trash. She immediately took the bag out to the can still waiting at the end of the driveway to be brought inside. Adam had always been the one to handle the garbage. How long had it been sitting there? Her neighbors would be upset.

Then she was weeping again, silent, racking tears that scalded her eyes and cheeks and left an acrid taste in her mouth. Sarah slapped the garbage can closed and left it there. Trash pickup would come around again. Her neighbors would have to deal.

She stopped just outside the front door, aware that she'd left it hanging open when she came out. She remembered the night before, the figure in the shadows. Her creeping sense of being watched. She turned to face the street, scanning up and down the sidewalks for any signs of a stranger lurking, but she didn't see anything out of place.

The planter next to the front door looked as though it had been shifted. Carefully, looking over her shoulder, Sarah bent to trace a finger over the rim of dirt that showed where the heavy concrete vase had been placed before. She strained to tilt it and look beneath it at the same time. The spare key was still there. She set the planter back in place and straightened. Maybe she was only imagining that the planter was in a slightly different spot.

When she stood up, the woman who'd claimed to be Adam's mother was standing at the bottom of the driveway.

5

"SHE'S BEAUTIFUL. BUT you know that, of course. All those dark curls. I bet they're a lot of work to take care of." Adam's mother hadn't been able to take her eyes off Ellie since the moment she'd stepped through the front door.

Candace Granatt had apologized over and over for how she'd behaved the day before. Sarah had asked Candace to come inside. She wanted time for the two of them to talk without anyone else around. The only problem was, Sarah wasn't sure what she wanted or needed to say.

Now the two of them silently watched Ellie play on the swing set. She twirled the pirate ship steering wheel and waved at them both from the small clubhouse's window. Candace seemed willing to allow Sarah to drive the conversation. Sarah appreciated that. She and Adam had rarely argued, but when they did, it was often because he was incapable of leaving her alone long enough to formulate her thoughts when she was upset. He'd claimed it was because he wanted to "fix things."

"He was always afraid we were broken," she said aloud finally.

"Who, Henry?"

"He called himself Adam."

Candace puffed out a breath and patted her sleek blonde updo, her fingers aglitter with rings. "Whatever he called himself, I named him Henry. He said you were broken?"

"He worried that we were. No matter how many times I told him that people could be angry with each other and that didn't have to mean they were going to break up, he always . . ." Sarah trailed off. Shrugged. She struggled and failed to keep her voice from breaking. "He always thought that if we weren't overflowing with joy, we were on our way to disaster. No matter how many times I tried to tell him that sometimes, being content is more solid than being ecstatic."

"So . . . you weren't happy?" Candace's lips pinched together.

"Most of the time, we were. But it could be exhausting, you know? Trying to convince him that not every minute had to be the Fourth of July."

"When Henry was a little boy, he'd work himself up into such a state before Christmas. Writing letters to Santa. Doing extra chores, asking me over and over again if he was being a 'good-enough boy.'" Candace sniffled and drew a tissue out of her fashionable handbag to dab her eyes and nose. "He wanted to know why it couldn't be Christmas every day, and I told him, if it was, well . . . it wouldn't be as special, would it?"

"We don't celebrate Christmas," Sarah replied quietly.

Candace stiffened, her shoulders squaring. She cleared her throat, her gaze focused on Ellie. "I wasn't sure. I thought maybe . . . for the little one."

"No. Adam converted before we got married."

Adam had been reticent about his life before they'd met, but he had told Sarah about his conservative Christian upbringing and how he'd cast it off before going to college. A small town; a small, strict church. Parents obsessed with their religion.

Candace puffed out a small breath and sat up straighter. "He accepted Jesus into his heart when he was a little boy. It doesn't matter what he did as an adult. Jesus still loves him and took him into his arms when he passed. That's just what I believe."

It wasn't what Adam had believed, but Sarah didn't argue the point. She didn't have to agree with Candace's religious beliefs to empathize with how it must feel to have your child turn his back on something you hold so precious. If it gave his mother comfort to believe, it would be an undeniable cruelty to take that away from her. And what did it matter, anyway? Adam had died; he was wherever people went after that, or he was nowhere and nothing at all. His life and what he'd done during it were what counted. It took nothing away from Sarah if Candace wanted to believe something that wasn't true. They sat in silence for a few moments longer before Candace spoke.

"He never spoke of me? Truly, never?"

The most he'd ever shared were the smallest of details, one at a time, always in passing and never with more than a minute or so of conversation. Sarah had told him early on about losing both of her parents, and he'd commiserated. It was supposed to be something they had in common. The only story he'd ever told Sarah in its entirety had been about the brother his parents had adopted when Adam was in second grade. The other boy had been the same age, or close to it, but had spent his early years in a Russian orphanage. He'd had behavioral problems so severe that Adam's parents had un-adopted him. Sent him back.

Sarah wasn't going to bring that up to Candace. The story had seem so far-fetched she'd had a hard time believing it the single time Adam had told it, and she'd never asked him about it again. The experience had obviously scarred him, and with both of his parents deceased, there'd never been reason to discuss it.

Except that Candace was here right now, clearly *not* dead, and that raised a whole other set of questions about Adam's past and the secrets he'd kept.

"He said he grew up in Ohio," Sarah offered.

"Shelter Grove. I still live there." Candace beamed.

Sarah almost hated to say it, but she had to. "He told me that both his parents had died."

Candace pressed a hand to her heart and drew in a soft, pained gasp. "Oh."

"I'm sorry."

"Why . . ." Candace's voice shook, the blonde curls that had escaped her French twist floating around her face. "He and his father had a falling-out. They didn't see eye to eye on a lot of things. Henry said I took Peter's side."

"Did you?"

"He was my husband," Candace said sadly. "The husband is the head of the household. To me it wasn't about taking sides, it was about being a good wife. And I'm sure you know how bullheadedly stubborn Henry could be when he was convinced he was right."

Stubborn was not how Sarah would have described her husband. Determined, sure. Confident. But certainly not bullheaded.

"What did they fight about?" she asked.

"Everything. I'm not sure what was the final straw. It might have been when Henry told us he wanted to go away to school, that he didn't want to follow in Peter's footsteps. He didn't want to be the church's next pastor. He rejected everything we'd always hoped for him." Candace gave Sarah a candid stare. "They never reconciled before Peter passed away. Henry told me if I didn't support him that he'd never see me again. I thought . . . foolishly, I know that now, that he'd come back around once he'd been out there in the world, when he'd seen how an ungodly life could tear away at your soul."

"He didn't live an ungodly life." Sarah braced herself for a comment about hellfire and burning, but Candace only stared at her.

There were so many questions left to answer, but movement through the sliding glass doors into the kitchen caught Sarah's attention. Linda had promised to come a little early to help set up. Sarah stood with a gesture toward the house. "I need to get changed for shiva. You're welcome to stay as long as you want, of course. Or not, if you don't want to."

"I'll be happy to stay and help in any way I can. I can watch Ellie for you. Or," Candace said quickly, perhaps at Sarah's hesitant expression, "if that doesn't make you feel comfortable, I can go in and help with the food. There's a lot of food spread out, isn't there? If there's one thing about funerals that everyone seems to have in common, it's food."

"That would be very nice. Ellie, come on over here to Mama. We're going inside."

For once the little girl didn't complain at being called away from her swing set and ran to her mother. She gave Candace a shy, curious glance. Candace made as though to reach for her but held herself back at the last moment. She gave Sarah a sheepish grin.

"I don't want to scare her," she said. "Since I'm a stranger and all."

The back doors opened, and Linda stepped onto the deck. "Everything all right?"

"Go on," Candace urged Sarah. "I'll introduce myself and help her with whatever needs to be done. You go get yourself squared away. Whatever you need. I'm here for you, okay?"

It seemed like a good time for the two women to embrace, but Sarah wasn't sure she could make herself. She'd been hugged a lot over the past few weeks, mostly by well-meaning people who thought it would be a comfort when in reality it always felt as though she were being strangled. Candace seemed to understand. She nodded instead, sharing a look with Sarah so full of compassion and care that Sarah was the one who reached first for the hug.

"It doesn't get easier," Candace said when the embrace ended. "You just get through it. But I'm sure you know that already, don't you?"

"I'm glad you're here," Sarah said, and meant it, to her own surprise.

Candace's eyes welled. "Oh, honey. I'm so glad to hear you say that. After the way I acted—"

"It's a weird time. I'm happy you came back so we had the chance to talk."

A small sob leaked out of Candace's polished lips. "You don't know what that means to hear you say. He always told me you didn't want him to . . . that you wouldn't let him . . ."

"That I wouldn't let him what?"

Candace swiped away her tears with her crumpled tissue. Her bracelets rattled as she dabbed her nostrils. It was obvious she was trying to get herself under control, but Sarah was getting impatient.

"Ellie, go with Miss Linda, okay? See if Bex or June are here to play with you."

Ellie's eyes had grown wide at the sight of Candace's tears, and she ran off with a backward glance. Linda waved at Sarah and took Ellie inside.

"Candace, what did Adam say I wouldn't let him do?"

"Talk to me." Candace's voice rippled and rolled.

"I'm sorry? What?"

Candace dabbed again at each eye before tucking the tissue back into her handbag. "He said you didn't want him to have anything to do with me. That's why I never met you."

"Why would I have ever said that?"

"Well. Because of what you made him do to marry you," Candace said, then added hastily, "I told him it didn't really matter, you know, all I ever wanted was for him to be happy."

"Adam told you I *made* him convert so we could get married? And that I wanted him to abandon his family?" Sarah let herself sink onto the lawn chair.

Candace took the seat next to hers. "No matter how many times I told him how much I love and support Israel—"

"I'm American," Sarah cut in, irked. "I have nothing to do with what Israel does or doesn't do."

"Well," Candace said softly, "I was trying to respect his wishes. That's all. I hoped he'd change your mind."

"I never told him he *had* to do anything." Revulsion at the thought choked her, and she swallowed hard.

Candace looked uncomfortable. "I didn't mean to upset you."

"Everything upsets me right now." Sarah pressed her hands to her belly and watched understanding dawn on the other woman's face.

"Oh," Candace said quietly. "Oh my goodness. Oh my dear."

They stared at each other.

"Candace, were you standing in the street watching my house last night?"

The other woman blinked rapidly. "You *saw* someone watching your house?"

"I thought . . . maybe. I don't know."

A headache throbbed at the base of Sarah's skull. What was next? Would she start covering the outlets with tape and tinfoil to keep the "spy cameras" from being able to see her in the shower? Would she regale her own daughter with whispered, frantic stories about all the people bent on stealing her away?

Except . . . someone did want to steal Ellie away, Sarah thought with a shudder at her mother's thoughts echoing in her own. Yet surely Ava wouldn't have been lurking in the front yard, dressed in black, watching for the opportunity to snatch Ellie. It was ridiculous to think she'd broken into the house and left the baby gate open . . .

Sarah sat up straight. "It was probably just my imagination," she said firmly.

"Well, it certainly wasn't me." Candace looked over Sarah's shoulder. "More people are here. I can see them in the kitchen. Should you go inside?"

The sliding door opened, and Ellie's wail of "Maammaaaaa" echoed into the backyard. Sarah stood. "I should, for Ellie. But you can stay as long as you want."

"I know you're busy and have so much going on, so if I duck out without saying goodbye . . . here. I wrote down my phone number. I'm staying at the Glenmark. I'll be here for another week or two; I haven't decided yet. The best shopping, you know," she said in a lowered voice bumpy with repressed giggles, "is on Rodeo Drive."

Sarah's brows rose at what she was sure had been meant as a joke, not an inconsiderate comment. People dealt with their grief in all kinds of ways. She took the piece of paper and folded it.

"After all this time, I'm so happy to have finally met you," Candace said.

"I'm sorry Adam told me you were dead."

Candace shrugged lightly. "No matter how much you love someone, you can never really know what they keep in their hearts. But we know each other now, and that's what counts, isn't it? We're family, Sarah. I'm in your life for good."

6

FOR THE FIRST morning in the past week, Sarah had not woken to an alarm. No shiva tonight, nothing to prepare for other than Shabbat. Usually, her Fridays were spent doing a top-to-bottom housecleaning, baking challah, crafting a delicious meal. So far today, she'd managed to take a shower and wash her hair. That was it.

Sarah's mother had been proudly Jewish without being religious. She'd trotted out an old menorah every Chanukah and spoke every year of going to shul for the High Holidays but never actually went. Sarah had never observed Shabbat until she went to college, where she became involved with Hillel. Most of the young adults would have Shabbat dinner at the rabbi's house before heading out for a night of regular college partying. She'd never been particularly adamant about full sundown-to-sundown observance, not using electricity and the like, but Shabbat had always been something she and Adam looked forward to. A delicious meal, good wine, a designated time to stay home and be together without other obligations getting in the way. It was the one night of the week he was guaranteed to be home for dinner.

It wouldn't be the first time she'd lit the candles and said the prayers without Adam by her side, but it was the first time since before they married that she was considering not doing anything at all. No lighting candles. No drinking wine, not even the sip she'd have allowed herself for observance during her pregnancy. She had a month's worth of bread and rolls in the kitchen already, so no need to bake something fresh. She didn't have to acknowledge Shabbat in any way; it would occur without her, the same way the world was still turning without Adam in it. Like making the coffee, was practicing her faith something she'd have to learn to do without him?

Without him, did she have any faith left?

The doorbell rang. A quick glance into the den showed her that Ellie had fallen asleep on the couch. Sarah had allowed her to watch cartoons all the way to nap time again. It was going to be hard getting them both back on a regular routine.

The doorbell rang again. She could ignore it. Whoever was out there would eventually go away.

Thinking of the lurking stranger from her imagination the other night, she decided to at least peek through the living room window and see if she could catch a glimpse of who was ringing. She recognized the tall man on the porch at once. Graham. He held a glass vase of flowers.

"You *are* here," he said when she opened the door. He sounded relieved.

She hesitated before stepping aside to let him in and shut the door behind him. "Ellie's sleeping."

"You know if you need a break, Ava can come grab her. Take her to the park, whatever." Graham held out the vase. "These were on your porch when I got here."

Sarah took them and put them on the dining room table without looking at the card. "*Grab* is an interesting choice of words."

She faced him. He hadn't moved from in front of the door. He gave her a pained look.

"Can we sit down?" he asked.

She shrugged and gestured at the living room. "Sure. Do you want anything? Coffee? Actually, I don't have any. I'm sure there are some sodas in the fridge or something."

"No, I don't want anything. Just . . . sit with me for a couple of minutes, okay?" He perched on the edge of the couch.

Sarah sat in the chair angled toward him. Graham leaned forward, hands on his knees. He rubbed them back and forth against the denim of his jeans.

"You took the day off?" she questioned.

He looked taken aback. "Yeah . . . ?"

"Jeans," she said. "Usually you're in a suit if you're at the office, Flash."

He smiled at the old joke—Graham had always been the face of FlashDrive, Inc., Adam more behind the scenes. Graham the flash. Adam the drive.

"I closed the office until next week," he said.

They stared at each other without speaking.

At last, Graham leaned closer. "I came to talk to you about what happened. Ava told me she upset you. I wanted to apologize for her."

"You shouldn't have to apologize for someone else."

"She's my wife."

"And she's not sorry," Sarah said. "Right?"

Another few seconds of quiet ticked past before he answered. "She understands it wasn't an appropriate time. I told her that."

"Oh, so you scolded her about it." Sarah laughed humorlessly under her breath. She narrowed her eyes to look him over. "But she's not *sorry*."

He shifted uncomfortably. "We've been trying for a while. She really, really wants a baby."

Sarah stood. "That doesn't entitle her to one, and it certainly doesn't entitle her to mine. How could you even think a request like that is reasonable, Graham? How could you think I'd just give away my child?"

Graham stood too. "I'm sure you want what's best for you and for Ellie. Adam wanted that—"

"Don't you dare try to tell me Adam wanted me to give our baby to someone else to raise."

"He *told* me he wanted that."

She took a step back, her mouth working but no words coming out. Graham stepped closer. He reached for her but dropped his hand when she put up her own in warning.

He sighed. "Let us just help you, okay? Me and Ava, we'll be happy to take care of you until the baby's born. You have to think of Ellie."

Everything around her shifted into sharp focus. Crystal clear. Small, electric zaps tingled along her arms and into her fingers, which twitched.

"You need to leave," she said.

Her calm tone seemed to surprise Graham. He didn't budge. He slipped an easy grin onto his face, both hands out in a placating gesture she'd seen him use on drunken frat boys acting up in the dorm study lounge. She'd also seen it in Adam's imitations of his friend and partner when he spoke about a business meeting, of how Graham had coaxed a recalcitrant client into renewing a contract they'd wanted to cancel. Adam had never tried such a thing on her, though. She wasn't about to take it from Graham.

"Sarah, c'mon. I'm sorry you're upset."

Wordlessly, she crossed to the front door and opened it. Pointed outward. Graham didn't move. A shadow crossed his expression, twisting his mouth momentarily before he raised it back into a smile.

"At least sign the guardianship paperwork," he said. "In case something happens to you, don't you want to know Ellie would be taken care of? The baby too? With Adam gone, you'll be a single parent. Anything could happen to you."

"Is that a threat?" Sarah demanded.

His shocked expression looked genuine, and that gave her a small, bitter satisfaction.

"What? No! Of course not. I'm just saying that you'll be juggling a lot. You'll have to go back to work. And honestly, who's going to hire a pregnant woman when they'll just have to let you go on maternity leave in a few months?"

"Adam made sure we'd be taken care of. Things will be tight, of course, but he didn't just *leave* us. We'll get his life insurance. The money from the business." At the look on his face, she slowly shut the door until it clicked. "He told me he'd arranged it all. He said it would put the business at risk if you had to buy him out, so instead of that, I'm supposed to get his salary for the next five years. He worked it all out with you. You get the business, all of it, and I get his salary. Five years, Graham. Until both kids were in school and I could get back on my feet."

"About that," Graham said, then stopped.

Sarah leaned against the door, eyes closed to prevent the floor from leaping up at her. "He said it was all worked out."

"There was paperwork drawn up, yes, but then he got so sick at the end, so fast . . . anyway, I don't know what he did with it, but I don't have it. Do you?"

"It's very convenient that his will states clearly that you inherit his half of FlashDrive, not me, his wife. Not his heirs. You. *That* paperwork isn't missing," she said, unable to tell if he was lying. When he didn't answer, she said, "Draw up more paperwork."

"Look, all I'm asking you to do is consider our offer for the baby, okay? You can decide later. But for now, at least, sign the guardianship paperwork. If you sign that, then we can talk about the rest of it."

"You're threatening me," she whispered. "How can you do this?"

"He was worried about you. How you'd handle the stress. Can you blame him?"

"What are you trying to say?" she challenged, knowing what he was dancing around.

If he was going to make her seem too incompetent to take care of herself and her children, she wanted him to have to say it out loud.

Graham looked uncomfortable. "He was worried you might end up like your mother."

"Adam would never have said such a thing."

"C'mon, Sarah. You know he had reason to worry. There was that time in college—"

Graham had not been there the night Sarah came home after a long night shift and punched her hand through a mirror because she'd been convinced she wasn't real. Adam, woken by the noise, had found her. He'd helped her to her feet. He'd listened to her explain how she wasn't sure she was here; she was dreaming, she had once existed but no longer did; she had never existed and never would.

It had been the anniversary of her mother's death, and once he'd pointed that out to her, she had returned to herself. He'd bandaged her hand, made her some coffee despite the late hour, and he'd sat with her at the table. He listened as she talked about the loss of her father and how her mother had never been able to deal with it and therefore had never been able to help Sarah with the loss. How her mother's hoarding and paranoia had escalated over the years until she'd no longer been able to mother Sarah and had instead become the child.

She'd told him how much she missed her mother and how terrified she was that she always would.

"I always wondered where you went," he'd said.

Hot shame had flooded her. "I thought nobody could tell."

He'd taken her hand. Pressed his lips to her knuckles. "I don't think anyone else can. You go kind of distant, that's all. But I can tell."

"It's a trauma response," she had whispered. It was the first time she'd ever said the words aloud.

"Because of your mom?"

"She was always so afraid someone was coming to get us. To get me—"

"If you aren't really here, nobody can take you away. Is that it?"

When she'd nodded, he had pulled her into his arms and rocked her while she cried. He'd taken her to bed, and they'd made love in the darkness. After, he'd held her again, her cheek pressed to his warm, bare chest.

"You're real, Sarah. You're here. No matter where you go, I'll be here when you come back."

She'd never known Adam had shared that story—or that he'd ever worried she was too unstable to be a mother herself.

"I *never*," she ground out, "gave him any reason to be worried that I couldn't take care of our children."

Graham shrugged. "You don't have to believe me. I'm just telling you what he said. That he wasn't sure you'd be able to handle everything on your own. He regretted agreeing to have another baby with you. He wanted me and Ava to be guardians of Ellie in case something happened to you. You don't have anyone else. That freaked him out."

"But the baby . . ." She heard her own voice, but it was like someone else was speaking. "That's all your idea, isn't it? Or at least *hers*."

"Is the baby even his?"

"How dare you," she said, voice shaking. Fists clenching.

"He was so sick. How could he even . . . I mean, look, it must've been really hard these past few years and months especially. I'm not judging you for taking whatever comfort you could."

Her mind tried to reel, but Sarah dug deep into whatever shredded reserves of strength she had. Adam had been the one to suggest they try for a baby, a sibling for Ellie. She hadn't believed she'd actually get pregnant. Even when their lovemaking ended in tears, she'd been grateful to have those final moments of intimacy, and when the test came up positive, she'd been relieved to find herself grateful for that too. This baby was going to be here before she knew it, and she was *not* giving it away to anyone else. She refused to believe Adam had wanted her to.

"I will not even address that disgusting accusation. Adam's final wishes were to make sure me, Ellie, *and* his baby were taken care of, to give me time to get back into working, to cover the cost of the bills, the mortgage . . . you *know* that."

Graham stepped forward. "Yeah, well, his other final wishes were for you to make arrangements to have me and Ava become Ellie's parents in case something happened to you. And if you're not willing to honor those wishes, I just don't see how you can expect me to honor the others. Adam made a very nice salary, but he also brought in business and took care of things to cover that. Without him . . ."

"Without him. Right. He's gone. And I'm the one without my husband. Ellie's the one without her father. My baby is the one who will never know him."

"We all miss him," Graham said. "You know he was family to me."

"This is how you treat your family?" Without looking at him or waiting for an answer, Sarah opened the door again and stepped back.

It took him a minute, but finally, Graham left. She closed the door behind him before he could say another word. Her knees wanted to buckle, but she forced herself to stand up straight. Ellie would wake up from her nap soon. And it looked as though Sarah needed to search the stacks of paperwork that had been sitting for weeks, untouched, on Adam's desk in his home office.

First, she went to the dining room to look at the flowers and the brief message scrawled on the card.

And we know that in all things God works for the good of those who love him, who have been called according to his purpose.

Sarah wasn't familiar with the words, but they sounded like a Christian Bible verse. It was signed *Mom*.

The card crumpled in Sarah's fist. She leaned on the dining room table to stare at it. The card and the verse made sense, but not the signature. *Mom?* The woman hadn't been in her son's life for at least a decade. She'd never met her daughter-in-law or granddaughter, supposedly at his behest, until he was dead.

Sarah looked through the doorway into the den, where Ellie still slept, sprawled in a boneless heap on the sofa. Sarah's heart ached. She couldn't imagine never seeing Ellie again, discovering she'd married, had a child, died, all without being a part of her life. Would she still refer to herself as Mom, despite all the years that had passed and whatever bad feelings had caused the rift in the first place?

She might.

Pulling her phone from her pocket, she typed in the number on the card Adam's mother had left.

CHAPTER

7

SARAH ALMOST TURNED around before the hotel room door could open, had even taken a couple of steps back in preparation, but within seconds of her hesitant knock, the door flung open to reveal a grinning, eager-looking Candace. The older woman looked Sarah up and down, then leaned out the door to look side to side before stepping backward into the room. Her expression went from joyous to uncertain.

"You didn't bring Ellie?"

"She's with a sitter." Sarah's chin went up. "I thought it would be better if I came by myself. Easier."

Candace's lips pursed briefly. She nodded and stepped aside with a sweeping gesture. "Of course. Come in, please."

The room was bigger than Sarah had expected. A suite, really, with two big beds visible through an arched doorway and a small sitting area complete with a kitchenette. White on white, fresh flowers on the coffee table, sheer curtains pulled back so you could look out over the city. Swanky, Adam would've said. Expensive.

Candace matched the hotel decor in a pair of white culottes and a crisp white blouse tied at the waist over a navy-blue tank top. Her pale hair fell over her shoulders in soft ringlets. Full makeup, full jewelry, for what? Sitting around in a hotel room? Or had she done herself up for Sarah's sake?

Sarah looked at her own dark leggings and the oversized sweater that hit her midthigh. Comfy clothes. Mom clothes, nice enough for public but in patterns that would hide the stains from grubby hands and made of fabrics that could be thrown in the washer without much care. She'd put on mascara and eyeliner. Maybe she ought to have made more of an effort.

"You look wonderful. Glowing," Candace said, as though she'd read Sarah's mind. "How are you feeling?"

"Fine."

"No . . . ?" Candace trailed off with raised eyebrows. She wiggled her fingers in the direction of Sarah's midsection, then hovered her palm over her mouth.

Sarah laughed lightly. "Not at the moment. But it comes and goes. I don't plan to stay long, so—"

"You just let me know if you need anything. Anything at all. I have some of the most delicious shrimp salad in the fridge. I've just been gobbling it up since I got here. Let me just tell you, Ohio is not the place to enjoy seafood." Candace chortled.

"No, thank you," Sarah replied. That was one mystery solved, anyway.

"I can ring for room service, quick as that." Candace demonstrated with a snap of her fingers. "When I was carrying Henry, my goodness, there were days I thought I'd never be able to keep anything down. I lived on ginger ale and saltines. To this day, I can't eat them, imagine that? Except I . . . well. Never mind."

Sarah cleared her throat. "What?"

"I just . . ." Candace looked shy. "Well, I hadn't been able to touch either of those things in years, bad memories, you know, but in the airport on the way here, the vending machine was out of all the pop I liked, and there was only ginger ale. And I had a package of saltines left from my soup at lunch, a small package, you know the kind that comes with soup? I'd tucked it away into my bag, not thinking about it. Anyway, I had a delay and the lines were so long at the café, so I sat myself down and drank that ginger ale and ate those crackers. And you know what?"

"No," Sarah said, fascinated by the string of words, spoken with barely a breath between them. "What?"

"They reminded me so much of Henry. Not the bad memories, of being so sick, but of being pregnant with him. Of him being inside me. The kick of his tiny little feet. I carried him inside me for nine months, you know, and there's something so special about that. About carrying a child. Nobody else will ever be able to share that with you except your baby. You understand what I mean, of course, don't you, Sarah? It was the most special thing I've ever experienced. *He* was the most special."

"Yes." Sarah nodded.

"How far along are you?"

"Twenty weeks. Almost twenty-one." She waited for Candace to ask if the baby had been planned.

"Halfway there," Candace said. "Are you sure I can't get you something? There's an electric kettle. Maybe some tea?"

"I really just came to talk about Adam."

Candace looked thoughtful. "Let's sit, at least. What can I tell you?"

"I guess I mostly want to try to understand why he'd lie to me. And to you."

"What kind of relationship do you have with your parents, Sarah? If I may ask." Candace settled onto the chair.

Sarah took the love seat. "My dad died in an accident when I was in first grade. My mom never remarried."

"Do you have a good relationship with her?"

"I did," Sarah said. This was both the truth and a lie. Her relationship with her mother had been complicated. "She died before I met Adam."

"Was she sick?"

"No. She killed herself."

Candace gasped softly and pressed a hand to her chest. "You don't have any brothers or sisters?"

"No." Sarah hesitated, adding, "That's one of the reasons we tried for a sibling for Ellie. Because we were both only children."

Except they both hadn't always been, not really. Sarah eyed Candace's expression, watching for any signs she meant to talk about the adopted son she'd returned. If the boy crossed her mind now, Sarah couldn't see any evidence. Candace nodded, looking a little sad.

"We tried, but the Lord never blessed us with another child. I had many losses before Henry came along, my miracle. And after him, well . . . we stopped trying. We'd been blessed enough. Didn't want to be greedy." Candace hid a smile behind her hand, but her tears glimmered.

"One of the reasons I haven't told many people about this baby is because I'm superstitious that something might happen. Because they'll be judgmental, you know? That we decided to try for a baby even though we knew Adam was dying."

"He might have recovered," Candace said sharply, then softened her tone to add, "The Lord does have his mysteries, you know."

Sarah didn't bother to correct her. They'd known Adam was terminal. Miracles could happen, sure, but neither of them had held out any hope of that. "Can you please tell me why Adam would have told me you were dead, not just estranged? It doesn't seem like something he'd do, especially since he knew how hard it was for me to have lost my own parents."

"Oh, honey, that must've been so very, very hard." Candace scooted forward to pat Sarah's hand. Her lipstick had feathered into the creases above her lips. For a moment it seemed as though she meant to link Sarah's fingers with hers, but she pulled away instead. "I wish I had an answer for you, but I just don't. Henry and Peter had their troubles. Maybe that was our fault for spoiling him. When you raise a boy like he's special, can you blame him when he believes it? I'm sure they both thought it would all get resolved, but they just ran out of time. And then, so far as I knew, *you* didn't want me around."

Sarah squinted, trying to process this information. "He actually said that?"

"He told me that since your mother had passed on, you were very fragile and couldn't really handle the idea of a mother figure in your life. He said he was working on you, slowly, until you were ready to accept another mother. I was patient, because I wanted the best for him, and for you, and for sweet little Ellie. The same way I want the best for your new baby."

Sarah did her best to take this all in. "So . . . he *did* tell that you my mother was dead?"

"I can't really remember what he said, exactly. Maybe he just told me your mother was not in your life," Candace amended. "I didn't dare to pry. I just hoped one day your heart would soften."

"But he called me *fragile*?"

"Maybe that's not the word he used. Delicate, maybe," Candace said quickly. "Out of respect, I never questioned. I knew he was doing his best to be a good husband to you. Since a man should leave his parents to cleave to his wife . . . I suppose I was just doing my best to honor that."

Sarah slumped in her seat. "I missed my mother terribly, but I would never have told Adam he had to abandon his family to shield me. It doesn't make any sense."

For the first time since Adam's death, Sarah allowed herself some anger toward him. Not for dying and leaving her but because he'd held the entirety of her heart in his hands. She had trusted him, and he hadn't done the same.

"Did he talk to you often?" she asked.

Candace looked sorrowful. "I saw pictures. He was so happy with you. I always was so glad to see him so happy. It doesn't matter how much they've broken your heart, so long as your child is happy."

Sarah straightened to look Candace in the eyes. "Did you know he was sick?"

Candace nodded hesitantly. "I prayed for his recovery. But sometimes the Lord just needs an extra angel up there at his side."

"People don't become angels when they die," Sarah said.

"You don't believe in angels?" Candace looked scandalized.

"Angels are completely distinct beings from humans," Sarah told her.

Candace's forehead wrinkled in thought. "Well. Yes, of course they are."

Sarah didn't want to get into a philosophical argument neither of them was going to win. "I'm sorry you didn't get to come out before he died."

"I wanted to," Candace told her earnestly. "He just said . . . it would be too much for you. I had to find out he'd died from an obituary. I came as fast as I could, but it was too late."

"We bury people as soon after they die as we can, but if I'd known, we could have delayed it by a few days. I just never knew," Sarah whispered, defeated.

"Nothing to be done about it now, and no need for you to beat yourself up about it . . ." Candace trailed off, studying Sarah's face. "Did he leave you in a good position? Financially, I mean?"

Sarah didn't want to share her conversation with Graham about Adam's salary, or the lack of it. "Once the insurance payment comes, we'll be okay for a while. We have some savings too. I'd always planned to go back to work once the baby was old enough, but it looks like I'll have to get a job much sooner than that."

"Who'd hire you right now with that baby bump?"

The women stared at each other quietly.

"Women bear the brunt of our men's choices. Even the good ones seem to end up doing what's best for themselves. I'm ashamed my son did so poorly by you."

Sarah started to wave a hand in protest but stopped herself. She'd loved Adam beyond any measure, but she could not deny that he had left her in the lurch. He'd kept secrets. He'd flat-out lied to her.

"I have a brilliant idea." Candace clapped her hands briskly. "You, Ellie, and the baby. You can come live with me."

8

"JUST THINK ABOUT it," Candace had said two weeks ago, when Sarah declined her offer. "At least come and visit. I have plenty of room. Would you promise me you'll keep in touch?"

That promise, at least, had been easy enough to make, even if Sarah wasn't sure she meant to keep it. She'd been without a mother for a long time, and in many ways, she had lost hers even before she died. What Adam had told his mother about her had stuck in her head, spinning her thoughts into tangles. *Was* she too "fragile?" Incapable of accepting a maternal relationship?

You know he had reason to worry.

Adam had been dead for a month. She wasn't ready to move on, but the world wasn't going to wait until she could. Bent over the sheaf of bills on the kitchen table, Sarah closed her eyes. After her graduation from UCLA, she'd taken a job as the front desk manager for a chain that catered to business travelers. Adam had still had three years of college left, but he and Graham had already been working on what would eventually become FlashDrive. She'd often come home after work to find the two of them bent over this same IKEA kitchen table, the remnants of fast-food containers spread out all around them while they dreamed big.

Adam had always been the dreamer.

"I want Ellie to have a brother or a sister. You might go on to have another husband—"

She'd hushed him, but he'd continued.

"But once I'm gone, Ellie will never have the chance for a full sibling."

He'd convinced her. They'd talked about it together for hours, days, months. What it would mean for Ellie to have a full sibling. What it would mean for Sarah to raise two children on her own. There'd never been any question that Adam was going to die. They'd made their choice together, but Sarah had always known she would be the one left behind to face the consequences of it . . . the one to make his dream happen.

But what about her dreams? They hadn't included being widowed, becoming a single mother, fretting about finances. All of that was what had driven her mom into instability. Or maybe it had always been inside her mother, and therefore it might be inside Sarah too.

Stifling a yawn, she wished for bed. She'd been counting on his salary being direct deposited, and, caught up in the funeral and shiva, she hadn't immediately pursued the life insurance payout. After her conversation with Graham, she'd turned everything in and received an email in response alerting her to watch for a packet in the mail that would give her all the information she'd need to proceed. Adam had set up the life insurance policy for her before they even had Ellie, before he'd even been diagnosed, not that it should have mattered. The money from the life insurance was supposed to be for future expenses; drawing his salary for five years was meant to keep her afloat until she could stand on her own. But now, while she waited for the payout, she needed to cut as many expenses as she could.

Sarah stared at the laptop screen and the bank balances and wanted to put her head down on the desk and weep and scream and pound it with her fists. Her life of sourdough starters and sewing her own curtains now seemed like the stupidest kind of cosplay. How, in this age, could she have trusted her husband to handle all the finances?

Because she had trusted him. And loved him. And believed in him. Because their bills had always been paid, they'd never lacked for anything, never lived beyond their means so far as she knew. The business had been making money, and their small family's needs and wants had been reasonable. Between the two of them, Adam had been the spender, and since he'd also been the wage earner, she'd never thought to question his expenses.

Sarah had never intended to be a stay-at-home mom. Adam had been the one to point out to her, gently and with love but also a firm honesty, that she didn't love her job as front desk manager. Her dream had been to own and operate a boutique bed-and-breakfast someplace near the ocean, with windswept views of the water. The work had paid the bills while Adam finished college and during those first couple of years while he and Graham built FlashDrive, but it did not and never had fulfilled her. The hours were long and variable, and she hated working nights.

"You'd be working to pay for day care," he'd told her in bed, one hand on her rounding belly. "And why work to pay someone else to raise our baby when you're going to be such an amazing mom? You can always go back to work when the kids are grown—"

"Whoa," she'd interrupted. "How many kids are you planning we have?"

"A couple of dozen, at least."

Then they'd laughed and kissed and made love, and the next day she'd given her notice. She'd never regretted it. Everything she'd dreamed of doing as the owner of a bed-and-breakfast turned out to be just as gratifying as she'd imagined, only she got to do it for her beloved husband and baby daughter instead of strangers. Cooking and baking from scratch, sewing and crafting, taking care of not only a house but a *home*.

Their home.

And now it was all being stripped away from her, one piece at a time.

When her phone screen lit up with a call from Ava, Sarah turned it facedown on the table. The Morgans really weren't going to quit. She opened a new browser tab on her laptop but hesitated with her fingers on the keyboard. What could she even search?

"Jobs that will hire pregnant women," she whispered without typing the words.

Her fingers moved in a different pattern. *Work from home* brought up an instant hundred links, most of which looked scammy. With her background in hospitality, she could do something related to booking cruises, she thought, cursor hovering over a link promising *Flex hours! Great pay! Equipment provided!*

She filled in the application on autopilot. She wasn't going to get that job. She didn't *want* that job. But she had to do something, anything, to convince herself she was moving forward. If she didn't . . .

But she would. She'd been able to take care of herself before she met Adam Granatt. She'd be able to take care of herself, and Ellie, and this baby.

She was not her mother.

A text came in from Linda next. An invitation for Sarah and Ellie to join the Ruttenbergs for both seders. *Oh, no. Passover.*

Sarah groaned. She hadn't forgotten about Passover, because of course she couldn't forget one of the major holidays. Nor had she forgotten the intensity of the preparation for Pesach's eight nights: cleaning the house to get rid of every stray scrap of chametz, cooking the seder meals and special holiday dishes that conformed to the rules about eating no leaven. Her mind had simply flown right over the fact that it was going to happen so soon. She hadn't done anything to prepare.

She didn't really want to either.

Adam's religious observance had always been a nonnegotiable part of his faith. He wouldn't have given it up for anyone or any reason, but he wasn't here. Sarah, on the other hand, had always been Jewish; she would always be, whether or not she celebrated a single holiday. There'd been many years of her life, before Adam, in which Sarah had not celebrated Shabbat or Rosh Hashanah or Yom Kippur, not even Passover, and this year, well . . .

The seder's final saying was "Next year in Jerusalem." For her, this year, it would have to simply be "Next year."

Typing off a quick acceptance to the dinner invitation, Sarah stifled another series of yawns. She wasn't sure what she could do about Graham reneging on Adam's salary but also not buying her out, but it was probably going to require a lawyer. For that, she'd need some money . . . and proof. So far, the only paperwork she'd found had been the copy of Adam's will stating that upon his death, his half of the business was to go to Graham. The file folder should have included the paperwork with the agreement between the two of them to pay Sarah his salary for the five years in lieu of a buyout, but all she'd found was a heavy-duty paper clip. Once the insurance payout came, she'd be in a much better place to deal with all of this.

For now, sleep.

Her first few months of pregnancy with Ellie had been just like this. All-day nausea interspersed with a raging, famishing hunger. Utter exhaustion to the point that her bones felt heavy as iron bars. At her last appointment, the doctor had said everything looked fine, but she didn't feel fine. She felt exhausted and overwhelmed.

She closed her laptop and left it on the table. Before going upstairs, she made the rounds. Making the coffee had been Adam's job; this had always been hers. She checked the doors and windows. Looked to be sure the outside light was on at the end of the driveway and, after a moment's thought, turned on the motion-activated porch lamp so it would remain lit all night. Their street had always been quiet. Low crime. Even so, darkness invited darkness, didn't it?

Sarah centered herself, focusing. The floor under her feet, the coolness of the wooden railing she gripped as she climbed. When she got to the top of the stairs, she was convinced once more that she was *here*. She was *real*. She *existed*.

Her phone lit up again. Another text. Sarah tapped the screen. Ava had sent a photo of a nursery.

CHAPTER

9

THE SOUND OF running water woke Sarah from a lovely, vivid dream in which she lay on a sun-soaked beach wearing a bikini and sipping from a frosted glass. It took her half a minute to blink hard enough to realize she was looking at the ceiling of her bedroom, not the hotel of the resort where she and Adam had honeymooned. It took her another few seconds to notice the sound of water was real.

With a panicked curse, Sarah wrestled herself out of bed. The faint rush of pouring water got louder as she went downstairs. She followed the noise to the kitchen, where she braced herself to see a spouting faucet or an overflowing sink. Instead, she gaped at the ceiling, where a flowing waterfall cascaded over the edges of the glass globe light fixture. As she watched, the ceiling softened and finally gave way, sending the entire fixture crashing to the tile floor. Sparks flew, popping and hissing, and a wire dangled.

Sarah ran upstairs to the Jack-and-Jill bathroom shared by Ellie's room and Adam's home office. It was directly above the kitchen. The toilet was overflowing from the bowl. The floor gave a bit under her feet as she edged toward the toilet, meaning to turn the water off at the floor valve, but when she twisted it, the entire knob came off in her hand. The water didn't stop. It continued its relentless, almost-silent running. No wonder she hadn't noticed. It could've been running this way for hours or even days. She hadn't used this bathroom in weeks—Ellie wore a Pull-Up to bed, and Sarah had been doing the bedtime routine of bath and final potty in the master bathroom since Adam had gone into the hospital. The door to this bathroom was kept shut and locked from Ellie's side to prevent her from wandering in there during the night.

Lifting the lid, she prepared to flinch at a mess, but it wasn't the sort she was expecting. Sodden bagels floated, disintegrating. More had sunk to the bottom of the bowl, and she could see even more crammed into the drain. It looked like someone had repeatedly flushed bagels until the toilet could hold no more. When she took off the tank lid, another bagel greeted her. This one had been shoved into a position that prevented the float from lifting to shut off the water. This explained why the toilet was running and running, but not who'd filled it with bagels . . . or why.

Sarah tried to fix the knob back on the shutoff, but it wouldn't stay. Water had puddled all over the floor, but much of it was slipping through the cracks around the back of the toilet where the vinyl flooring had lifted up. Enough was draining through those spaces that the flood hadn't reached Ellie's room, far across on the bathroom's other side, but she could see it flowing toward the carpeted floor of Adam's office, which squelched when she stepped on it.

Back downstairs, she went into the kitchen to grab a bucket from beneath the sink, but it wasn't going to do much to catch the torrent of water gushing from the ragged hole. More sparks sizzled from the dangling wires, and glass crunched under her heels from the shattered light fixture.

She ran to the garage. In the event of an earthquake, she knew, there was an automatic shutoff for their gas, but not for the water. The manual valve for the water shutoff lived nondescriptly behind some storage bins in the garage, but the wrench needed to twist it closed was missing. It had been hung on a nail, which was now bent, with a permanent marker outline on the wall to show where it was supposed to be. She looked for it on the floor. Not there. She shoved the bins out of the way in the opposite direction. Also not there.

By the time she got back into the kitchen, more water had eaten away the hole where the ceiling light had been. Sodden drywall scattered across the floor and countertop. It covered the laptop she'd left on the table. Water no longer cascaded like a waterfall but steadily and relentlessly trickled. The puddle beneath the hole had doubled.

Sarah ran back upstairs, where she managed to adjust the float so it would at least stop running fresh water into the tank, down into the bowl, and out onto the floor. She wanted to kick herself for not thinking to do that immediately. For a moment, she allowed herself to lean against the sink, head down so she didn't have to see her own reflection.

She'd weathered Adam's illness, the doctor visits, the treatments, the hospitalizations while she "held down the home fort," as he'd said. She'd kept up with taking care of Ellie, paying the bills, taking out the trash, arranging for lawn care. She'd made sure the vehicles got the oil changes and other maintenance needed when her husband had been too ill to see to it.

Now Sarah was at an utter loss.

If this had happened a few weeks ago, she'd have called Graham. No way was she going to do that now. She went back to her room to grab her phone and called Barry Ruttenberg, who gave her the number of a plumber he recommended and promised he'd be over as soon as he could get there.

In Ellie's room, she found the little girl playing with her dolls in the corner. She looked up when Sarah came in and gave her a sunny grin that normally would have made the whole day brighter. Sarah barely mustered a small smile in return.

"Ellie. Come here." She passed the closed bathroom door, still locked, and pressed her toes onto the carpet. Damp. She sat on the bed and patted it. Ellie joined her, cuddling up on her lap. Sarah took her daughter's cheeks in both her hands and looked into her blue eyes. "Did you put bagels into the potty?"

Ellie frowned. "Daddy did."

"Ellie, I know Daddy did not put bagels into the potty." Sarah bit her tongue to keep herself from snapping and sounding harsh.

Her daughter wriggled. Her small brow furrowed, and her lips pursed. She looked so much like Adam most of the time, but with that "pouty" on, she was the image of Sarah as a little girl.

"Daddy did." Ellie pointed at the bathroom door, then put a finger to her lips and made a *shush-shush*.

Sarah's heart twisted. She rocked Ellie against her. There was no way, of course, that Adam had been the one to fill the toilet with bagels, but she didn't believe Ellie had done it either. That mess had taken an effort the little girl couldn't have made—she didn't even go up and down the stairs by herself, much less while carrying an armload of bagels.

So who had?

If Ellie thought it had been her father, that meant a man. Graham could have come up here at any time during shiva, but anyone else could have too. But why? To ruin her house? To prove she wasn't capable of providing a safe place for her children so she'd be forced to give them up? She thought for a moment about the wedding vows Graham and Ava had exchanged. He'd vowed to "do whatever it takes" to keep her happy, and all the guests had sighed and wiped their happy tears, but that statement sounded a lot more ominous when it related to his wife wanting to steal Sarah's children.

Fearing Ellie could be taken away was like something her mother might have thought.

The doorbell rang. Sarah lifted Ellie onto her hip, aware the time was fast approaching when she'd no longer be able to carry her this way. Barry was at the front door, a wrench in hand and a sympathetic expression on his face.

"I left a message with my buddy about coming over," he said at once as Sarah let him in. "Did you already call a plumber?"

"I hadn't yet—"

"Don't worry about it, then. Let's see if my friend can help first. He owes me a favor," Barry said with a firm nod, already looking toward the back of the house. "Water shut off in the garage?"

She settled Ellie in front of the TV with a bowl of dry cereal, a banana, and an order not to come into the kitchen. The kid had watched more television in the past few weeks than she had in her entire life. No help for it, though. Sarah closed off the kitchen with the baby gates to make sure Ellie didn't wander in and cut herself on the fallen glass. Then she showed Barry to the garage.

He found the wrench used for the shutoff high on top of the storage shelves and held it out to her. "Hard for you to see it way up there."

"It's usually there, on the wall." She pointed. "I don't know how it got up there."

Back in the kitchen, he and Sarah surveyed the damage. His shoes crushed glass and squished on the sopping-wet drywall. Water *plink-plink*ed from the hole in the ceiling. When she showed him the toilet bowl full of disintegrating bagels, he looked flummoxed.

"Did Ellie do this?"

"She says no."

Barry frowned. "That would be a lot of bagels for a little girl to carry upstairs, especially without anyone noticing. But why would anyone do such a thing?"

"I guess I have an enemy I don't know about," Sarah said.

"I find that hard to believe."

She rubbed her forehead but gave him a rueful smile. "That I don't have an enemy? Or that I don't know who it is?"

His phone rang, and he pulled it from his pocket. "That's my buddy."

Barry chatted with his friend for a minute or two, laying out the problems, and then he handed the phone to Sarah so she could arrange for the guy to come over and take a look. While she was talking, Barry managed to get the valve on the bathroom floor to close. He refused to allow Sarah to run down to the garage to turn on the water so they could be sure the toilet no longer had water flowing into it and instead did it himself.

By the time they both got downstairs again, the ceiling had almost stopped dripping. Ellie had opened her toy chest and strewn the den with princess dresses and other toys. She'd helped herself to more cereal from the box Sarah had left on the coffee table. She greeted them both with a beaming grin that lit up her face.

Barry ruffled Ellie's hair and gave Sarah a solemn look. "You should be good for the leak. I turned off the circuit breaker to the kitchen ceiling. Your fridge is still running, but you won't be able to use your stove for a bit."

"I have enough food left from sitting shiva. It'll be fine. Thank you so much again for everything."

She wasn't going to tell him she'd lived in far worse conditions than this. Her mother's house had fallen into such disrepair that at one point they'd been cooking all their meals on the grill out back and using a cooler with ice from the gas station. Compared to that, this was practically a gourmet kitchen.

"How's . . . everything?" He eyed her belly. Even if Linda hadn't told him about the baby, there was no hiding it by now.

Sarah put her hands on the bump. The baby pushed at her palm with a tiny foot. "We're all right."

As much as they could be, anyway. After Barry had gone, Sarah went into the den. Ellie had been busy stacking a set of wooden blocks to make a tower, which she kicked over in triumph, clapping her hands. Sarah winced at the loud noise. She took her daughter by the arms and looked into her face. Sticky banana covered her cheeks and had collected smudges of dirt on her skin. "Tell me about seeing Daddy."

Ellie ducked her head and shook it. She put a finger to her lips. "Shush, shush, shush."

"Did Daddy tell you not to say anything about him being there?"

The little girl gave Sarah a cautious look. Her lips worked as she tried to put her thoughts into her limited vocabulary. Finally, she nodded.

"You stay here while Mama cleans up, okay?"

Sarah got to work in the kitchen, mopping, sweeping, clearing away the glass. The bucket beneath the hole in the ceiling would catch any errant drips. She filled a couple of trash bags and set them out on the deck to take to the garbage can. Her laptop was so thoroughly trashed, no bag of rice was going to dry it out. Fortunately, she could access her email from her phone. A peek at Ellie confirmed the little girl was still happily playing with her toys.

Sarah fixed a plate of leftovers, aware that she'd been so busy she hadn't had time to feel nauseated, and now she was starving. Settled at the table, she tucked into her haphazard meal, forcing herself to eat slowly so she didn't upset her stomach. Her efforts turned out to be useless, though, once she saw the message from the insurance company. She stared at it stupidly.

"No," she said. "Oh, you have to be kidding me."

10

"I DON'T UNDERSTAND. I'M supposed to be the primary beneficiary." The words dropped one at a time from Sarah's lips, but
no matter how hard she tried, she couldn't feel her mouth. Not her
lips, not her teeth, not her tongue. Someone else might've been
speaking for her, that's how distant she felt from herself.

She had to draw herself back. This was not a dream. She was
really here in the office. She curled her fingers into her palms, pressing the nails deep into the flesh to cause a sting, being careful not to
cut the flesh.

The woman sitting on the other side of the desk gave Sarah a
pained grimace she probably meant to be a smile. Her name was
Pam, and she'd already expressed her condolences profusely when
Sarah arrived without an appointment, Ellie on her hip. Pam had
given the toddler an equally strained smile but had not looked at
her since.

"Your husband made some changes to the policy regarding the
recipient of the dea . . . the ah, benefit." Pam coughed lightly into
her fist.

She couldn't even say the word *death*. No wonder she couldn't
bring herself to look at the child of the man who'd died. Sarah shifted
Ellie's weight from one knee to the other. The little girl was content-
edly playing a game on Sarah's phone with the sound turned off, and
Sarah put her onto the chair next to hers to give her legs a rest.

"But . . ." Sarah tried to gather her thoughts, to stay coherent. She gave Pam a long, hard stare. "When did this happen?"

"About four months ago, according to the transaction records."

Four months ago, Adam's doctor had first talked to them about hospice care. They'd planned for him to spend his last days at home, but instead a rampant bacterial infection had sent him to the hospital. He'd died there.

"And he changed the beneficiary to who?"

Pam looked even more pained, if that were possible. "A trust."

"And I'm not the whatever you call it. The person who's in charge of the trust."

"The trustee."

"It's Graham Morgan, isn't it?"

"The recipients of a life insurance policy are confidential. I can only tell you that you are *not* listed as the beneficiary." Pam leaned forward and lowered her voice. "I'm so sorry for your loss."

"Yes, you said that. Thank you," Sarah added to soften the hardness in her voice. She rubbed at her eyes with both her hands, pressing the lids until colored blossoms bloomed.

"Is there anything else I can do for you?"

"I guess not. Sorry to barge in on you like this." Sarah stood but didn't offer her hand to shake.

Pam stood too. "I'm really sorry, Mrs. Granatt."

"That and a pack of matches will still burn a house down," Sarah said, taking no pleasure in Pam's expression. "Sorry. My mom used to say that, but it was rude. You're just doing your job."

Pam smiled kindly. "I'd say you're entitled to be a little rude right now. It's okay."

Sarah had another thought. "Is there a way to look up if I am the beneficiary on *any* policy? If he took out a new one, maybe? He could've done that."

"I don't have that information, I'm sorry. I can only access what I have in my files. My best advice would be to look through any bank accounts or credit cards to see if there were any payments made to an insurance company. You might be able to track it down that way. Oh, and there's a website you can check to see if you're listed as the beneficiary on any policies. Hang on. I'll write it down for you." Pam scribbled some information on a sticky note and passed it to Sarah, who put it into her pocket. Pam hesitated, then added, "It's none of

my business, really, and I'm not authorized to offer advice or anything, but . . . do you have to go through probate?"

"No. We settled all of that before he died. Community property
with right of survivorship, all of that. He . . ." Sarah's breath hitched,
and she drew herself up. "My husband wanted to make sure we were
taken care of. That's why this doesn't make sense. There has to be
another policy."

"I hope you find one." Pam sounded genuine.

"Yeah," Sarah said. "Me too."

*   *   *

Ellie had fallen asleep in her car seat. Sarah considered waking her
up, but battling a cranky toddler woken from a nap was not on her
list of things she wanted to deal with. She carried the little girl into
the house and, too weary to make it all the way up the stairs, put her
on the couch in the den. Then she went to the kitchen to make herself some tea.

The hole in the ceiling didn't look any better than it had this
morning, but at least it didn't look worse. Cleaning up the debris had
made the kitchen usable, but she'd have to get the hole repaired. She
refused to live surrounded by broken things. When the microwave
beeped to alert her that the water was hot, she steeped a peppermint
tea bag but couldn't muster the energy to sip.

She was just so tired.

And she hated tea.

She went to the mailbox to bring in a handful of junk mail along
with a few square envelopes, hand addressed. Condolence cards.
They just kept coming. At least the food basket deliveries and flowers
had stopped—Adam had been well liked by his clients, but Sarah
was completely over the stink of dying flowers.

She didn't even want to open any of the cards, but she did anyway and immediately wished she had not. Ava's letter rambled, slop-
ing lines declaring how sorry she was that everything had become "so
complicated" and that she was "there" for Sarah and Ellie and she
was so sorry for anything she might've done to "cause harm."

"So sorry, so sorry, everyone's so fucking sorry," Sarah
muttered.

She put the card through the shredder, along with all the others.
Then the junk mail. Finally, she opened an official-looking envelope

addressed to Adam. The mortgage statement, a harsh reminder of how perilously close to being broke she was.

"Not even close. Already there." Talking to herself didn't help.

Crumpling the statement, she considered shredding it too, but then she smoothed it out and put it on the counter. She'd find the strength to call tomorrow, see about getting an extension for extenuating circumstances. Something. Anything.

Pulling the sticky note from Pam out of her pocket, Sarah started typing in the website address on her phone browser, then put both the note and her phone on the counter. This would be better researched on a computer. With her laptop destroyed, that meant using Adam's, which meant going into his upstairs office, something she had to do soon anyway. She had to take care of the wet carpet. She had to box up his things.

One of those tasks, she was ready to face. The other was still too daunting.

"Mammmaaaaa!"

"In the kitchen, ketzeleh."

Ellie came in, scrubbing at her eyes. "I hungry."

"Go turn on your 'toons. I'll bring you some apples and peanut butter, okay?"

Her own stomach gurgled, but whether that was an alarm that she was going to throw up or a plea to be fed, Sarah had a hard time telling. She gave it a second or two. Hunger.

No matter what else was going on, bodies needed food and sleep. She'd feel better with some of both, but for now, a meal would have to suffice. Later, she'd get Ellie into bed and sink into her own, where she could hope to lose herself in dreams that hopefully wouldn't become nightmares.

Her phone rang, a loud and startling jangle that had her hand jerking. She knocked the phone off the counter. It landed on the floor, screen cracked.

"Of course," Sarah grumbled.

It was broken, but it still worked, and there was an analogy she didn't want to dive too deeply into. A notification popped up for a voice mail, an unknown number with a local area code. In case against all odds it was Pam with some information about another life insurance policy, Sarah tapped to listen.

"Hi there, this is Julie Anderson, and I'm a local Realtor, just checking in to see if you'd thought about selling your home. I have over twenty years of experience, and this is a great time in the market for sellers. If you or anyone you know is looking to sell, please give me a ring and I'd love to chat with you."

Surveying the mess of her kitchen, Sarah could only let out a burbling series of strangled chuckles. It was the kind of phone call she never would have answered before, simply deleting the voice mail and moving on with her life.

Judaism had literally hundreds of brachot, blessings to be said for everything from seeing a rainbow to hearing an ambulance passing. Sarah's conversations with G-d tended to happen only during Yom Kippur services, and she rarely send up pleas. But what about now? What if this was a sign? What if this was the three rowboats and the helicopter from that old joke about the man waiting to be saved from a flood?

"Hashem," she murmured, "are you trying to tell me something?"

She thought of her dwindling savings. Of Ava's determination to get her hands on her children. Graham's refusal to abide by the agreements Adam had made with him.

"Hi there, Julia," Sarah said when the woman on the other end of the line picked up. "I got your message."

11

THE HOUSE SOLD immediately.

Even a year or so before, there would have been a bidding war, cash buyers, no contingencies. Sarah accepted an offer for ten thousand under the admittedly inflated asking price to account for the repairs and necessary upgrades to get the house to market value, and she agreed to an accelerated closing date of a few weeks instead of months. The money was enough, barely, to satisfy the outstanding mortgage and put aside a small nest egg for her and Ellie. Not enough to buy a new house. Not enough to pay off the medical bills starting to trickle in or put aside money for the future. Enough to support them for a year, though, while she rented a place to live, looked for a job, and got on her feet. She had a small condo all lined up, and an estate sale company was coming tomorrow to assess the house and all her stuff so she could dump most of it before the closing.

Everything was moving at warp speed, but that was what she wanted, wasn't it? To be rid of it all? This house she'd loved so much had become a jail, holding her prisoner to her memories.

At six, Sarah been able to understand that her daddy was gone but not why he wasn't coming back. It had been even harder to comprehend why she and her mother had needed to move out of the house they'd all shared overlooking the Atlantic ocean and into one close by, but much smaller. A rental house stuffed so full of their belongings that navigating the living room and dining room was like walking through a maze. The two small bedrooms upstairs shared a bathroom, and for a long time, Sarah and her mother also shared the slightly larger room so that the other could be used for storage.

It wasn't until Sarah turned thirteen and demanded her privacy that Mom had cleared out the second bedroom, moving its contents into other places in the house. For the next four years, Sarah had kept her room meticulously clean and minimalistically bare. A single bed, a dresser, a desk and chair. She pinned decorations on a corkboard but otherwise left the walls blank. She had shut herself in that room for hours simply to keep herself away from the ever-growing piles and stacks in the rest of the house. Periodically, she'd come home from school to find a box or bag inside her room, and without fail, she'd watch herself from a distance as she tossed it into the trash without even looking at the contents.

Those were the only times she and her mother ever fought.

Sarah's senior year of high school, Hurricane Sandy devastated the East Coast. Brigantine flooded, including the house her mother had rented for the past twelve years. Mom had refused to evacuate until the waters got so high she and Sarah had used an empty ice cooler to float to safety.

Everything in the house had been ruined.

Sarah's mother had died shortly after that. Losing her husband had not broken her heart; losing her "things" had shattered her irrevocably. Sarah had been in her freshman year at UCLA. She'd gone home for the funeral and to take care of her mother's estate. After that, she'd never returned to Brigantine. She rarely even thought of her life before leaving home, but when she did, it was always through a filter. She remembered, but it was as though the events had happened to someone else.

She'd vowed long ago that she would never hang onto "stuff" and "things" to the point where they became a burden. A home was not the house but the people who lived inside it. She would never allow herself to become so attached to a physical building or belongings that losing them could break her the way her mother had been broken.

Now, sitting at the IKEA kitchen table from her and Adam's first apartment, Sarah put her face in her hands and wept. She'd found herself in tears countless times over the past few months, but this was different. She wept for her loss, so much of it, but mostly for how devastated she was at losing something she'd always promised herself she wouldn't hold on to.

"Sarah?"

With a shriek, Sarah flew out of her chair, sending it skidding along the tile floor with a crash. The baby kicked and punched, maybe startled at the sudden jostling. Ava, hands holding a cardboard file box, stood in the doorway. What the fuck was Ava doing in her house?

Which is exactly what Sarah said aloud.

Ava flinched and held up the box like an offering. "I hope you didn't wake up Ellie."

"I asked you a question."

"Graham cleaned out Adam's office. I thought you might like his personal effects."

"That is not the answer to what I asked, and I think you know that." Sarah fought to keep her voice steady, even though she felt poised to run. Fight or flight, wasn't it? Living with her mother, she'd grown numb to being constantly poised to flee for her life. She didn't like being reminded of how that had felt.

If her shriek had woken Ellie, the girl wasn't yelling for her mother. Not yet, anyway. Sarah took a deep breath and squared her shoulders as Ava set the box on the counter and pulled something from the pocket of her creaseless linen palazzo pants. She held it up, turning it side to side so it caught the light. She set it on the kitchen table with a light *clink*.

Sarah stared at it for a moment. "Why do you have a key to my house?"

"Adam gave it to Graham." Ava's chin went up, and her voice steeled.

Sarah snatched it up. "That does not give you the right to use it to waltz in here whenever you like."

"I knocked. You didn't answer. Look," Ava cut in when Sarah began to retort, "I wanted to make things okay with us. *Please*."

"Letting yourself into my house like you own it is not a good start."

Ava's pale-pink lips stretched into a smile. "About that. Owning the house, I mean."

Sarah went cold. "What are you talking about?"

"We bought it."

"An LLC bought it," Sarah said, but she already knew she'd been played.

Ava shrugged and pulled out a kitchen chair. She settled into it and smoothed her creamy trousers over her thighs before fixing Sarah with a calm and infuriatingly triumphant look. "Oh, I know. Graham set that up for me when I was thinking of starting up my life-coaching business. Could I get a cup of coffee?"

"I don't have any." Sarah leaned against the counter, wishing desperately for something stronger than coffee.

"Tea?" Sarah's expression must've been answer enough, because Ava sighed and shrugged. "Fine. Nothing, then. I'll make this quick. I feel terrible about how things happened. I never meant to hurt your feelings, Sarah. I hope you believe me."

"No matter what you wanted, you insulted me beyond measure. And now I find out you bought my house? For what purpose?"

"To help you. We heard about the leak. Water damage is the worst, isn't it? So expensive to repair, and if you don't take care of it properly, the mold issue can completely ruin your entire house."

"Did you do it?"

Ava looked taken aback. "Beg pardon?"

"Did you do it? Stuff the toilet full of bagels, I mean."

Ava let out a startled huff of laughter that she quickly cut off behind her palm. She shook her head, eyes wide. When she took her hand away, her lipstick had smeared. Sarah had been wearing the same clothes for the past couple of days, hadn't washed her hair in longer than that. Lipstick? Forget about it. Even at her best, she'd never begin to compare to Ava's cool and effortless style. That messed-up lipstick wasn't going to level the field, but even so, it gave Sarah a small bit of satisfaction.

"You're serious." Ava's expression turned solemn. "You think I sabotaged your plumbing? Graham was right. You've got some real problems."

Saying the words out loud would sound combative, if not paranoid. "Why would you buy my house under an LLC and not your own name?"

"I thought you'd refuse our offer."

"Your offer was shit, Ava, and you know it. I only took it because—"

"Because you really have little choice, right?" Ava inclined her head as though imparting some terrific bit of wisdom.

"You knew about the trust."

Ava's brow creased, but she nodded.

Sarah gritted her teeth. "What are you planning to do with the house?"

"Rent it to you. So you and Ellie can stay here, in the only home she's ever known." Now Ava's smile turned sly. "For a very reasonable rate, of course. Graham and I really want to help you out. We loved Adam. We love Ellie. We'll love your new little one too."

"This 'reasonable rent.'" Sarah made air quotes. "Does it happen to come along with the stipulation that I sign guardianship paperwork to you and Graham? Or maybe it's an adoption agreement. You let me and Ellie live here, in our own house, in exchange for my baby."

"It's not your house anymore. You sold it."

"Yeah, well, I'm not selling you either one of my children, so you might as well just show yourself out." Sarah pointed toward the front of the house.

Ava drew herself up and out of the chair, her posture regal and lean and glamorous, and Sarah hated her for that cool composure. She hated her for daring to try and take her children. For buying her house. For having a living husband.

"It's not your house until we sign all the papers," Sarah said as she followed Ava from the kitchen and toward the front door. "I can change my mind."

Ava paused, hand on the doorknob, to look over her shoulder. "You won't. You need the money. You have Ellie to think of. Adam always said you were stubborn, but I never thought you'd be so . . . stiff-necked."

Sarah hissed in a breath. She didn't believe her husband would've ever said such a thing about her, certainly not to Ava, but she was not at all surprised at the other woman's casual but cutting use of a phrase long meant as an antisemitic dig. Ava gave Sarah a long, assessing look tinged with pity.

"See you at the closing," Ava said finally.

"I've arranged to do it all electronically. I won't have to sit in the same room as you. I don't have to be there at all. I want nothing to do with either one of you ever again."

This set Ava back a literal step. She drew in a harsh breath and her expression became wounded. "Sarah."

When Sarah didn't reply, Ava shook her head, gave her another woebegone look, and opened the front door.

"By the way," Sarah said, placing a hand on the door when Ava had stepped through the doorway and onto the porch. "Your lipstick is smeared."

Then she shut the door before Ava could reply. She locked it and watched through the sidelight window for the other woman to walk away. For a moment, she did consider calling her Realtor and telling her the deal was off. There would be other offers. She could make it another few weeks if she had to. She'd gone so far as to pull out her phone before she stopped herself.

The house. The stuff. They weren't taking it from her; she was giving it to them, Sarah thought. *Let them have it.* Because they sure as hell weren't going to take her children.

And if they didn't back off?

She'd make sure they regretted it for the rest of their days.

CHAPTER

12

IN HER ROOM, in the dark, Sarah stretched her arms and legs wide. A starfish. She couldn't stay in that position very long and had to turn onto her side with a pillow tucked between her legs. The baby rolled around, thumping her internally with a fist, and she rubbed her belly. How long would it be until she didn't feel guilty for enjoying the bed all to herself? Adam had been a heavy sleeper, hot as a furnace, prone to flinging out a hand or a foot in the night to startle her awake as though someone had pounced on her.

How long would it be before she could remember him without crying? She was no stranger to the length and breadth of grief, and still she didn't know the answer. If not never, at least not for a long, long time.

At twenty-four weeks, her baby was the size of an ear of corn, growing as it should. Her glucose screening showed no signs of diabetes. All good news.

"We need to talk about your health insurance," the receptionist had said to her discreetly as Sarah was making her copay after the visit.

The health coverage from FlashDrive had been exemplary. She was supposed to be covered for the length of the buyout agreement, another promise Graham had backed out on. It turned out the coverage from her new plan was not as extensive. The copays were higher. The out-of-pocket costs too. The new numbers on the list the receptionist handed her were so much higher that Sarah had laughed right in the woman's face.

Her back hurt. Her feet had swollen this afternoon, but at least she could still see them. Her eyes were grainy with sleepiness, but she had to use the bathroom. She'd be lucky to get any decent sleep tonight.

The rep from the estate sale company would be there at nine with the paperwork, and she'd promised to give Sarah an estimate of what she thought the sale could bring. It wasn't going to be much. Even including Adam's car, they didn't have anything collectible or particularly valuable. People would buy her mismatched silverware and her collection of battered paperbacks, but they wouldn't pay a lot for them, and she was paying a higher commission for the sale to be held on such short notice.

Swinging her legs over the edge of the bed left her huffing and puffing. Her spine crackled. The pangs in her bladder deepened, and she went to her bathroom in the dark. On her way back to bed, she paused in her bedroom door to listen for any sounds from Ellie's room. She thought she heard a small giggle—Ellie often sleep-talked, still mostly in a babble even as she gained a greater vocabulary. This sounded like full sentences.

But what was she saying?

Tiptoeing down the hallway, Sarah focused on the soft lighting from Ellie's nightlight. A few feet before she got to the doorway, the shadows shifted. Movement.

"Ellie?" That wasn't Ellie; Sarah knew it in her gut, and she ran to the doorway to hurtle through it, both her hands raised to fight whoever was in there. Her eyes scanned the room, finding only more shadows and her daughter sitting up in bed, surrounded by a pile of her stuffed toys. "Who were you talking to?"

"Daddy."

"Oh, honey." Sarah sat on the edge of the bed to pull her daughter close. "Remember what Mama told you? You must've been having a dream."

Yet even as she cuddled Ellie close, Sarah's gaze went to the bathroom door. It was ajar. It had been closed and locked from the inside when she put Ellie to bed, she was sure of it.

Was that footsteps? The creak of another door? Someone was in Adam's office. She put Ellie back onto the bed and grabbed a unicorn hobbyhorse, turning it to hold the soft end so she could strike with the pole. She threw open the bathroom door with a bang. The door to Adam's office was open, and she leaped through it with a hoarse shout, swinging the makeshift weapon hard enough to knock the wind out of . . . a stack of file boxes. The top one shifted enough to topple over, spilling stationery supplies.

Nobody was in there.

But someone had been. She was sure of it. The door from his office into the hallway was also ajar, and she couldn't recall if it had been that way when she went into Ellie's room, couldn't convince herself she *would* have noticed, since she'd been focused on her daughter.

Breathing hard, Sarah yanked open that door, still half expecting to see someone standing there, ready to fight anyone who stood between her and Ellie. The hall was empty. Ellie's door was open as Sarah had left it.

"Mama?"

"Be right there, ketzeleh."

"Meow, meow," Ellie called, and Sarah replied with a murmured "Meow" in response.

There. Downstairs, footsteps, creaking along the front entryway. The click of the front door opening, shutting. She ran for the stairs and pulled up short at the gate, which stood closed at the top of the steps. She didn't dare to climb over it and lost a few seconds fumbling with the latch and pulling it to lock behind her, well aware that Ellie was up and might come after her.

Would a fleeing intruder have bothered?

Yes, Sarah thought, if the shadowy stranger pretending to be Ellie's daddy didn't want the little girl to fall down the stairs. If the person who'd crept into her house in the night believed they had "Ellie's best interests at heart." By the time Sarah managed to get herself to the front door, she knew she wasn't going to find anyone.

She knew who it had been, though. Ava had left a key on the kitchen table, but clearly she'd made a copy before doing so. She'd come back when she thought Sarah was sleeping and gone upstairs to creep on Ellie. Maybe, Sarah thought with a chill horror working its way through her, to steal her away.

No. She shook her head. Ava wouldn't be stupid enough to abduct the child. So why sneak in?

To mess with Sarah's sanity.

Hadn't Graham said as much? He'd told her Adam had been worried about Sarah being too much like her mother. Unstable. Unfit.

His wife wanted children. They had paperwork that proved at least one of Ellie's parents wanted the Morgans to be her guardian. If something did happen to Sarah, who'd be first in line to take her?

They come in the night, Sarah. And do you know what they do? They dress up like your dad, and they try to make me go away with them.

Sarah had shared a lot of stories about her mother with Adam, but had she ever told him about that? If she had, might he have shared those words, her mother's fears, with Graham? The stuffed unicorn hobbyhorse suddenly weighed more than a brick, and she leaned it against the wall in the entryway. She tried the front door. Locked. She pressed her hands to it and let her forehead rest against the cool metal.

"Get. Your. Self. Together," she gritted through her teeth. Her jaw ached.

But she couldn't. Every breath seared her lungs. A stormy sea pitched waves in her stomach. Sweat gathered on her palms, her upper lip, her armpits, the small of her back.

Ava wasn't going to give up.

She was going to keep finding ways to pursue them. To make their lives miserable. She had the money and time to do it too. And what did Sarah have but debt?

No, she thought with a grim burst of triumph. She had something more than that.

She had an escape hatch.

13

"ARE YOU SURE you want to move all the way to Ohio? It's all so sudden." Linda pushed a glass of ice water across the table toward Sarah.

The seder had finished half an hour before, and Ellie, hopped up on sugary desserts, was happily playing with Linda's daughters. She'd crash soon, but that was all right. Sarah was taking advantage of the chance to sit and digest the enormous meal.

The Ruttenbergs' kitchen was as bright and warm as Linda herself. It wasn't her fault Sarah's insides had gone icy, that she felt on edge and unable to sit still. Her bouncing knee jostled the table and the drink. She forced herself to settle by pressing on it with her hand and gave Linda a dry smile.

"It's only temporary. A place to stay until the baby's born. Candace was generous enough to cover the cost of the movers and the flights, and I can start looking for remote work once I have a place to settle in. Adam loved it here, but I'm from the East Coast. California never really felt like a good fit."

This was true.

It was also true that she had to get far, far away from California and the Morgans. In Linda's comfy kitchen, it was easy to tell herself she'd been imagining the nightly trespassers, to talk herself out of believing Ava and Graham were going to actually *steal* her child and not just harass her into giving it up. Sarah had spent years fighting off worries that she was going to become like her mother, but she couldn't let that fear convince herself it wasn't really happening.

Linda sighed. "Please feel free to tell me to mind my own business. But didn't Adam . . . ? I mean, it wasn't unexpected."

"If you're trying to gently point out that we had plenty of time to prepare, you're absolutely right. I thought we had; he told me it was taken care of, and as far as I knew, it was." Sarah blinked away tears. The words slipped out of her before she could hold them back. She told Linda everything, watching the other woman's expression become more and more shocked with each revelation. The only thing she didn't reveal was Graham's rationale for why she might not be a competent mother.

"That's a lot to deal with," Linda said when Sarah finally fell silent.

"He left us, Linda, and not just because he died. He totally left us."

"He must not have been thinking clearly. Illness can do that to people—"

"That's a very nice and very kind way to put it."

Linda's brow wrinkled. "You don't think so?"

"He lied to me. For years. And even at the end, he kept lying to me. I'll never know why. To be honest, I don't think I even want to know. He's gone." She gave Linda a bald, honest stare. "If I'd found out any of this beforehand, I would have strongly considered it a test of our marriage."

"You think you'd have left him?" Linda looked surprised.

Sarah's shoulders hunched. "I don't know. It's been a huge betrayal. Not just finding out that his mother is, in fact, very much alive, but that he essentially sold our unborn child and our three-year-old to his business partner. They aren't even Jewish. I mean, if nothing else, what does that say about how little he valued our entire life together? Was it *all* a lie?"

"Hey. You can't think like that. Okay?" Linda reached across the table to take Sarah's hand. She squeezed gently.

"He always said he didn't convert for my sake. He did it because he really felt like it was the right choice for him. I never asked him to do it. I would never have done that!" Sarah's voice rose, and she looked into the family room, where a fading Ellie was firmly ensconced in front of a cartoon.

"Do you think he didn't really want to?"

"I never thought so before. Now I just don't know." Sarah sipped the cold water, but it didn't do much for the sweaty feeling in her palms, her armpits, her upper lip. "It was so much work to convert. Why would he have done it if he didn't really want to?"

They sat in silence for a moment.

"He loved you very much, Sarah. Anyone who knew the two of you could see that. Can you hold on to that?" Linda asked finally.

"I don't know." Sarah hated herself for saying so out loud, but any other answer would've been a lie, and there'd been far too many of those in her life lately. "Have you ever heard the saying *Never trust the man who tells you all his troubles but keeps from you all his joys?*"

Linda laughed softly. "Sure."

"Well, what about the man who shares all of his joys but keeps all of his troubles to himself? How is that a partnership? How can I trust anything he ever said or did, knowing that he kept so much from me? It's like I didn't know anything about him at all."

"I don't know, hon. I wish I had an answer for you." Linda patted Sarah's hand. "Is there some other way? I know people at the shul would be willing to help out—"

"I need to leave California, Linda. I don't trust Ava Morgan not to do something awful. She could call CPS, she could find out my new address and stalk me there, she could . . ." Sarah drew in a hitching breath. "She could pick up Ellie from preschool. I mean, Ellie would go right to her."

Saying it out loud sounded worse than thinking it, but if Linda thought she was being dramatic, she didn't show it on her face.

"You really think she'd do something like that?"

"She bought my *house* as a way to get closer to us," Sarah said. "I think she's capable of anything."

"You're not worried that Adam had good reason to cut his mother out of his life?"

Sarah took another sip of water, hoping it would ease the constant pressure of emotion in her throat. "She wasn't awful enough for him to stop sending her pictures of our child or updating her on our life or making me out to be some kind of horrible witch who didn't want him to have a mother. He's been in touch with her all this time, and I never knew it. He lied to us both. Candace wants the chance to know her grandchildren. I don't have any family of my own left . . . Ellie deserves a grandmother, I think."

Linda looked sad. "You deserve a soft place to land, that's what I know. Far away from that mamzer Graham and his wife. When do you leave?"

"The day after tomorrow. The movers packed up and shipped out a couple of days ago. I'll finish packing for me and Ellie tonight. Whatever didn't sell at the estate sale or get sent to Candace's house, I'm leaving behind. The Morgans can deal with it." Sarah let out a hoarse chuckle. "We're basically fleeing in the night. I don't want them to have any idea where we went."

"I won't tell anyone, if anyone asks." Linda sighed again. "You'll keep in touch with us, though? Let us know you're doing all right?"

"I will. Of course. Thank you for everything."

Linda clearly wanted to say something more but hesitated. Finally, she said, "His mother isn't Jewish."

"No, but she told me all about the Easter seder her late husband had held for their church."

Linda grimaced. "Ah. One of those."

"Yeah." Sarah laughed hoarsely. "Anyway, Adam was always the one who wanted to be more observant. He said keeping kosher was hard but important, *because* it was hard."

"You weren't religious when you met?"

"Spiritual. Religious, but not observant. I was raised more Reform than anything else. And barely that. My mom never belonged to a synagogue." Sarah spun the glass in her hands—slowly, so it didn't splash. "Now I wonder if he really believed anything he told me or if he was somehow just trying to do what he thought his parents would hate the most."

"Does it matter?"

"Not anymore," Sarah said.

"I've never heard of Shelter Grove. How are you going to like living in Ohio? It's not the East Coast either. You're going to be a nice midwestern girl." Linda smiled.

Sarah returned the smile. "I'll take up casserole making and start calling soda *pop*. How bad could it be?"

"Not bad at all, I hope."

"It can't be any worse than it is here," Sarah said.

* * *

An entire life, distilled into a small moving truck and a few suitcases.

Sarah's mother had always declared she didn't hold on to things for memory's sake. The towering boxes of old junk mail, stacks of books, and plastic grocery bags stuffed with other garbage kept anyone from being able to break in at night and "get her." Tossing even a single grocery story flyer could bring down the unnamed malevolent forces supposedly trying to lure her from the protection of her garbage fortress and out into . . . wherever it was she thought they meant to take her. Her stuff somehow kept her safe.

Safety for Sarah and Ellie meant dumping everything but the necessities, Sarah thought as she made one last pass through the kitchen to make sure she hadn't left behind anything she really wanted to keep. Maybe she shouldn't take such satisfaction in picturing Ava's face the next time she let herself into the house, only to find it barren of anything important and still chock-full of a bunch of stuff she'd have to get rid of. She wanted the house? Let her deal with the four years' of accumulated junk, outdated furniture they'd meant to replace, half-used bottles of floor cleaner. Oh, and the hole in the ceiling, Sarah thought with a chuckle. They could have it all.

The car would be here in a couple of hours to take her and Ellie to the airport. Candace had already flown home and would pick them up in Columbus tomorrow afternoon. All Sarah had to do was get herself ready to go.

She'd jokingly told Linda they were fleeing in the night, but that was literally what they were doing. She'd changed all of the information on their bills but had also secured a mail-forwarding service that would hold all of her mail and packages and allow her to screen it and choose what she wanted sent. It had an address in California, so if either Ava or Graham did manage to find out the forwarding address and try to show up at her "new house," they'd end up at an office building.

Maybe she was being a little extreme, but she didn't trust them. If Adam truly had told Graham he was worried she was mentally unstable, she wouldn't put it past him to use that information as leverage. Children were taken from their parents every day. She wasn't being paranoid. She was being . . . careful.

She was doing whatever it took to keep her children safe.

14

"WE HAVE TWELVE acres," Candace said proudly as she turned off Shelter Grove's Main Street and onto a smaller state road that led them out of town.

"How far from town are you?" The drive from Columbus had taken almost two hours. The state route was rapidly turning into a rural, two-lane road wending its way into a sparse forest growing thicker by the minute.

"A few more miles," Candace said as she took another turn, this time onto an even narrower road. "We're almost home."

Sarah looked out the window. They hadn't passed any other cars since leaving town. A small break in the trees revealed another, even-smaller road. It looked paved, but barely, with a lot of gravel and potholes. A large white sign painted with black letters stood at the end of it.

Candace slowed as they passed. "That's where our church was. See that sign? Blood of the Lamb. Look out the window, Ellie! That's where Nanna and Pop-Pop's church used to be!"

Ellie didn't care about a man she'd never met, and she didn't even know what a church was. Sarah craned her neck to watch, though, as the sign fell out of sight behind them. "Used to be?"

"There was a fire," Candace said after a moment.

Sarah looked at her. "Oh, I'm sorry."

"Vandals did it," Candace said. "The police said it was an accident, kids messing around with firecrackers, but I think they knew exactly what they were doing."

"And you didn't rebuild?"

"Peter was already gone. Henry wasn't here to take his place. That arrogant Pastor Steve swooped right in with his promises that he'd only 'take care' of the flock until Henry came back . . . well. Henry never did come back, and Steve's got a fancy big church and modern sermons. One day we'll rebuild ours, but congregations need someone to lead them."

"You couldn't lead it?"

Candace burst into laughter. "Me? Oh my, no. That's not a job for a woman. I can't even imagine it!"

Sarah didn't have much of a reply to that. She didn't have much experience with pastors poaching church congregations, but she'd been in a few board meetings when the synagogue committee was voting on which new rabbi to hire. It wasn't quite Battle Royale, but it did get heated.

What she couldn't wrap her mind around was the concept of Adam being a pastor for a church called the Blood of the Lamb. Adam, the man who'd belonged to the Men's Club at Temple Beth Or so he could study the Daf Yomi. He'd led their seders every year with a Haggadah he'd put together himself. A memory of him in his kippa and tallit, swaying as he prayed during Yom Kippur services, was overlaid with another of him standing in front of a giant crucifix like a television evangelist . . . she could *imagine* it, but it didn't feel realistic. Her husband had embraced his chosen faith with enthusiasm, passion, and commitment. If he'd done it for her, he'd also done it with his whole heart.

The road narrowed, the trees closing in as they turned a final sharp corner. The house rose up, up, up, beyond the trees that had shielded any sight of it until now. More stately evergreens surrounded the sparse and patchy lawn. Some even spread their sweeping, needled branches close enough to brush the house, and more than a few were so tall their tops inched above the roofline.

"Home sweet home!" Candace twisted in the driver's seat to grin at Sarah.

Sarah murmured her response, watching through the car window as they pulled into a circular driveway in front of the massive house. What she'd taken for a narrow country road had been entirely

the driveway, she realized now. Adam had rarely spoken of his childhood, but when he did, he'd always said he lived in a "cottage." This
was an enormous brick-and-stone building set into a slope so that it
had three full stories of living space. A McMansion cobbled together
from several different architectures, none of them particularly well
represented. It was ugly but undeniably grand.

"Did Adam grow up in this house?" Maybe Candace had moved
here after her son left for college. Maybe Adam really had grown up
in a small house the way he'd said. Maybe this wasn't yet one more
lie he'd told her. Yet another deception.

"Of course he did. His father built this house for me as a wedding gift. We spent our wedding night here, and our honeymoon.
And poof!" Candace laughed. "Exactly nine months later, on the
dot, out popped Henry!"

Pregnancy didn't really work that way, but Sarah wasn't going to
argue with her. "Wow."

Candace shut off the ignition. "I'll pull into the garage when
we've unloaded. Sarah, honey, you go ahead into the house. I'll bring
in Miss Princess."

"She'll be cranky if you wake her," Sarah began, then dropped it.
If Candace wanted to deal with a tantrumming toddler, fine with
her. She desperately needed the bathroom.

The morning sickness that had plagued her in the first months
still tried to get her now and then, when she'd gone too long without
eating or because of motion sickness. Her acupuncture wrist bands
and ginger chews had fought off her nausea well enough for her to
get through the trip without needing her mother-in-law to pull over
so she could puke, but now the gravel stones of the driveway threatened to roll under her feet. No, it was the ground itself, swelling and
rolling and making her steps unsteady. Sarah put a hand on the top
of the car door, hesitant to let go in case she fell over.

It's all going to be okay.
You're going to be safe here.
They won't find you.

All the windows on the lower floor were barred. Sarah hesitated,
looking around the yard of patchy grass and the trees surrounding it.
The first house she and Adam had owned featured bars on the windows and doors, but it was in an urban neighborhood with a bad
reputation. This place was in the middle of nowhere. They hadn't
even passed any other houses along the driveway.

"Vandals," Candace said again when she caught Sarah's curious look. "They come around, causing trouble."

"It's so rural, I didn't think you'd need anything like that."

Candace pressed her lips together. "Well, we're out in here in the middle of nowhere, I'm sure you understand. Two women out here all by ourselves. Four now. Those hooligans from the town like to cross my property so they can get into the woods, where they drink and cavort and get up to all kinds of shenanigans. They already burned down the church. I can't take any chances."

"Are they violent?" Sarah frowned.

Candace softened. "They like to play pranks. Ring the doorbell and run, put bags of dog waste on the porch and light it on fire. Stupid things. It was never an issue when Peter was alive. They knew better than to cause trouble out here then. But since he's passed, they've gotten . . . bolder. I don't trust any of them. I've had things go missing. There's been vandalism."

"They've broken into the house? Stolen things?" Sarah's nose wrinkled at the thought.

"I could never prove it, but I know it was them. Don't you worry about it, though, honey," Candace added quickly at the sight of Sarah's concerned expression. "They might sometimes still make a ruckus outside, but they know better than to try and get in here again."

Sarah closed her eyes. Drew in a breath. Blew it out. She appreciated the cool, early May breeze fending off the imminent nausea, but she was also a little too cold. She reached into the back seat for the Adam's cardigan and shrugged into it, pulling the fabric collar up to take another long, deep breath. His scent had begun to fade. Tears prickled. She ought to have sealed it up in plastic, taken it out only to take a whiff, then put it back. She should have preserved it, but putting it on had always reminded her of having his arms around her. Not a substitute. Only memories.

"Come on, then, Miss Princess, come to Nanna. There's my darling girly."

Sarah bent to look into the car. She expected Candace's coos to be torn into shreds by Ellie's shrieking protests, but the little girl simply blinked and looked around, saw her mother, and seemed comforted. She didn't fuss as Candace struggled to unbuckle the car seat.

"I can help," Sarah offered.

Candace handed her a set of jangling keys. "You go on inside, honey. Aren't you about dying for the private room? I would be, if I were you."

Sarah watched her mother-in-law tug the complicated series of buckles and straps. "It's hard unless you know how to do it. Let me show you."

"Things are only as hard as you let them be," Candace said, and let out a satisfied noise when the buckle finally popped open. She shot Sarah a triumphant grin. "See? Nanna knows how to do it. Come on, my precious little one. Let Nanna take you inside."

Sarah was going to pee her pants if she didn't get to a toilet soon. She headed for the house.

Flanked by sidelight windows and an overhead transom, the heavily carved double doors would've been well suited to a medieval castle. Each bore an elaborate brass knocker in the shape of a man's face framed by leaves and ivy.

Sarah's heart twisted at the sight. "The green man," she whispered. Adam had once shown her an identical door knocker in a catalog and had spoken so longingly of it that she'd bought him one just like these for his birthday. She'd left it behind on the door she no longer owned.

None of the keys were marked, so it took her a minute to find the right one. The pressure on her bladder had grown intense enough that she had to press her thighs together and take mincing steps. She sent up a plea that she wouldn't let loose right there in the foyer and hobbled as fast as she could into the small powder room, fumbling to pull her leggings and panties down to her thighs as she sat. A flood of urine was already cascading out of her as her bottom met the wooden seat, and it rang out against the porcelain loudly enough to be embarrassing. She couldn't care too much, though; the relief was so intense she let out a little moan, stifled it with both hands, began to guffaw. Her laughter sounded rough as sobs, so she pressed her hands harder against her lips, mashing them into her teeth. As her bladder emptied, she noticed for the first time the framed portrait hung over the mirror at the sink.

At least sixteen by twenty, the print featured a man with flowing, flaxen hair, soulful blue eyes, and an Elvis pout. White robes hung from broad shoulders draped with a red sash, and one hand lifted in a gesture she supposed was meant as beneficence but looked to her like Obi-Wan Kenobi convincing the curious Stormtroopers these were not the droids they were looking for.

Now she was shrieking with silent, gut-wrenching laughter. She tasted salt and bitterness. Jedi Jesus looked down at her with a smug little smirk, and she had to look away or else she'd never get herself under control.

The rest of the room was no better. Carved crucifixes hung on the wall above the towel rack. More frames held single words in an ornate script.

Faith.

God.

Home.

The soap dispenser was in the shape of a Bible, the pump rising up from its open pages. Sarah finished with the toilet but hesitated about using a holy text to squirt soap into her open palm. Since it wasn't a real Bible, she finally did. She also took a second or so to run the water from the cold faucet. It was shockingly frigid straight from the tap, and she cupped it in her hands to splash onto her face, then drank greedily. Then again. She used one of the hand towels to blot her face dry.

"Sarah? You all right in there, honey? You're not sick, are you?"

Quickly, Sarah gave herself a glance. She looked . . . not great, but passable. The shadows under her eyes weren't any bigger anyway, even if her hair looked as though she'd combed it with a whirlwind.

"I'm fine." She opened the door, a smile pasted on her lips. "Phew, did I ever need that!"

Candace hitched Ellie higher on her hip. The little girl looked rumpled but wide-eyed. She held a sucker in each hand but didn't seem to know what to do with them.

"Nanna gave her little precious a treat from the candy jar, for being such a good girl." Candace rubbed her nose against Ellie's cheek, then looked at Sarah. "I had Honor start taking all of your things upstairs. I know you'll want a house tour, but let's get you a little treat too, what do you say? You have to keep up your strength!"

As if on cue, Sarah's stomach rumbled, and she put her hand on it. Her last full meal had been a meager sandwich on the flight. "That sounds great. Thank you, Candace."

Candace dipped her head in a nod. As she turned, Sarah reached to snag her sleeve. The older woman turned back, eyebrows raised.

"I mean it," Sarah told her. "You've been beyond kind. I'm not sure what we'd have done without you."

This time, Candace's nod was slower. Solemn. She kissed Ellie's cheek.

"Honey, you don't have to thank me for doing my motherly duty. What kind of horrible person would I be if I didn't do everything I could to help my babies? You and Ellie," she said, and added with a look at Sarah's belly, "and our little prince."

Sarah laughed self-consciously. "We don't know if it's a boy or a girl. I chose not to find out."

Candace's eyes twinkled, and she winked. "I just have a feeling, and when I tell you it's one of my gifts, you should believe me, honey. I always know."

At the sound of footsteps behind her, Sarah let out a soft, startled sigh and turned. Standing in the kitchen doorway was a young, blonde woman wearing an apron over a modestly cut, long-sleeved gown in a soft floral pattern that looked like it had been popular when this house had been built. She carried a vacuum, which she set down with a thump that made Sarah jump.

Candace didn't even turn. "Oh, that's Honor."

"Hello," Sarah said.

Honor grunted a response and turned on her heel.

"Don't mind her," Candace said in a low voice, with a dismissive wave. "She'll get used to you."

Looking at the size of the house, Sarah couldn't be surprised Candace had a housekeeper, but it did seem like something she'd have mentioned before, if only in passing. Maybe, Sarah thought dryly, Adam had learned the art of omission from his mother. *A don't ask, don't tell* sort of policy about life. She'd just have to be sure to ask, then, wouldn't she?

That way, she wouldn't be surprised again.

CHAPTER

15

"How about a nice omelet? You need a good breakfast." Candace jounced Ellie on her hip before settling her into an oversized high chair next to the round, blond-wood table centered in the breakfast nook.

"No!" Ellie squirmed in the chair, fighting Candace's attempts to slide the tray into place.

"She's too big for that, Candace. She can sit at the table."

Candace frowned. "I don't have a booster."

"Mamaaaaaa!"

Sarah moved forward, gently moving Candace to the side and taking the high chair tray from her. "If we leave this off, we can pull the chair right up to the table, then. Ellie, look. You have your own special chair."

"I not baby!" Ellie growled, crossing her little arms.

"Of course you are a baby, you're my precious baby," Candace said, earning a scowl from Ellie.

Sarah took a deep breath. Her daughter had been strong-willed since birth, much the way Sarah had been, according to the complaints Sarah's own mother had often made. Or stubborn the way Adam's mother had described him? Either way, the kid had no problem making her wishes known.

"Ellison," Sarah said firmly, making strong eye contact. "This is not a baby chair. Nanna doesn't have a booster seat, so this is where you'll sit. And if you don't behave and sit like a big girl, you won't be allowed to have any more treats."

"Oh, don't tell her that, Sarah, of course Nanna will still give her treats."

Sarah drew herself up to face her mother-in-law. Ellie had settled down already, both from the use of her full name and the threat of not getting treats, but Sarah couldn't let Candace's interference slide. "Candace, we don't reward bad behavior, and especially not with treats."

Candace blinked. A swift but dour expression twisted itself across her face before a sweet, soft smile replaced it. She inclined her head. "Of course." A pause. "You called her Ellison."

"That's her name."

Candace coughed lightly into her fist. "I thought it was Eleanor."

"Did her father tell you that?"

"No, but . . . Eleanor was my mother's name. I suppose I just assumed Henry would have named his daughter after someone in his family. Especially since he . . ." She coughed again and straightened her shoulders, not meeting Sarah's eyes. Her cheeks had gone pink. "Well, never mind."

"We named her after my mother." Sarah kept her tone gentle, hating the awkwardness, empathizing with Candace's hurt feelings. Her son had clearly had his reasons for shutting her out of his life, but that didn't mean she wasn't entitled to feel whatever way about it that she did.

"Your mother was named Ellison?"

"My mother's maiden name was Ellison," Sarah explained.

"What was her Christian name?"

"Her *first* name was Amy."

"And her middle name? Ellie's, I mean."

"Her full name is Ellison Charlotte," Sarah said.

Candace beamed. "Oh, then he might have named her after me too! C for Candace!"

"He might have," Sarah conceded without adding that Adam had certainly never mentioned it. In Jewish tradition, it was bad luck to name your child after someone still living. But, knowing now how very many things her husband hadn't mentioned, it was entirely possible that he'd agreed to use a C name for the sake of a mother he'd said was dead.

Candace zipped over to the fridge to pull out a container of eggs, then a package of cheese and another of mushrooms. "Will all of this be okay?"

"Yes. That'll be fine, Candace. I can make it, if you want."

"No, no, it'll be my pleasure to cook for you. You've had such a long day, all that overnight travel, and then our long drive. And besides"—Candace dipped her chin toward Sarah—"I'm fussy about my kitchen."

"Fair enough." Sarah took a seat next to Ellie and watched Candace bustle.

She had very expensive stainless-steel pots and pans, and she cooked up the omelet with the practice of someone who had culinary training: swirling the butter in the pan, beating the eggs just so, folding the creation without breaking it.

"Were you a chef?"

Candace laughed as she slid the omelet, cut in half, onto two plates. "I was a labor-and-delivery nurse for years and years, and then I trained to become a licensed midwife. I suppose Henry never mentioned that."

"It's going to feel awkward for a long time, isn't it?" Sarah said. It was a statement, not a question.

Candace looked at her. "Yes. I guess it will."

"We'll have to get through it together, that's all."

"Yes," Candace said after a second. "Together. Exactly."

With breakfast finished, Candace took them on a tour of the house. Kitchen, family room, formal living room, laundry room, garage, a four-seasons room toward the back of the house. Many of the rooms were shadowed, the blinds drawn over the barred windows, and had the quiet air of spaces left usually unoccupied. Candace took them out a set of French doors from the kitchen and across a large, shaded deck to stare out at the woods.

"It's so peaceful here," Sarah said. She thought of the barred windows. No way Ava or anyone else would be able to let herself into Candace's house. She felt much safer here already than she ever had with her mother's booby traps made from broken kitchen utensils.

Ellie tugged at Sarah's hand, and Sarah released her. The little girl ran to the edge of the deck but stopped at the top of the three steps. She looked over her shoulder.

"You can play in the yard, but stay away from the woods," Candace called. "You don't want the boogeyman to come get you!"

"Candace," Sarah protested, but her mother-in-law laughed.

"Look, she's not even scared. Henry never was either. Both of you need to stay out of the woods, though. That's the truth. We have bears. Coyotes. Snakes. And *skunks*." Candace waved a hand in front of her face. "Pew. You surely don't want to tangle with one of those. When did you say the moving truck would be here?"

"They said it would take about a week. They'll text me updates."

"Why don't we go inside and you can see your rooms? I bet you want to settle in."

Upstairs, they passed a closed door Candace casually pointed out had been Peter's office. Honor's door was also closed. The room Candace showed off for Sarah was furnished with high-end, classic pieces and a decor so neutral it was clear the room had been meant for guests, not family. A familiar bentwood rocker graced one corner.

"Adam bought me one of those when I was pregnant with Ellie." It was on the moving truck, one of the few pieces of furniture Sarah had kept.

"That's the one I sat in when I nursed him," Candace said.

A tender silence fell between them.

"Let's finish the tour," Candace said abruptly.

Ellie's room was far at the other end of the hall near Candace's bedroom.

"And here. This is the room all set up for Nanna's little princess." Candace opened the door with a flourish and led Ellie by the hand into it.

Sarah heard her daughter's cry of delight before she could see what was inside, but as soon as she entered the room, she let out her own low cry of surprise. "Oh. Wow."

Pale-pink walls sparkled with some kind of opalescence. A pink-draped canopy bed angled out from the corner next to the deep-set window alcove, featuring a stuffed window seat laden with a pile of pillows in all shades of pink. Pink, plush rugs dotted the hardwood floor. A large toy box revealed a cascade of games, dolls, stuffed animals, and what looked like costumes. A tall dresser and vanity, both of white wood, matched the bed. Heavy, ornate furniture suited for a . . . well, Sarah thought wryly, a French provincial princess.

"Did you get all of this just for Ellie?"

Candace smiled broadly. "Oh, the bedroom suite was mine from when I was a little girl. *My* princess furniture. I was my daddy's princess, wasn't I, my sweet Ellie? Just like I bet you were yours."

Ellie had beelined straight for the toy box, and now she turned with wide eyes. "I can play, Mama?"

"Of course you can, sweetie-girl, these are all for you. Nanna had quite a shopping spree before you got here." Candace knelt beside the toy box with a heavy groan. She started sorting out toys from it, handing a doll to Ellie, then a princess dress. She looked over her shoulder at Sarah. "What about you?"

Sarah had been peeking into the closet, which was hung with racks of clothes, all brand-new and in Ellie's size. She went to the window now to look out across the backyard. It took her a moment to answer—brain fog. She'd barely slept on the red-eye flight, and the rush of travel was wearing off. Somehow it had become the afternoon, but she was ready for bed. "Hmm?"

"Your father," Candace said. "Were you a daddy's girl? A little princess?"

"Ahh . . . no, not so much. Although my name does mean princess." Sarah's laugh scratched in her throat, which had gone thick with self-consciousness.

Candace got to her feet with a concerted effort. "Oh? But what about your relationship with your father? Before he passed, I mean."

Sarah crossed the room to help Ellie wrestle a frilly dress over her head. She tugged the fabric over the little girl's shoulders, straightening it. She stroked Ellie's tangled hair, which was in need of a good scrub. "He was great."

All these years later, and talking about her parents still choked her up. It was why she'd never pressed Adam to speak about his mother. He'd told Sarah she was dead, and she'd sympathized. As she thought of that now, a fresh claw of anger scratched at her throat. A new slice of sorrow.

"What kind of people do you come from, Sarah?" Candace pulled a glittery fabric star stuck to the end of a stick from the toy box and pressed it into Ellie's hand. "Here, sweetie-girl. A fairy princess needs a good wand."

Sarah frowned. "What kind of people? I'm not sure what you mean."

Candace fussed with Ellie's hair, then pulled out a cone-shaped princess hat with a trailing, sparkly ribbon coming out the top. She slipped it onto Ellie's head and fit the elastic strap under her chin, which she chucked gently. Without looking at Sarah, she said, "Oh, you know. Where were they from?"

"New York. New Jersey."

Candace gave Sarah a sideways glance. "Do you still have family there?"

"My parents were both only children. My grandparents . . . well, they were all very young when they came here with their own parents. They'd left their families behind." Sarah cut herself off, not wanting to get into more explanation with Ellie right there.

"Where'd they leave them?"

"Germany. Poland."

"So you have people overseas," Candace said.

Sarah pressed both hands to her belly and the baby inside it. "No. My great-grandparents' families were all lost in the Shoah. The Holocaust."

Candace gasped, her French-manicured fingertips flying to cover her mouth. "Oh! How terrible!"

Ellie gave them both a curious glance. Sarah tried to give Candace a silent warning, but her mother-in-law didn't seem to get it. She pulled Sarah into an embrace Sarah didn't want but didn't try to fight.

"Oh, what a terrible thing," Candace said over and over, patting Sarah's back. "Oh my goodness. What a tragedy."

Sarah's tears surprised her—she'd grown up knowing about her family's loss, of course, in stories told by all four grandparents as well as her mom and dad, but she'd rarely wept over it. The ending of a family line because of the Holocaust was something many of her friends growing up had also experienced, something to be recognized, of course, but not fresh like an open wound. Not like the loss of Adam had been and still was and would be for a long time.

"I know what will make you feel better," Candace said cheerfully, pulling away with a bright smile. "Come on. I have a surprise for you."

CHAPTER

16

SARAH MARVELED AT the closet full of brand-new clothes. Maternity dresses, leggings, tunic tops. Packages of cotton panties and soft bras in the dresser drawers. Nightgowns. Even a soft robe and slippers had been hung on the back of the door the way a fancy hotel would do it.

"Candace . . . I don't know what to say."

"If a new outfit can't make you feel better, what can?" Candace continued showing off the items in the dressers. Adam had often used that same phrasing, if not the exact words. Candace opened the armoire door and turned with another broad smile. "And in here, well, I just went a little wild."

Sarah looked around her to see racks of baby clothes, mostly in blues and greens and yellows. Her mouth gaped before she thought to close it. She covered it with a hand.

"You don't like it?" Candace asked anxiously.

"It's just . . . we don't buy new things for an unborn baby." Like naming a child after someone still living, preparing a nursery before a baby's birth was considered to be bad luck. "Because of ayin hara . . . um . . . evil eye."

Embarrassment tickled Sarah's cheeks.

Candace put a hand to the base of her throat, clutching nonexistent pearls.

"We just try not to invite envy," Sarah tried to explain.

"Well, who on earth would envy you in this house? Your baby is a blessing, who would envy that?" Candace looked disgruntled. "But if you don't want any of this, I guess I could just throw it right into the trash."

"You don't have to do that," Sarah said hastily as Candace moved toward the armoire. "It's superstition, that's all."

Candace sounded stiff when she replied. "You can just keep it locked up in here and not look at it until he gets here."

"I can. Absolutely. Thank you, Candace. You've been beyond generous."

Her mother-in-law looked mollified. "I wanted you to have everything you could need, that's all. Especially since the moving company won't be here with your things for a while. I thought I was helping, but what do I know? I'm just an anxious Nanna."

"I really appreciate it. I do. All the help with the moving expenses, having us stay . . . I hope you'll at least let me contribute to the household while we're here," Sarah said.

Candace let out a delicate snort. "Don't be silly. You're *family*. You let me take care of you and Ellie, all right? Now, why don't you take a nice shower and put on something fresh and comfy? I know after I've been traveling, I always want to get out of my dirty clothes. You can toss them in the basket, and Honor will wash them for you. Ellie's too."

"I should make sure she's—"

"I'll go play with her," Candace said. "She's right down the hall. You take your time."

"Thank you," Sarah repeated.

This was what she needed. Another set of hands and eyes, another heart to love and care for her child. To assist her, not replace her. Ava and Graham had both insinuated that Sarah couldn't handle motherhood on her own, but instead of truly helping her, they'd tried to take it away from her completely.

When Candace left the room, Sarah gathered the robe and slippers and some clothes from her suitcase. On second thought, she put them back and pulled a new pair of leggings and a tunic top from the hangers in the closet and held them up to herself, looking at the mirror hung on the back of the door. They were the right size, and the muted navy and gray tones were flattering. She held the soft fabric to her cheek for a moment, eyes closed.

She could let herself be taken care of, couldn't she?

In the bathroom down the hall, she luxuriated in the shower, which had been outfitted with high-end shampoo and conditioner and body scrub all arranged in a rack hanging over the shower head. A smaller basket full of clearly used products rested on the tub's corner. Fresh lavender towels that matched the flowered wallpaper had been laid out on the double sink's counter. A pale-yellow set, not threadbare but definitely not new, hung on one of the towel racks. Next to the right-hand sink was fresh toothpaste and a toothbrush, both still in their original packaging. The medicine cabinet over that sink was empty, but when she peeked in the other one she saw deodorant, face cream, and other personal items. Honor's things. Sarah left them alone.

Ellie's laughter lilted down the hall to her when she came out of the bathroom, so Sarah went directly to her room. She took her time combing out her hair and dressing, her door open so she could listen for any signs of distress. Candace had been right; a shower and fresh clothes had done wonders.

"Your laundry?"

Sarah looked up to see Honor in the doorway, holding a basket she thrust forward.

"Oh . . . yes, hang on a second." She tossed the clothes she'd been wearing into the basket. "Thanks. I appreciate it."

"What about that?" Honor jerked her chin toward the cardigan on the bed.

"That was my husband's. I don't want that to be washed right now. Thank you."

Honor backed up a step, the basket held close to her. "If there's anything else, you can just put it your basket and leave it in the hallway, and I'll take care of it."

"Thank you."

"Candace said we're having dinner soon." Honor took another step back so Sarah had to move forward to keep her in sight.

"It feels like we just had breakfast." Sarah patted her belly with a laugh. "But that sounds great. Can I help with anything, or . . . ?"

"No." That solid single word left no room for argument, and Honor ended the conversation by leaving.

All righty, then. That was not a likely friendship in the making. As Sarah turned to her carry-on to pull out Adam's laptop, hoping to get online and check her emails, Candace knocked lightly on the doorframe. She held out a small, square book.

"I thought you might like to look at these." She moved closer, flipping the pages to show off the photos.

Together, they sat on the edge of the bed. Sarah opened the photo album carefully, holding her breath. A very pregnant Candace stood in front of this house, a tall, blond man next to her. The next were baby pictures, and then some of toddler Adam. Sarah traced his tiny face, seeing Ellie there. She looked at Candace.

"These are wonderful. Thank you for showing them to me."

"I can make copies of them, if you'd like." Candace tilted her head, looking quizzical. "He never showed you any pictures of himself as a little boy?"

"He said he didn't have any."

"You didn't think that was weird?"

"I don't have any photos from when I was young either. My mother's house flooded during Hurricane Sandy. Everything was ruined. I figured something like that might've happened to his baby pictures too." Sarah paused. "We just never talked about it."

Candace gently took the photo album from Sarah's hands and flipped through it again before closing it. Her shoulders hunched for a moment. Then she straightened and stood. "I've got to get down there and supervise Honor making the dinner. She tries hard, bless her, but she's more apt to break something than make it, and oh my, she's slower than a snail with a blister on its toe."

"Sounds great. If you need me to do anything, just let me know, okay?"

Candace patted her shoulder. "Not tonight. You get settled in. I'll call you down when it's ready."

"I'll go see what Ellie's up to," Sarah said.

Ellie was happily playing with the large dollhouse in the corner of her extravagant bedroom. Sarah carefully eased onto the floor with her, watching as the little girl had the mama doll tuck the baby doll into its miniature crib. Ellie rocked it with one chubby finger and looked at her mother.

"Baby sleepin'."

"That's nice. What's the baby's name?"

Ellie's face screwed up as she thought. "Pancake."

Sarah laughed. She and Adam had planned to tell Ellie about the new baby together, but he'd faded so fast at the end they hadn't had the chance. Now she scooted forward to pull Ellie onto her lap. "What would you think about having a new baby brother or sister?"

Ellie looked up at her. "No."

This should be interesting. "You don't want a baby brother or sister?"

"No," Ellie said, snuggling into Sarah's embrace. She still held the mama doll in her fist. "I Mama's baby."

"You'll always be my baby. But there's another baby in Mama's belly."

Ellie leaned back to look at Sarah's stomach, then tugged up her top to poke it. Sarah laughed and held Ellie's hands to stave off another poke. Ellie struggled off Sarah's lap and bent back to the dollhouse. She walked the mama doll over to the baby's crib and bent it over.

"Laila tov, baby," she said.

So much for unbridled enthusiasm, Sarah thought, but didn't pursue the conversation. There'd be plenty of time to get Ellie used to the idea of a new sibling. For now, just as she'd said, *she* was Sarah's baby.

While Ellie played, Sarah unpacked her suitcase—not that she really needed anything they'd brought, since Candace had provided far more than Ellie could possibly wear or use. There were the favorite stuffies to be placed just so on the bed and some books, including Adam's childhood copy of *The Little Prince*, which Sarah put in the bookcase. After that, she took the luxury of her free time to sit and play with Ellie and the dollhouse. It had been a long time since she'd simply played this way, without distractions, without feeling torn in several directions at once. Since before Adam had gone into the hospital.

Before she knew it, a couple of hours had passed as she and Ellie explored all the delights of the giant toy box. Sarah had pulled the girl into an embrace for a ticklefest, both of them laughing, when she looked up to see Honor standing in the doorway. Whatever expression the housekeeper had been wearing before Sarah faced her, it faded quickly away into blankness.

"Dinner," Honor said.

"We'll be right down."

"I'm not going to clean up all that mess," Honor said after a second.

"Of course not. I'll take care of it."

They stared at each other while Ellie looked back and forth between them. Honor reached a hesitant hand toward the little girl, then let it fall back to her side. She squared her shoulders.

"I can take her downstairs, if you want."

"I'll come down now. I can clean this up at bedtime. She might play some more after dinner." Sarah heaved herself to her feet, noticing how much harder it was to do that than it had been even a few weeks ago. "C'mon, ketzeleh. Time for dinner. Are you hungry?"

She carefully feigned nonchalance and wouldn't even look at Honor as she took Ellie's hand. She didn't need to exacerbate any tension between them—the housekeeper had already seemed totally put out by being given new responsibilities. Honor was gone by the time Sarah and Ellie came out of the room.

Candace peppered the dinner conversation with questions about Adam and their life in California. Because she seemed starved for that information, Sarah did her best to answer without asking too many questions of her own. There'd be plenty of time to ask Candace about her son and his life before Sarah met him.

"You sit," Candace commanded when Sarah started clearing the table after they'd finished eating. "Honor will take care of all that. And I'm going to take Miss Princess Sweetie-Pie upstairs to play while you relax yourself."

Sarah laughed at Candace's shaking finger and mock scowl. "No arguing from me."

When she started to open the French doors to the deck, though, Candace startled her with a screamed "No!"

Startled, Sarah backed up a few steps, hands in the air. "Sorry! What's wrong? I was just hoping to go sit outside for a bit to get some fresh air."

"If you want to go in and out, you need to disarm the system."

"I'm sorry, I didn't know." Sarah paused. "You leave it on all the time?"

"I'm a silly old woman, I guess, jumping at my own shadow." Just like that, Candace's grim expression lightened up. "If you want to sit out on the deck for a little while, it couldn't hurt. Just remember, you can't go out any of the doors without tripping the alarm. I'll have to turn it off for you. It's getting dark, though . . . and it's probably chilly. Are you sure you want to sit out there?"

"I don't have to go outside tonight. I can relax with a book or something." Tomorrow she'd ask for the code and instructions on how to use the system. Tonight it might be best to let them all settle in and get used to being here, Candace included.

"I'm so glad you're here. I really am. I want you to feel welcome here, Sarah. You and Ellie are a gift I never thought I'd be blessed with. I'm so grateful." Before Sarah could say anything, Candace let go of Ellie's hand to take both of Sarah's. Squeezing them, she lifted her eyes to the ceiling and said, "Thank you, Jesus, my Lamb and Savior, for bringing me Sarah and Ellie to love and care for. Watch over my dear Henry, and all of us. Jesus' name, amen."

She gave Sarah an expectant look.

Sarah gently extricated her hands from Candace's grip. She pulled Adam's cardigan from the back of the kitchen chair and shrugged into it. "I'll go grab my book. It'll be time to get Ellie ready for bed soon."

"Are you cold? I can turn up the heat. Or bring you extra blankets. I always ran so hot when I was pregnant with Henry."

"I've got my sweater. Well, it's my husband's sweater. *Was* his." The words tumbled around before clumsily falling off her tongue. Referring to him that way felt precious and pretentious, but she couldn't bring herself to call him Henry, and it was clear Candace wasn't going to start calling him Adam.

Candace's upper lip quivered. She pressed a hand to her heart. "Oh. I see. That must be a comfort to you. Having his things."

"I didn't keep everything. But this was one of his favorites." Sarah drew it around herself, hoping Candace wasn't going to burst into tears, especially not in front of Ellie. Sarah would join in— they'd both dissolve into grief, and there would be awkwardness about who was supposed to comfort whom.

Candace's mouth turned down at the corners. She touched Ellie's hair. Then, quickly, before Sarah could stop her, she pressed both hands onto Sarah's belly. "You had more of him than I ever had."

Sarah chuckled uncomfortably, inching away from Candace's hands. What was it about pregnant bellies that made people think they could touch without asking first? And what could she even say to Adam's mother in reply? Candace had had him for eighteen years, Sarah only ten.

"Come on, my precious princess, let Nanna take you upstairs. We can play with your dollies." Candace didn't seem to need a reply from Sarah and instead swept Ellie up into her arms and carried her off while Sarah watched, bemused.

As she pulled her cardigan around her throat, though, she thought about their earlier conversation. *Who on earth would envy you in this house?*

Candace did.

17

T HE SLANT OF morning sun through the window wasn't right.

Sarah blinked slowly. Sleep drifted back into her eyes. Then all at once, she sat up, throwing off the blankets in a panic, her heart pounding until she recognized where she was.

She groaned and fell back onto the pillows. How did jet lag work, anyway? Could you be lagged if you went forward in time? Last night, Ellie had fussed and cried and screamed about going to bed until Sarah had almost broken down herself. She'd thought about letting Ellie sleep with her but hadn't wanted to set that precedent— her own sleep had been so terrible lately, and it wasn't going to get any better the farther along she got with this pregnancy.

Carefully, Sarah sat up again, a hand on her belly. The baby greeted her with a few thumps. Everything else seemed inclined to stay in place, at least for now. In fact, she felt empty, hollow. Hungry.

"Good morning, little one," she whispered.

Her stomach rumbled. Her phone, the screen still cracked but functioning, showed her the time. Almost nine thirty. She hadn't charged it last night and it was on low-power mode. She'd have to dig up the cord as soon as she could . . . or not. What did she really need her phone for, anyway? Way out here in the woods of rural Ohio, it didn't even get a signal. That was kind of nice, actually. She hadn't blocked either of the Morgans, preferring to know if they were still trying to contact her so she could keep track of their harassment. Ava had sent her a few texts over the past couple of days that Sarah had ignored, but no cell signal meant no calls or texts to upset her.

In the mirror, Sarah expected her reflection to look as haggard and drawn as she'd become accustomed to looking. Apparently a good night's sleep and knowing she and Ellie were far out of Ava and Graham's grubby, greedy grasp had made a difference in Sarah's face. She looked positively aglow.

Candace commented on it as soon as Sarah came into the kitchen. "Sit yourself right down here. Ellie, tell your Mommy what you ate already for breakfast."

"Pan. CAKE!" Ellie banged her fork on the table and gave her mother a syrupy grin.

"Looks delicious. Smells good too. I'm so hungry." Sarah slid into the seat at the table and looked for a coffee mug. "Is there coffee?"

Candace slid a stack of pancakes onto her plate. "Oh no, honey. I never drink the stuff; it's as bad as drugs with how addicted you can get to it. Besides, coffee's so bad for the baby. I have some nice herbal tea. Or milk. Or lemonade."

"Oh . . ." Sarah covered her disappointment with a smile. Her OB had told her a cup of coffee was fine, a treat in moderation. "Ice water will work for me, then."

"No tea? Honor," Candace said abruptly, "go into the basement and fetch me that other box of pancake mix. I used up all of the one from the pantry. Miss Sarah needs a hearty breakfast."

Sarah hadn't heard the housekeeper enter the room and gave her a smile. "You don't have to do that on my account. Three pancakes is more than enough."

"Honor. Go." To Sarah's discomfort, Candace snapped her fingers in the young woman's face. Honor, who'd been staring at Sarah with big eyes, startled and ducked her head before scurrying away toward the basement door. Candace turned back to Sarah with a bright smile.

Ellie was too busy stuffing her face with sweet pancakes and syrup to notice that she was covered in it. Candace deftly took a washcloth from the side of the sink and swiped it over one of Ellie's hands, then the other, without interrupting a single bite. She kissed the top of her head.

Sarah cut into the stack of pancakes and took a bite, letting out a groan of pleasure as the sweetness burst on her tongue. "Oh. Wow. These are amazing, Candace. When I was pregnant with Ellie, I craved spicy, sour things. But this time, it does seem like I'm craving the sweet stuff more than anything else."

"I was the same with Henry." Candace nodded. "Eat up."

Suddenly ravenous, Sarah fell to and demolished the food fast enough to almost—not quite—embarrass herself. How could she be ashamed when she saw how happy her consumption had made Candace? Candace grinned and patted Sarah's shoulder, proud, as if Sarah had done something special instead of simply polishing off a stack of pancakes.

"Look at you." Candace set a steaming, fragrant mug in front of Sarah and sat across from her with one of her own. "Good job."

"I miss my mom," Sarah said suddenly. Unexpectedly.

A shadow flickered over Candace's expression. She reached for Sarah's hand and pressed it. "Oh, honey. I'm sorry."

It wasn't the first time she'd missed the mother she *wished* she had, but for the first time in years, Sarah longed for the mom she'd been given, the one with all the flaws and faults and frustrations, the one who'd been too caught up in her own problems to be maternal . . . but also the one who'd loved her daughter fiercely, all the same, and had always believed she was doing her best to protect her.

"She never made pancakes when I was growing up, but she did make a killer matzah brei that I've never been able to re-create just right." Sarah took in a shaky breath.

"I don't know what that is."

"Oh. Basically scrambled eggs with matzah broken up and mixed into it. Some people like to make it savory with spices and onion, but my mom always did a cinnamon-sugar blend, and she served it with syrup. Like this. Makes me miss her right now." Sarah sniffled.

"Matzah. That's those special crackers your people eat for Jewish Easter."

"For Passover," Sarah corrected.

Ellie looked concerned. "Mama, 'kay?"

"I'm fine, ketzeleh." Sarah took another bite. "Mmm, didn't Nanna make us the best breakfast ever?"

"Ketz . . . what-a-la?"

Sarah laughed. "It means little kitten. It's something Adam started calling her when she was a baby, because she'd make these little mewing noises."

"Meow meow!" Ellie banged her fork on the table.

Candace looked taken aback. "He knew how to speak Jewish?"

The basement door opened, revealing Honor holding a box of pancake mix. She set the box on the counter and left the kitchen without speaking. Candace didn't even give her a glance. Sarah leaned forward in her chair to watch where Honor had gone.

Candace noticed Sarah's attention. "Don't you worry about her. She's got chores to do. If she's hungry, she'll eat. Now. After breakfast, I want you to make me a grocery list of anything you and this little princess need, and I'll make a big shop today."

"You don't need to do anything special for us. You've done so much already." Sarah tried a sip of tea. It was hot. It was minty. It was not coffee.

"Hush. You deserve to be treated. You came all this way! And with such a big change to your lives. You make me that list. I want to make sure you feel welcome." Candace patted Sarah's hand again and sipped her own tea.

"I can come with you," Sarah began, although heading to the grocery store with Ellie in tow was at the bottom of her list of things she wanted to do today.

"Don't you worry about it. I've got a nail and hair appointment I need to get to anyway."

"I do need to spend some time on my laptop taking care of some things. You have Wi-Fi, right? I wasn't able to get a signal on my phone."

Candace made a face. "I never use it. I couldn't tell you anything about it."

"But . . . you have it, right?"

"Peter used the internet. It was all bundled in with the cable TV and the wall phone and my cell phone. That awful thing. It doesn't get a good signal way out here. And I like it that way. Everyone's just got their noses stuck in their screens all the time." Candace made another face and dipped her chin toward the old-school rotary phone attached to the wall. "That old thing is better."

"Oh."

"Is that going to be a problem, honey?"

"I was hoping to look for a job, something remote I could do part-time for now. And I need to be able to access my email and accounts for bills, things like that." Sarah couldn't eat another bite, and Ellie was now simply pushing around the final bits of her pancake. "Let me get her cleaned up."

"I'll take care of it." Candace took away Ellie's plate and left it conspicuously on the counter while she wiped the little girl's face and hands again, then lifted her down from her chair. "Honor! Come take Miss Ellie upstairs so she can play in her room."

"I can—" Sarah began, but Honor had appeared, silently, like magic.

She held out her hand to Ellie, who took it willingly enough. Sarah watched them go. She warmed her hands on the cooling mug. "Ellie's settling in."

"Of course she is. This is home now. Finished? Are you sure you don't want me to make you more? You look like you know your way around a stack of pancakes." Candace giggled and waited for Sarah to shake her head before sweeping her plate away to stack it on top of Ellie's.

"I could go into town with you. There must be a coffee shop or a library or something with Wi-Fi that I can use. I need to make an appointment with an obstetrician." She needed to do a lot of things.

"Oh, don't you worry about that. I got you an appointment with Dr. Maple's office. You'll love her, Sarah, she's fantastic. And she's right here in town."

Sarah sat back in her chair, both relieved and a little irritated that she apparently had no say in the matter of who'd be taking care of her for the rest of her pregnancy. "I have a list of providers my insurance will cover."

"You have an appointment with her tomorrow, but I suppose if you want to try to go somewhere else . . ." Candace shrugged. "It'll be a much longer trip anyplace you try."

"And I might not be able to get in to see anyone right away," Sarah said after a second.

"If you don't like Dr. Maple's practice, you can try someplace else. How about that? And you can find yourself a place to use the internet too, if you really have to."

"I really do have to." The pancakes were sitting heavily in Sarah's stomach now, and she regretted being so greedy. A faint headache was building behind her eyes. She rubbed the spot.

"Uh-oh," Candace said. "Feeling sick?"

"Just a little headache. I'm okay." She wasn't drifting, but she took a few seconds to employ the same tricks she used to keep herself anchored. She paid attention to the cool table under her fingertips. The lingering smell of pancakes and, fainter, Candace's perfume. The golden light sparkling among the trees she could see through the French doors.

"Write me that list," Candace said. "I'll leave in a little while. You rest up. I can take Ellie with me, if you want?"

Sarah hesitated.

Candace waved a hand at once. "Never mind. She can play with her toys, or I have all of Henry's old DVDs from when he was little in the den. All the Disney cartoons. And *VeggieTales*, of course."

They were definitely not going to be watching that show.

"I'm sure she'll love that. Thank you, Candace."

After Candace left, and with Ellie occupied upstairs, Sarah busied herself cleaning up the kitchen. It seemed wrong to simply let the dishes sit on the counter, especially when she didn't have anything else to do. When she'd finished, she went to the French doors and grabbed the handle. Stopped herself. *Bother.* She'd forgotten to ask Candace about the security system code.

She looked up to the top of the door—yes, there was a small sensor there, shining a solid red. If she opened it, would an alarm sound? The police arrive?

She wasn't going to test it out. Instead, she looked through the glass, out over the deck and the patchy grass of the yard, and into the trees beyond. She and Adam had often hiked the trails they could get to from behind their house. He'd been the one to tell her about the Jeffrey pines and how their trunks smelled like butterscotch. Had he learned that here, behind his childhood home? Or were these different trees? she thought, shielding her eyes to see if she could identify them from this distance. They were some kind of evergreen, but whether they were hemlocks or pines or fir, Sarah had no idea. A breeze moved the feathery branches, and that was *not*, she told herself with a self-conscious laugh, a shadowy figure standing there watching the house. Watching her.

And then it moved.

18

Sarah cried out and stumbled back from the door. Her heel caught the edge of the throw rug. She was going to fall. The thought passed through her mind with a calm clarity as she imagined herself hitting the tile floor. Cracking her head open. There would be blood . . .

She caught herself. Heart pounding, she leaned on the table. Nausea swam up her throat, not morning sickness but the aftermath of her fear. She shook it off and went back to the doors to look out.

Nothing. Of course, nothing. The shadowy form moved again, but now she could see it was the tree branches, not a person.

"You're being paranoid," she chided herself.

"What did you do?"

Sarah whirled to face Honor, who was looking around the kitchen with a scowl. The housekeeper went to the drying rack and looked over the dishes Sarah had washed. She opened the dishwasher and looked inside. She stood up straight, hands on her hips.

"You should have left that for me," Honor said. "That's my work to do. Not yours."

Sarah licked her top lip and tasted sweat and a remnant of syrup. "I didn't mind."

"I mind," Honor said. "You can't just come in here and take over."

"I'm sorry. I have no intentions of taking anything away from you." Like doing dishes and laundry was some kind of privilege,

Sarah thought, then mentally scolded herself for being unkind. There was nothing wrong with taking pride in your job and not wanting someone else to mess it up.

Honor drew herself up. "Are you okay? You look really bad."

"Thanks," Sarah said dryly. She looked out the back doors again. "I thought I saw someone out there."

Honor pushed past her to also look out. Back and forth, her gaze swept the yard. She turned back to Sarah. "Why would someone be out there?"

"I don't know. I just thought I saw someone. Maybe it was a bear," Sarah joked.

Honor didn't laugh. "Why were you trying to go outside?"

"Why is it such a big deal?" Sarah shot back.

The housekeeper visibly bristled, then softened. "Your little one is a sweetie. She's having a great time up there, playing with her dolls. But I have other things I need to do, so I can't be babysitting her all day long."

"I wouldn't expect you to. Thanks for taking her up. I'll check on her in a bit."

Honor nodded stiffly, then spun on her heel and left the kitchen. Sarah went upstairs to find Ellie in her room, playing as happily as Honor had described. She went back to her own room and grabbed Adam's laptop.

Sarah settled at the desk in Ellie's room. Her phone had only a bar of service, but she hoped the laptop would be able to find a network connection. All of her files, and his too, were backed up to FlashDrive's cloud server—which she couldn't access without the internet. She typed his password into the lock screen.

!!ILoveSarah!!

"Oh, Adam," she whispered to the screen as the laptop unlocked. Her heart twisted at this, his final message to her. When she clicked on the Wi-Fi icon, no choices for a network showed up. She muttered a curse, mindful of Ellie across the room.

Who lived their daily lives without the internet?

Sarah sat up straight on the hard desk chair to give her aching back a break. Her butt was getting numb too. Almost twenty-eight weeks, the start of the third trimester. She was glad they'd moved when they did, before she wasn't allowed to fly. She hoped she liked Dr. Maple.

"How you doin' over there, ketzeleh? Come here."

Ovah theah. Come heah. It was her mother's voice, that slight Brooklyn accent. Sarah had only picked it up for a few key phrases. Adam had teased her that she sounded like Tony Manero from *Saturday Night Fever*.

Obediently, despite the allure of the dollhouse, Ellie hopped up and ran over to her mother. Sarah cupped the little girl's face and leaned to kiss her forehead. She studied her daughter for a few seconds. Adam's eyes. His smile.

"I love you, Ellie."

"Luff you, Mama."

"Do you need a snack or anything? How about the potty?"

"No, no, no." Ellie yearned toward the toys, her small hand caught in her mother's grip.

Sarah peeked quickly into the waistband of Ellie's leggings. They'd been doing Pull-Ups instead of training pants because of all the upheaval, but now that they were getting situated, it might be time to try again. "If you need the potty, you let me know, okay?"

"Wanna playyyyy." Ellie wriggled, and Sarah released her.

Sarah closed the laptop and got up as Ellie ran back to the dollhouse. They'd get back into their puzzles and learning the alphabet soon, she promised herself as she kissed the top of her daughter's head. And they'd go on walks in the woods, keep this big old pregnant body active. Or not, because of the bears. Sarah sighed. She would, but not today.

Her stomach grumbled, the enormous breakfast already forgotten. Some peanut butter toast with a slice or two of cheese on it sounded like it would be both disgusting and delicious. "Ellie, Mama's going downstairs to get a snack. Do you want anything?"

"Nononono . . ."

Sarah laughed and kissed the top of Ellie's head. There were no child gates here, but on the other hand, Ellie had gotten the hang of going up and down the stairs by herself right before they left California. Soon enough, Sarah wouldn't think twice about it, but for now, she said, "You stay here and play, okay? I don't want you going near the stairs."

Downstairs, it took her a few minutes to orient herself in the unfamiliar kitchen. Glasses, plates, pots and pans, but no food in the cupboards. The tall door she thought might be either a broom closet or a pantry was locked.

So was the fridge.

Sarah touched the metal hasp that she hadn't noticed before. Adam had childproofed their house, and they'd had something similar on their fridge. This was no child lock, though. It was heavy-duty, drilled into the fridge doors, and secured with a padlock.

Her stomach growled again, and Sarah did a slow turn around the kitchen to see if there was anything out on the countertops. A bread box, fruit basket, something. Anything.

This morning, Candace had told Honor to get more pancake mix out of the basement. When she tugged that door handle, it too was locked.

"What the actual . . ." She cut herself off before she could drop another f-bomb. Ellie had started repeating too many words, and Sarah had been trying to break herself of the swearing habit.

She tried the door handle again, but it didn't budge. Honor would have the key, right? Or maybe it was on the ring Candace had handed her to unlock the front door. There was a plaque hung by the door to the garage with hooks on it for keys, but they were all empty. Candace must've taken them with her.

"Honor?"

Sarah found her in the glass-paned four-seasons room at the other end of the house. She sat at a table laid out with fabric scraps, baskets of embroidery floss, and skeins of yarn. The younger woman was bent over an embroidery hoop, studiously stabbing a needle into the cream-colored fabric and pulling out a red thread before repeating the stitch. Red roses, it looked like, from what Sarah could see.

"Honor," she repeated.

Honor looked up. "What do you want?"

"I need something in my stomach. Is there a way you could get me some crackers, maybe some peanut butter toast or something like that? Ellie's about due for a snack too."

"You'll spoil your appetite."

Sarah pressed the tip of her tongue to the sharpness of her front teeth, not biting exactly but being careful with what words she let slip out. "I'm sure we won't."

Honor frowned, her gaze falling to the bump swelling from Sarah's loose-fitting top, one of the new ones from her closet. "Candace should be back soon. She'll have snacks for you."

"Isn't there anything here until then?" Sarah took another tack. "The doors are locked. Even the fridge."

"Peter used to get into it at night, when he wasn't supposed to," Honor said. "He was supposed to be on a diet. For his heart, you know? And the diabetes. But he'd get into the sweets."

That didn't explain why the doors were all still locked so many years after his death, but Sarah didn't pursue that line of questioning. "I didn't know he'd been in such bad health. Is that why . . . how . . . ?"

"You want to know how he died?" Honor asked bluntly. She set down her embroidery. "Well, he got into the sweets and ate himself into a diabetic coma. You can get diabetes when you're pregnant, you know."

"I know that." Sarah's stomach gurgled, and she put both hands on it. "But I'm not, and I have to eat something or else I'm going to start to feel sick. I might even have to throw up, and I'd really rather not. Please. Do you have the keys?"

"Candace took them with her."

Sarah couldn't hold back her annoyed sigh. She rubbed at her forehead to press away the caffeine-withdrawal headache. "Why would she do that?"

Honor got up from the table without answering the question. "I have some protein bars in my room. I could give you one. For the little one too."

"That would be great. I'd be so grateful, Honor. Thank you."

"I'll bring them." Honor pushed past her.

Honor looked over her shoulder as they both went up the stairs, seemingly vexed by Sarah walking behind. Honor went into her room and closed the door after her. Sarah waited in the hall until Honor came out and handed her two protein bars. Sarah's hands were shaking as she opened the first and took a bite, chewed and swallowed. The chalky peanut butter flavor caused bitter saliva to squirt into her mouth, and she forced herself to slow down so she didn't choke.

Sarah was very aware of Honor hovering, watching, but she didn't say anything. The girl—because although she was only a few years younger than Sarah, she seemed more like an adolescent than an adult—shifted nervously.

"Are you going to throw up?" Honor asked finally.

"I don't think so. Thanks. This did the trick."

"Good." Honor seemed lost and looked with yearning toward the stairs.

Beep-boop.

Sarah reached automatically for her phone, but the noise hadn't come from hers.

Beep-boop.

Honor put her hand in the pocket of her dress. Her hand moved slightly, probably turning the phone to silent. A deep crimson flush spread up from her square neckline, over her throat and into her face. Her gaze went hard and glittering, and her chin lifted like she was daring Sarah to say anything.

Sarah did not. She knew that sound, even if she hadn't heard it in years. The alert was for a popular messaging app. By the look on Honor's face, she was embarrassed about using it, but Sarah couldn't have cared less about who the housekeeper was hooking up with. She just wanted access to the Wi-Fi.

"I wasn't able to get my computer on the internet." Sarah kept her voice casual and nonaccusatory. "And my phone doesn't get any kind of signal out here at all. Do you know if Candace even has Wi-Fi?"

"Candace hates the internet."

Sarah took another bite of the protein bar, a tiny one. A nibble. She chewed and swallowed. Her stomach was settling, but her heart beat a little faster.

"What service does your phone use? If you're able to get service out here, I might be able to switch—"

"I don't have . . . I mean . . ." Honor choked off the words and gave Sarah a wild-eyed stare. "Don't tell on me. Okay?"

Sarah nibbled again. There was nothing to savor about this protein bar, but she pretended it was so delicious it was taking up all her concentration. She even made a little *mmmmm*. No worries, no pressure, just a pregnant lady eating a mediocre snack. Nothing for Honor to get stressed about. No reason for her to think Sarah would "tell."

"Please," Honor repeated. "She's so strict about cell phones; she says they're just worldly, sinful temptations. Worse than the internet."

"She has one," Sarah pointed out.

"She barely uses it. And if you tell her I have one, she'll . . ." Again, Honor stopped herself. "I just don't want her to know about it, all right?"

What would Candace do? Fire her? That seemed extreme, but clearly, Honor was upset about it. Sarah tried one last time.

"I won't tell her. But if you can tell me what service you have, I can get mine changed, and then I'll at least be able to use my phone out here. I could even get a hotspot." Sarah gave an embarrassed chuckle. "I really can't get by without the internet for longer than a few days."

Honor frowned at her. "You might have to learn to get along without a lot of things here."

19

CANDACE HAD DROPPED Sarah off in front of the small building. She was taking Ellie to the playground so they could enjoy the gorgeous May weather. She'd be back in three hours—long enough for Sarah's doctor appointment and also a visit to the coffee shop across the street. Wi-Fi and coffee. Sarah couldn't wait.

"Hi, I'm here to see Dr. Maple." Sarah's enthusiasm for the upcoming coffee shop time spread over her face in a wide grin.

"She's running a little behind. You'll have to take a seat." The woman tapped a paper appointment book with a pencil and gestured toward the four seats circled around a battered wooden coffee table laden with magazines. She swept Sarah with a look, and her expression lit. "Oh, you're Candace's daughter-in-law, aren't you?"

Sarah nodded, wondering when that title would ever stop feeling awkward. "That's me."

The woman craned her neck to look behind her. "Where's your little one? Candace told everyone all about her. What a precious little lovebug she is. Eleanor, right?"

"Ellie. Short for . . . her name's Ellie." Launching into an explanation about the confusion over her daughter's name was going to take more effort than Sarah had the energy for.

The woman blinked rapidly, her smile fading into a look of confusion. "When I ran into Candace at the grocery store, she said—"

Sarah cut her off with a fake, bright laugh. "Nope. She's Ellie."

"That's Candace for you, I guess," the receptionist said after a second, leaving Sarah to wonder what that meant. "You have to fill out these release forms. There's information in there about the fees. Also information about the home birth requirements."

She gave a delicate pause.

"Dr. Maple has a very reasonable cash plan, if you don't have insurance."

Had Candace told the entire town of Shelter Grove about Sarah's financial trouble?

"I've got coverage," Sarah said. "But I can also pay the fees. And I'm not interested in a home birth."

"Oh?" The receptionist looked surprised but said nothing else.

Sarah took the clipboard and its thick sheaf of papers, along with a pen bearing the name of a local bank, and found a seat. She bent over the paperwork, filling in her name, birth date, pertinent medical history. When she got to the section about her emergency contact, she stopped. A sob crushed her throat. *Adam*, she thought, *it ought to be Adam*. She filled in Candace's name and number—the barely used cell phone—instead. She scanned the home birth information. She'd never been that crunchy.

By the time she'd filled out the paperwork, a nurse in a set of cheerfully patterned scrubs stood in the doorway. "Sarah?"

"That's me." She got to her feet and handed the nurse the clipboard as she followed her down the hall to a small exam room at the end.

"I'm Patricia, and I'll be helping you out today." Patricia began the routine of getting Sarah's weight and blood pressure, her temperature, all the usual. She didn't spend much time in extraneous chitchat, which Sarah actually preferred. Finally, the nurse swiveled on the stool to look at her. "You're coming to us from California, huh?"

"Yes. I . . . well, I'm living with my mother-in-law until after the baby's born. So she can help me out."

"You're very lucky to have such a kind-hearted woman in your life," Patricia said with a small smile.

Sarah barely kept herself from quoting Magenta from the *Rocky Horror Picture Show*—*I'm lucky, she's lucky, we're all lucky!* Instead, she said, "The universe sends us what we need."

"God does that," Patricia said briskly, emphasizing the word. Her gaze flicked the Star of David pendant nestled at Sarah's throat, but she didn't say anything.

Sarah sat up straighter but kept herself from touching the necklace. Her expression remained neutral even as her cheeks burned. She
refused to look away.

"We're still waiting on the records from your previous practice to
get here, but your paperwork says you're about twenty-eight weeks?"

"Yep. Somewhere around there, anyway."

"This says you're *not* interested in the home birth?"

"Definitely not. I'm hoping for an easy birth with no complica-
tions, but I still want to be in a hospital for it."

Patricia scribbled something on the paperwork. She looked again
at Sarah's necklace. "Hope is fine, faith is better."

"Even better than that," Sarah said sharply, "is an epidural."

After a moment, the nurse gave an almost indiscernible shrug
and stood. "Dr. Maple will be in shortly."

The poster on the far wall had been drawn in pale colors, peaches
and soft yellows and beige. It showed an illustration standard enough
for an OB/GYN office, a pregnant woman gazing lovingly at her
belly, with a cutaway showing the tiny floating embryo. What was
not as expected was the text surrounding it: Boldly lettered state-
ments about fetal heartbeats and development. In the poster's bottom right corner, a small line drawing of a church and a list of one,
two, three . . . Sarah counted six church names boasting of sponsor-
ing the artwork. The Blood of the Lamb was one of them, which
showed how out-of-date the poster had to be.

The door opened, and the doctor stepped in. She wore her dark
hair in a bun at the base of her skull. Her kind blue eyes and smile
immediately set Sarah at ease. She took the swivel stool across from
Sarah and clapped her hands on her knees.

"Mrs. Granatt," she said. "I'm Dr. Maple. Nurse Patricia tells me
you're here from California? And you're twenty-eight weeks?"

Tired already of having to explain her situation to everyone over
and over, Sarah only nodded. Dr. Maple smiled and twisted to look
at the tablet the nurse had left behind. She tapped it for a second or
so, scanning the screen, before looking back at Sarah.

"You're Candace Granatt's daughter-in-law."

Sarah managed a smile. "Does everyone know that?"

"Shelter Grove's a small town, so . . . yes." Dr. Maple chuckled.
"But I happen to know Candace because she and Dr. Bender
worked together for years before he retired. The practice needed a
family doc to replace him. His wife's cousin goes to church with

my wife's mom and dad. We thought it would be great to move closer to family. She wanted to be near her mom for help with the kids. I'm sure you know what that's like." Dr. Maple gave her a friendly smile Sarah didn't have to fight to return. "There are some practitioners I'd hesitate to recommend, but not Candace. You're in good hands."

Sarah bit her lower lip for a second. "I'm not planning on a home birth. I think there's been some confusion."

Dr. Maple tilted her head. "Really? Huh. When you called to make your appointment, you didn't say you were?"

"Candace called for me. I'm not sure why she'd have said I wanted a home birth. We never talked about it."

"Well, that changes things, certainly. But it's not a problem at all. I don't want you to worry about that."

"Is that what most everyone around here does?"

"Honestly, no. Most of the women in the area prefer to have their babies in the hospital. I take care of the ones who choose otherwise. They see me for their checkups and the midwife for their actual birthing plans. Or, if they're seeing an OB, then they only come to me for their regular care."

Sarah's brows went up. "You're not an OB?"

"Family med. But family docs do it all. It might not be my primary specialty, but I have delivered a lot of babies." Dr. Maple's gaze held Sarah's as though she was waiting for her to protest or complain. "But I can refer to you one of the docs I work closely with, if you'd rather see an OB."

Sarah'd had doctors who rushed through their exams, and she'd had some who'd taken their time. She'd never had a physician seem as though she had no other patients waiting and nothing else to do other than sit and chat with her all day long. Her OB back in California, as a matter of fact, had often been rushing from the room almost before she'd finished asking Sarah how she was feeling.

"Do you like it here?" Sarah asked instead.

"I do. Mostly. Living in a small town can be a challenge." Dr. Maple's gaze dropped to Sarah's necklace, then met her eyes again. She scooted forward on the stool and placed two fingers over the pulse point on Sarah's wrist. "Especially if you're a little . . . different. But I do like the slower pace here. I like knowing my neighbors. I like seeing my patients as part of the community, and I like seeing the few babies I do deliver growing up. I guess if anything, the fact I deliver so few makes them even more special to me. Are you planning to stay in town?"

"Only until the baby's born and I've had some time to get back on my feet." Sarah tipped her chin upward as the doctor palpated the base of her throat, then felt the sides of her neck and slightly behind her ears. Dr. Maple pushed back on the stool to give Sarah space and gestured for her to stand.

"It's good to have a support system. Do you have other family?"

"No," Sarah said quietly.

"Take a careful hop up here and let me check out your heart and lungs, okay? And, Mrs. Granatt," Dr. Maple said firmly, confidently, catching her gaze and waiting to be sure Sarah was looking before she continued, "I just wanted to reassure you that you're in good hands."

Her words were exactly what Sarah needed to hear in that moment, and the rush and swell of tears overtook her. Sarah pressed her fingertips to her closed eyelids, breathing deep, embarrassed even though she was sure a doctor who took care of pregnant people had to be used to her patients experiencing emotional havoc. At the comforting weight of Dr. Maple's hand on her shoulder, Sarah shivered.

"Thanks. Sorry. I have a lot going on."

"No need to be sorry." Dr. Maple pressed a tissue into Sarah's hand.

Sarah wiped her face and blew her nose. Gave the doctor a watery smile. "I'm all over the place."

"Understandable. And I'm sorry for your loss." The doctor gave her a solemn look. "Shelter Grove is a community. We stick together. Good times, bad times. Thick and thin. We watch out for each other."

"Even if you're . . ." Sarah gave the same pause the doctor had earlier. ". . . different?"

"The people here are as good or as bad as anywhere else. You have some who lead with hate and some who lead with love," the doctor said.

"How long did you say you lived here?"

"Two years. But my wife's family has lived here for generations."

"It's just that . . . well, I know that Candace and her husband had a church on their property, but there was some trouble with it after he died. Vandalism, I guess? It burned? I was hoping maybe you knew more about it. I don't want to upset Candace by asking." She wasn't going to probe Honor for answers either, but she did want to know what had really happened. She wanted to meet someone who'd known Adam before he left Shelter Grove, someone who might be able to give her more insight into why he'd told her his family was dead.

Dr. Maple frowned. "I don't know anything more about that than what you just said. My wife's family didn't belong to that church. The most I know is that it was very . . . niche."

"Huh. The way Candace talks, it was well attended and popular."

A fleet of changing expressions marched across Dr. Maple's face. She lowered her voice. "All I can tell you is that it was very small. Unaffiliated with a larger diocese or any kind of council. Peter Granatt was supposedly very charismatic, involved with the local community, that sort of thing. But when he founded the church on his property, it caused some tension with the town. That's really all I know. And I know that Candace is a competent midwife. If you change your mind," Dr. Maple said easily, as though she weren't also quite conveniently changing the subject.

"I doubt it," Sarah said. "The only way I want to give birth at home is if I don't know it's happening until it's too late to leave for the hospital."

Dr. Maple grinned. "Babies come whenever they want to. You never know what might happen."

CHAPTER

20

A TALL COFFEE, RICH with cream and sugar. A loaded bagel. And, of course, the Wi-Fi. Sarah had found a nice seat in the window of the coffee shop and wasted an embarrassing amount of time scrolling her social media feeds. She lingered on Ava's Connex post, a meme about Mother's Day.

The gist of it seemed to be that people shouldn't post happy things about the holiday, because some people struggled with it. Sarah had completely forgotten about the day, and guilt twinged her. She didn't care so much about being acknowledged herself, but it would've been nice to do something for Candace.

Tension coiled inside her as she scrolled through the rest of Ava's posts, each one tagged with her location. All of them were from California except the week of posts made from Punta Cana. Lots of bikini shots, frosty drinks, Ava and Graham looking tan and fit and happy.

Her phone pinged with a text, and her heart twisted. Ava's message was brief. *Hope you're doing well. Please get in touch. We worry about you.* With frantic swipes, Sarah closed out the Connex app, her throat tightening. Had Ava somehow been able to see that she was looking at her profile?

A second later, a flurry of texts came in. Linda. The old OB/GYN office. A few from spam numbers. Sarah's breathing eased. No, Ava hadn't magically been able to sense Sarah's snooping. Something with the lack of cell service, probably, keeping her phone from connecting and getting messages until it was using Wi-Fi. Heck, maybe she'd broken more than the screen when she'd dropped it.

Cautiously, she opened her Connex app again, this time clicking through to Graham's profile, careful not to accidentally "like" anything. He didn't post as much as his wife did, but he had shared a few of the same pictures from their recent vacation. Like Ava, he'd kept his location display on. His latest post was a simple shot of a blurry view of bright lights and a glimpse of water and sand and the caption *On the Road Again*. Not Punta Cana this time.

He was in Atlantic City.

It meant nothing. Graham traveled all the time. Atlantic City was far from Shelter Grove . . . but very, very close to Brigantine, where Sarah had grown up. Graham knew that.

At the honk of a car horn, she looked up to see Candace waving at her from the parking lot. Quickly, Sarah packed up and headed out, grateful for the air conditioning even though she'd had to walk only a short distance from the coffee shop to the car. She put her seat belt on.

"Did you get everything taken care of? Ellie and I had the best time on the swings, didn't we, princess girl?" Candace gripped the steering wheel tight with both hands and kept her eyes on the road. She was an anxious driver.

"Yep," Sarah said. "I was able to get online and take care of some things. But I'd like to possibly change my phone plan to whatever service you have that gets a signal at the house. And would you consider getting internet installed? I'd of course be happy to pay for it."

Candace slowed the car at the town's single intersection as the light turned red. She puffed out a breath. "There is no good service out where we are."

"Oh, but . . ." Sarah stopped herself from giving away Honor's secret. She didn't want to get the poor kid fired. "I thought you said Peter used it?"

Candace gave her a little pout but quickly turned her attention back to the street as the light turned green. "Peter only used it for church business. He's been gone for quite some time, Sarah."

"Of course. I'm sorry." Sarah looked out the window to the brown fields showing their first hints of green. The weather was warming, full-on spring. Soon the summer would be here, and after that, the snow would come. What was it like out there in the middle of the woods when it snowed? Quiet, she thought. Private.

Sarah did not want privacy. She wanted Wi-Fi. She shivered and told herself it was the blast of air conditioning. Anyway, the baby would be here in early August. By the time the snow came, she and her children would be settled into their own house somewhere.

The car rumbled and bumped over the much-rougher road as they left the town and its surrounding fields behind and started entering the forest.

Twisting around to look at glazed-eyed Ellie, Sarah said, "Did you have fun with Nanna?"

Ellie yawned broadly and didn't answer. If she was kept up past nap time, would she go to bed tonight without so much fuss? Sarah was still wondering that when Candace slammed on the brakes hard enough to lock Sarah's seat belt. Candace cried out.

Sarah managed to face front despite the tightened belt across her. "What happened?"

"They just won't leave us alone!" Candace's usually impeccable blonde updo had tousled a bit. Her eyes were bright and her cheeks were flushed. She bared her teeth at the sight in front of them.

"Who?" Sarah looked from side to side but at first could see nothing. "Oh."

The sign that Candace had pointed out the day they'd arrived had been defaced. A fuzzy form hung limply from the top of it. Sarah strained to see what it was. A lamb? Crimson splashes covered most of the words on the sign.

Blood.

Candace slammed her foot onto the gas, jerking the car forward, tires spinning, engine revving. Gravel spattered as she whipped the wheel to pull the vehicle into the church driveway. The car fishtailed. Sarah cried out, gripping the door handle.

The car stopped in front of the sign. Candace got out, leaving the engine running and the driver's side door open. She ripped down the fuzzy white lump and threw it behind the sign. She yelled incoherently, shaking her fists at the damage.

"What Nanna doing?"

"Somebody messed up her sign, ketzeleh. She's mad, that's all." Fortunately, it didn't seem as though Ellie understood exactly what the vandals had done. Cautiously, Sarah opened her door and stepped out, keeping a hand on the door in case she needed to get back in the car quickly. She scanned the vacant lot, which was surrounded by the same evergreen trees as the backyard. No sign of anybody. She didn't even imagine a shadowy figure this time.

"Candace?"

Her mother-in-law spun around. Tears streaked bare-faced lines through her makeup and smeared her mascara. "The church already burned right down to the empty ground! Wasn't that enough? They had to come out here and do this?"

From her vantage point, Sarah could see the sign much better. Relief fluttered in her belly. "It's a stuffed toy, not a real lamb."

"Yes, and paint. They think it's funny." Candace spat the words, but her fury seemed to be fading. Her shoulders slumped.

A mean prank, and a gross one, but still just a prank. Kids, not menacing shadow men. Sarah had seen worse back in California. She moved to put an arm around Candace. "Let's get home, okay? You can call the police and make a report. Can you get someone to come and clean it up?"

In addition to the "blood," someone had spray-painted a penis and testicles. More than one, actually. Sarah pressed her knuckles to her mouth, not meaning to find any of this funny, since it clearly upset Candace. She could see other, older graffiti that had bled through the white paint meant to cover it up. Words. She leaned closer to see what they were, but most were so faint and obscured by the red paint that she could only make out a few letters.

EDOPHI

It meant nothing. She turned back to Candace, who was silently weeping as she stared at the desecrated sign. Sarah touched her shoulder. "Kids in small towns get up to mischief when they don't have anything else to do, Candace. I'm sorry. Let's get home, okay? It's after lunchtime."

Candace clenched her fists and shook them at the sign. Her voice went stifled. Guttural. "They'll *all* burn."

Uncomfortably, Sarah tugged Candace back toward the car. "I can drive us the rest of the way, if you're too upset."

Like a dog shaking the water out of its coat, Candace trembled. "No, no. I'm fine. I can get us home. It's only another mile and a half. It just makes me so angry, Sarah. The disrespect. It was Henry's birthright. It was meant to be his son's too."

Instinctively, Sarah's hands went to her belly. A breeze filtered through the trees, whispering. Sunlight shafted into the clearing, highlighting the remains of the foundation, and she imagined a hint of smoke. Maybe it wasn't such a bad thing the church had burned down.

The rest of the drive took only a few minutes, and by the time Candace pulled the car up to the front door, she was as bright and cheerful as ever. She insisted on taking Ellie out of the car seat. In the house, she called out for Honor, who appeared with the beginnings of what looked like a beanie cap in one hand.

Candace pulled a jingling ring of keys from her purse and waved them at Honor. "Go make them some lunch."

Honor held out her hand to the little girl. "Want to come with me, Ellie? You can help."

Ellie gave Sarah a quizzical look and, at her mother's nod of agreement, took Honor's hand and skipped off with her. Sarah put a hand on Candace's elbow to stop her from going up the stairs. Candace turned, eyebrows raised.

"I meant to talk to you about this before," Sarah said. "It's about the lock on the fridge."

Candace tilted her head. "What about it?"

"I wanted to make a snack for myself and Ellie while you were out shopping, and I couldn't, because of the lock."

"I have to keep it all locked up when I'm away, Sarah. She steals."

Sarah chewed her lower lip for a second. That wasn't the explanation Honor had given, but would she have admitted such a thing to Sarah? "She steals food?"

"More than food," Candace said.

"Why don't you get rid of her, then?"

Candace blinked rapidly, her lips parting in a small O. Then she burst into laughter, shaking her head. She patted Sarah's arm. "Oh, honey, I could no more get rid of that girl than I could get rid of you. Just like you, where else would she even *go*?"

Sarah stepped back, stung and upset with herself for feeling that way. Yes, she'd taken Candace up on her offer, but, while there were other places they *could* go, this had seemed like the best, most practical choice. A *choice*, not something she'd fallen into without other options.

"It's just that I do need access to food," she said.

Candace's expression turned solemn. She nodded. "Of course, honey. Of course. You're pregnant, you need to eat."

"I'm not trying to be a pain—"

"Of course you're not." Candace took both of Sarah's hands and swung them back and forth. "I want you to feel like this is your home."

Carefully, Sarah disengaged herself from Candace's grip. "I do. And I'm grateful to you. I'd love to help out by making dinner sometimes. Or taking care of the house, at least picking up after myself and Ellie."

"Don't you worry about that. Honor takes care of all that. You let yourself be a lady of leisure." Candace chuckled.

"I'm not used to doing nothing all day, that's all." Sarah stepped to one side to look around Candace, down the hall toward the kitchen. She could hear Ellie giggling and Honor saying something in a singsong lilt, although she couldn't make out the words.

"I don't mean to cut you off, hon, but I really need the private room. And I need to take care of this mess." Candace circled a finger in front of her face. "You go on into the kitchen and have your lunch."

"You don't want us to wait for you?"

"Don't you worry about me. I'm not having anything for lunch today." Candace patted her slim frame. "I'm reducing."

"And I'm expanding," Sarah joked.

"You sure are. If I didn't know you had a baby in there, I'd never be able to guess," Candace said.

Sarah laughed hesitantly as she watched Candace go upstairs. Had that been a joke, or a jab at her weight? She looked down at the bulge of her belly, slightly tenting the maternity top.

Ellie was already seated at the table with a sandwich cut into triangles, no crust, on a plate in front of her. Apple slices and some cubed cheese rounded out the meal, and she sipped from a cup of milk.

"You can make your own," Honor said stiffly with a gesture at the platter of deli meat and a loaf of bread left out on the counter. "I'll put everything away when you're done."

"Is that turkey?" Sarah already knew it wasn't and moved swiftly toward Ellie to remove the sandwich from her plate before she could bite into it.

"It's ham. Why are you taking it away?"

"We don't eat that. I told Candace before we came here." Sarah slid Ellie's plate onto the counter. The rules of kashrut were so complex, she didn't expect Candace or Honor to understand all of them. She'd decided to look the other way when it came to eating meat that hadn't been prepared kosher, since there was really no way to get it here, but she drew the line at eating pig. "Is there something else?"

Honor frowned. "I can make some tuna salad. Or peanut butter and jelly."

"You don't have to do that. I can make us PB and J, no problem. Are you eating?"

"I'm not hungry. She bought it all for you." Hope opened the refrigerator and showed Sarah the deli meat drawer, stuffed with plastic packages of ham and sliced cheese. The drawer had a sticky note affixed to it.

FOR SARAH AND ELLIE **ONLY!!**

"I don't like ham and cheese anyway." Honor sounded aloof.

Sarah looked a little deeper into the fridge and spotted a few other labeled items, some with Honor's name. A few with Candace's. "Why does she still lock the fridge?"

"She doesn't want me to eat the special things she buys for herself. Or for you two. I'm sure she'll be just *fine* with you eating whatever *you* want," Honor said. "You can just help yourself, I guess."

Sarah took another quick peek. "I hate to waste food, but we aren't going to eat that ham."

"Are you vegetarian?"

"No. We just don't eat certain things."

"Allergic?"

"No," Sarah said again, trying to think how she could explain even the basics of keeping kosher, especially since she wasn't following most of them.

"Look, I want to get back to work on my projects. Can you handle your own lunch?"

"Of course. I always wanted to learn how to knit," Sarah called after her as Honor turned away.

The housekeeper looked over her shoulder. "It's not as easy as anyone thinks. Crocheting is so much easier. Embroidery is even harder."

"I could use a hobby," Sarah said.

Honor faced her, hands on her hips. "It's not my *hobby*. I do custom orders for people. I have a store."

"That's great," Sarah said, adding, "Especially that you can do it around whatever Candace needs from you."

Honor shrugged. "It's my free time. I can spend it however I want to."

"Sure. Of course. I didn't mean any offense. I'll just . . . make myself a sandwich now."

"You're eating for two." Honor looked stiff, her back and shoulders straight. Her jaw set. "When's the baby due?"

"The end of August."

"Candace says you're going to stay here until then, and after that too."

Sarah nodded. "That's the plan."

"Plans can change," Honor said, and turned on her heel, her dismissal obvious and irrefutable.

This time, Sarah didn't try to call her back.

CHAPTER

21

THE DAYS PASSED faster than Sarah had expected them to. They'd only been here a little over two weeks but had fallen into a pattern—hours of play with Ellie or reading books from the selection of pulpy paperbacks lining the family room shelves. Around five, they'd eat the dinner Honor made, and the housekeeper would disappear to work on her crafts. Sarah would put Ellie to bed and be fought every second, or Candace would would do it and Ellie would go right to sleep in her "pwincess bed," no arguing or begging for another drink, another book. Sarah and Candace would watch a movie from a selection of literally a thousand or more DVDs, and Sarah would take herself to bed.

Today was Friday, tonight the start of Shabbat. Sarah had considered asking Candace for two candles, a glass of wine, and some bread so she could say the prayers. But then what? She'd be saying the blessings over unkosher food, the only person observing. Ellie wouldn't know any different. Adam would have been disappointed in her, but Adam wasn't here. If he had been, maybe she'd have lit the candles and he'd have laid his hands on Ellie's head to bless her for the week; maybe he'd have said the blessings over the wine and bread and shown his mother he was not living a life far away from faith.

Instead, Honor had served a platter of pork chops. Candace had scolded her vigorously, apologizing to Sarah, but there'd been something off about her apologies. It was like she was watching to see if

Sarah might change her mind. Make an exception. If it was a test of her convictions, Sarah had passed, declining the meat gracefully and serving up the mashed potatoes, corn, and salad for her and Ellie without complaint. She might not be as observant as she and Adam had been together, but she was doing the best she could.

Now she was in bed, having a hard time settling in. This bed was harder than the one she'd sold, the pillows flatter. The creaks and noises of this house had not yet become familiar enough to soothe her to sleep instead of keeping her awake, staring at the ceiling, wishing she could count enough sheep to drift into dreams.

Sometimes she still missed her connection to the outside world—an hour of scrolling through stupid thirty-second videos had never done much for her intellect, but she'd always been entertained. Slowly, though, Sarah had begun to appreciate being off the grid. It wasn't going to last forever, just like this pregnancy. She found herself sinking into her gestation, her days and nights moving along but also feeling as though they stood still. In some ways, she'd never felt so centered, as though the life inside her had fully fastened her to reality.

All of their worldly possessions now resided in the storage shed in the backyard. She hadn't yet had the emotional strength to deal with checking any of the boxes, but she'd have to get to it soon, before she got too big and the days got too hot. It was already June, and August would be there before she was ready for it.

Life in Shelter Grove wasn't perfect, but not having to worry about money, even for a short time, was a genuine comfort. It gave her the chance to think about what she wanted to do after the baby came. What kind of work she might be able to find. Where she wanted to live. Philly could be nice. Maybe she could take Ellie to visit Brigantine . . .

The book in her hands slipped forward as her head nodded. She'd been drifting. A flash of light from outside her window woke her up, and she grumbled, looking to the window and expecting to hear the rumble of thunder. None came. Another flash swept through the glass, brief but also definitely not lightning.

Someone was outside.

She swung her legs over the side of the bed and went to the window, but with the lights on inside, her reflection blocked any view. Cupping a hand over her eyes, she leaned close to get another look but still couldn't see anything.

In half a minute, she'd crossed to the nightstand and clicked off the lamp. The room fell into darkness, the window a black square while her eyes adjusted. This time when she stood next to the glass, she could see a light bobbing on the far edge of the yard, almost around the corner of the house. It swept the yard, revealing the patchy grass and forest beyond it. The faint sound of rising laughter filtered through the glass. Teen boys, she guessed. The bobbing light headed for the trees. Sarah glimpsed scampering shadows disappearing into the woods. When the security alarm began blaring, she stumbled back from the window and hunched immediately, hands over her ears.

She heard indistinct shouting from downstairs and headed for it, checking first on Ellie. The little girl's door was open, so Sarah could see her from the hallway. She curled like a comma with her arms wrapped around one of the new stuffed toys Candace had bought her. She stirred as the alarm's shriek cut off abruptly, but didn't get up.

Sarah shut the bedroom door behind her. At the top of the stairs, she hung back a moment. She could see Candace standing at the open front door.

The woman had a shotgun. She shook it, shouting out a jumbled stream of threats, before slamming the door shut. She entered the security code, and Sarah flinched at the shrill beep of the system being armed. Candace looked up and saw Sarah.

"Oh, honey, did those nasty vandals wake you up?"

"Did you . . . shoot something?"

Candace frowned. "Believe me, if I could get a clear shot at those little . . . jerks . . . but no. The alarm didn't wake up Ellie, did it?"

"I can't believe it, but no. I guess she's growing out of being a light sleeper." Sarah paused. "Her door was open, though. I'd closed it when I went to bed."

"Oh, I checked in on her earlier. She was crying a little bit. Must've been a bad dream." Candace let the gun drop to her side. "I guess you didn't hear her with your door shut. But don't you worry about it, I got her back to sleep."

Sarah took the stairs slowly, eyeing the gun. "It's much safer for children, everyone, really, to sleep with their doors shut. In case of fire. Candace, I have to ask you, where do you keep that gun?"

Her mother-in-law waved a hand and gave a small laugh. "I have it under my bed."

"In a locked box, I hope?"

Candace frowned as Sarah reached the bottom of the stairs. She looked at the gun and shrugged. "It wouldn't be much good to me if I had to get it out of a locked box every time those hooligans showed up, would it?"

Sarah winced. "That's so dangerous. I don't feel comfortable about that at all, not with Ellie in the house. What if she found it?"

"Now, how on earth would she manage to do that?" Candace looked affronted.

"She's a kid. Kids get into things. It's just not safe. Could you get a gun safe for it? Something?"

Before Candace could answer, a swath of red and blue lights swept through the front windows. No sirens, but as Sarah peered out, she could see a patrol car with two officers getting out of it. She stepped back from the windows.

Candace hurriedly shoved the gun into the coat closet next to the front door. She used the mirror to quickly smooth her hair and pinch her cheeks. She caught sight of Sarah in the reflection and turned.

"There, it's locked away in the closet." Candace patted her house-coat just as the knock came at the front door. She leaned close and spoke in a fake, trilling voice. "Who is it?"

"It's Officer Daniels, Mrs. Granatt."

"Just a minute. I have to turn off the alarm." Candace sauntered to the security system panel and took her time entering the code to disarm it. She gestured for Sarah to step back, her mouth pinched.

She opened the door to reveal two police officers, both young. Sarah's age or even a year or two younger. Both looked uncomfortable.

"What's going on tonight, Mrs. Granatt?" asked the taller one. "We got a call that you were threatening someone with a shotgun again."

"Those little jerks are running rampant on my property. It's not like I shot anyone."

The officer peered in around Candace and saw Sarah. "Who are you?"

"This is my daughter-in-law."

"Did you hear anything?" the shorter cop asked. He took a step back off the concrete front porch to shine his flashlight into the trees.

"I saw some lights and maybe some people running across the yard," Sarah said.

The taller officer, Daniels, cocked a hip and leaned on the door-frame to give Candace a charming smile. "Now, Mrs. Granatt, you know the local kids like to come out here and do what kids do in the woods. I know it's annoying, but there's no need to threaten—"

"It wasn't kids." Honor spoke up from the hallway behind Candace and Sarah. She sounded breathless, and her hair was coming loose from its usual braid. She wore a thick robe, too heavy for the early-summer weather, that she clutched closer to her throat. She repeated herself forcefully, adding, "It looked like a man and a woman to me. Adults. Not kids."

"Now, why would two adults be running through my yard at night, unless they were doing something they weren't supposed to?" Candace demanded of the officers.

Sarah froze inside. "Did the woman have red hair? Short, in a bob?"

Honor hesitated, then nodded firmly. "It was dark, but yes, I think so."

The cop with the flashlight swung it around, and Sarah put up her hand to keep from being blinded. "You have any idea who it might've been?"

"I told you, Officers, it was the local brats who like to come out here and cause trouble. We're lucky they're not burning my whole house down this time," Candace said before Sarah could speak.

Both cops looked at Sarah steadily. She shook her head. "I only saw flashlights and shadows. I have no idea who it might've been."

"Why'd you ask if one was a red-haired woman? You think you know who it was?" Daniels asked.

"Now, Eddie, how would she have any idea what the local kids look like?" Candace clucked her tongue. "She's only been here for a few weeks."

"Honor said it wasn't kids," Daniels said matter-of-factly, his gaze never leaving Sarah's face.

She did her best not to look guilty, because she wasn't, even if she wasn't telling the entire truth. But what was she going to say? That she'd fled California because she didn't want her dead husband's business partner's wife to know where she was and come after her for her unborn child? That Ava and Graham were out there running around in the woods at night instead of simply ringing the doorbell? The truth could sound more like insanity than the craziest made-up story.

Anyway, she thought as she pasted a bland smile on her face, she didn't know if she could trust these cops. They clearly didn't take Candace seriously. After promising her they'd take a look around, the cops left and Candace shut the door. She armed the system again and insisted that "after all the excitement," they go upstairs to bed—but not before making a show to Sarah of locking the coat closet.

Upstairs, Sarah lingered in her bedroom doorway, watching as Candace peeked in on Ellie before going into her own room and closing the door. When Honor sidled past, Sarah took a step toward her. Not quite blocking her. Not . . . quite.

"Did you really see a man and a woman?"

Honor nodded. "Yes. They were sneaking around the back of the house."

"What do you think they were doing?"

"People like to come out here into the woods to get into trouble."

Sarah frowned. "I can see why kids would come out here, although why they wouldn't avoid the house, I'm not sure. Unless it's just to get on Candace's nerves—"

"Yes. That's why they do it."

"But why would *adults* be sneaking around in the woods?"

"I don't know," Honor said, after a pause.

"But you said you thought one was a red-headed woman. You saw that? For sure?"

"I don't know what I saw. It was dark. And they were . . . well, they were sneaking, weren't they? *Someone* was out there." Honor's voice rose into a squeak. "But it's lucky that Candace has the security system set. To keep us safe."

"Right," Sarah said. "Safe."

But were they, really?

It wasn't until later, as she settled into the too-hard mattress and tried to get herself to sleep, that it finally jumped out at her. What had seemed so off about Honor tonight? Not her shifty gaze or twitchy reactions; those were all her usual. No, something else had been strange. Sarah thought again of Honor's tousled hair. Her breathless and sudden appearance, long minutes after the alarm had first gone off. The robe clutched around her throat, hiding whatever she wore beneath it. She'd also been wearing shoes.

Why wear shoes unless you'd been outside?

CHAPTER

22

SARAH HADN'T CONFRONTED Honor about sneaking out of the house. Now she had two secrets of Honor's she was keeping, and they both knew it. That was probably the reason Honor had started warming to her. They weren't friends or anything, but at least the housekeeper had stopped glowering at her all the time.

"Candace wants to show you off to her ladies. Lunch will be served in the dining room, with tea and dessert in the formal living room after."

"That's nice." Sarah smiled hesitantly. "There's no need to go to all the trouble. I'd be fine in the den with some cheese and crackers."

"It's for them. To show you off. She's so happy to become a grandmother."

"She already is a grandmother."

Honor rolled her eyes. "She'll get to spoil this one from the start. That's all I meant."

"She's very good at spoiling," Sarah agreed.

"Candace is very generous to the people she loves. She's someone I aspire to be, such a heart full of love and acceptance, and . . ." Honor drew in a quick breath, as though trying to keep her voice from shaking. "She's an angel right here on Earth."

Again with the angels.

"I'm certainly very grateful to her for everything she's done."

The women stared at each other. Honor ducked her head, finally, and mumbled, "I need to get into the kitchen and finish making the salads. We're having egg and tuna and deviled ham. The egg and the tuna are for you."

"I appreciate that, Honor. Is there something I can help with—?"

"No," Honor cut in quickly. "Of course not. You can just go get yourself ready."

"I *am* ready." She stopped herself from saying *I was born ready*, certain Honor wouldn't get the joke, but to her shock, the younger woman said those exact words aloud.

They stared at each other.

"*Big Trouble in Little China*," Sarah said. "It was one of Adam's favorite movies."

"Candace threw that DVD in the trash because of the magic in it." Honor spoke over her shoulder as she headed for the kitchen. "You'd better make sure she knows you're planning on wearing . . . that."

That. Sarah laughed and looked at her leggings, oversized tunic, the ballet flats. She'd showered that morning and washed her hair before tying it into a thick braid that hung over one shoulder. She'd even put on some mascara. She'd thought she was looking cute.

In the doorway to her bedroom, she stopped cold at the sight of the clothing laid out on her bed. She covered her mouth with one hand to keep the sudden flurry of giggles trying to escape. She moved closer, thunderstruck.

Laura Ashley had exploded all over the bed.

Flowers. Puffy long sleeves. That signature bib front. Sarah held the dress up in front of her. The hem hit her at the ankle. She turned to face the full-length mirror. Yellow was *not* her color.

"Don't you just love it?" Candace came into the room to stand behind her and look over her shoulder at Sarah's reflection. "Oh, it's so you."

"You don't have to lend me your dress," Sarah began, but Candace tutted her to silence.

"Don't be silly; I'd swim in that. It's *your* dress. I bought it for you. Surprise!"

"Oh, Candace. I don't know what to say. You really shouldn't have." Frankly, the dress was . . . not cute.

"I'll leave you to get changed. I have to go put my face on. These eyebrows are giving me such trouble this morning." Candace already wore full makeup, but she gestured at her face as though it were bare.

"Sisters, not twins, am I right?" Sarah quipped.

For a moment, Candace looked blank. Then her contentious eyebrows rose, and she laughed. "Oh, Sarah. You're a stitch. Hurry, now, get your face on. The ladies will be here any minute."

A few minutes after Candace left the room, Ellie appeared. "Mama?"

"Come in, ketzeleh. Don't you look nice?" Ellie nodded shyly from the doorway and twirled to show off the flowery dress. It matched the one Candace had left for Sarah. She ran into Sarah's open arms.

"Aren't we just going to be adorable," Sarah said.

That was one way of looking at it.

Despite everything, wearing the not-cute dress, Sarah did feel different. She'd never thought of herself as an optimist, not exactly, but she did have a lightness inside her that hadn't been there before. Yes, her life was weird, and yes, she'd discovered a lot of things that could have kept her down, but she wasn't going to let them. She'd adapt, thrive, be resilient.

At the sound of the doorbell, she took Ellie's hand, very aware that she'd have scooped her up even a few weeks before. "C'mon, let's go downstairs and meet Nanna's friends, okay?"

Candace's dining room was a glorious ode to a midnineties aesthetic. Plush, pale-mint carpet had been vacuumed in long lines no footprints dared to sully. The dining room table, long enough to easily seat eight, matched the sideboard and china cabinet, all in white laminate with curved edges and blunt handles. Walls of seafoam green, window valances of mauve. Pastel art prints of shells and sandcastles decorated one wall. The other featured family portraits in brass frames.

"Look," Candace declared as Sarah and Ellie came in. "We all match!"

The five women she'd invited for lunch cooed and exclaimed over how cute they all looked while Sarah smiled and kept her opinion to herself. Candace's dress was in the same flower fabric but in a different style. She, Honor, Ellie, and Sarah looked like a set of throw pillows. All they needed were some doilies.

"Honor, you take our little princess into the kitchen for her lunch, okay? Sarah, Honor will entertain her; you just relax and enjoy yourself," Candace urged as Honor led Ellie away by the hand. "Now, let me introduce you to everyone."

RuthAnn, a bubbly brunette with a stylish haircut, wore a diamond on her finger so big it cast a shadow on the tablecloth. Peg was
an older woman with soft gray curls and a pantsuit adorned with a
button featuring a picture of her grandkids. Heather and Jennifer
were look-alike sisters, both in their late forties. Rounding out the
group was Rebecca, who wore purple glasses with rhinestones at the
temples and looked to be closer to Sarah's age of early thirties. They'd
all been members of Peter's congregation. Their current pastor, Sarah
learned, couldn't hold a candle to Candace's Peter, rest his soul, but,
well, this new one was what they had.

Sarah hadn't forgotten what it was like to have a set of good
friends. She'd lost touch with her college group. There were people at
Temple Beth Or she was friendly with, and every so often before
Ellie was born, she'd gone out for drinks or met friends from her
hotel job for lunch. The COVID-19 pandemic had made it difficult
to join any mommies' groups, and by the time she felt ready to do
social things again, Adam was sick. With this group, she felt welcomed, but very much aware of the differences between her friends
and Candace's.

"Would you like some of this?" Peg had been serving herself from
the bowl of deviled-ham salad and now started doing the same
for Sarah.

Sarah put a hand between the spoon and her plate. "No.
Thank you."

"Too spicy?"

Everyone at the table looked at her.

"I don't eat pork."

Peg laughed. "Oh, but this is ham."

"Peg," RuthAnn said under her breath. "If she doesn't eat pork,
she won't eat *ham*."

Sarah looked around at each of them, then at Candace, who was
shooting black looks toward Peg. "I'm Jewish. In case Candace didn't
mention it."

Peg still looked confused. "Oh, she did. But . . ."

"Just put it down, Peg," RuthAnn said.

"I worked with a Jewish lady once," offered Heather. "She was
very nice."

Jennifer looked at her sister. "You never told me that."

"Oh, yes. She ate pork, though." Heather turned toward Sarah.

Again, everyone looked at Sarah expectantly. "Well, I don't."

"But you celebrate Christmas, don't you? You *have* to," Peg said.

Sarah kept her expression and her voice both light. "Christmas is not a Jewish holiday."

"Your little one never had Santa? I just don't see how you could deny your child Santa," Peg said earnestly while Candace gave her another dirty look. "It's not religious at all."

"Jesus *is* the reason for the season, Peg," RuthAnn put in.

"But Santa isn't *religious*," Peg insisted. "And it's such a shame to deny a child the joy of Christmas."

"We have our own holidays. We don't feel denied by not celebrating yours," Sarah replied, adding, "Just like you don't feel denied by not celebrating ours."

"But—" Peg began.

"Dessert's ready if anyone wants it," Honor said from the doorway, and to Sarah's relief, all the ladies turned their attention and discussion to that.

Rebecca held Sarah back with a hand on her elbow as they all filed out of the dining room and across the foyer to the living room. "Peg didn't mean anything by any of that. I hope you won't hold it against her."

"Of course I won't." Sarah had met many a Peg in her life, and she was sure there'd be many more.

"It's just that she's never really gone anywhere or seen anything. I can guarantee you she's never met a Jewish person in her entire life."

"Really, it's fine." Sarah forced a smile.

Rebecca stepped closer, her voice lowering. "Candace was devastated, you know. When she found out that Henry had married you. And Peter, oh, he was beside himself—"

"Sarah! Come in here, honey!"

Sarah's smile had slipped away. "We'd better go in."

"We'll never hear the end of it if we don't. Candace likes to have her own way." Rebecca's light tone carried an undercurrent of snark, and Sarah realized something. This woman was not Candace's friend. Not a true one, anyway.

"Sit here." Candace led Sarah to a straight-backed chair positioned between the love seat and the sofa. "Now, ladies, who wants to go first?"

"First for what?" Sarah asked.

"I'll go first. I need your wedding ring." Heather held up a piece of yarn.

Sarah closed her right hand over her left, protecting her ring finger. "Why?"

"We're going to predict whether you're carrying a boy or a girl," Heather said. "So I need your ring. I'll give it right back."

"My fingers are too swollen." Sarah held up her hand to show off her knuckles, too big for the ring to get past. She could force it off if necessary, but she didn't want to.

"Fine, we'll use mine," Candace said, already slipping off her diamond ring and the plain gold band beneath it. She handed the plain ring to Heather, who strung it on the yarn and made a loop.

"All right, Sarah, if the ring spins clockwise, that means it's a girl. If it's counterclockwise, it's a boy."

"What if it doesn't spin?" Sarah asked.

Heather frowned. "Don't even think such a thing."

That was not the answer Sarah had hoped to elicit. She decided to keep her mouth shut as Candace's friends each trotted out an old wives' tale method for determining the unborn baby's gender. These ranged from looking at the pattern of blood vessels in her eyes to asking her about cravings and whether she was getting stretch marks to determining if she carried high or low. And of course the ring test, done two different ways.

"Well?" RuthAnn asked Peg, who'd been scribbling down the results of each test on a piece of scrap paper. "What's the verdict?"

"It's a boy," Peg proclaimed, and held up the paper so everyone could see the column marked with a B. Only two of the tests had resulted in a check mark for G.

"I knew it!" Candace cried, and hugged Sarah. "Didn't I tell you that I always know?"

"You sure did."

"How wonderful. You'll have one of each," Jennifer said.

"Our special new little prince," Candace crowed.

Sarah paused. It wasn't the first time Candace had referred to the baby that way, but something in all the *oohs* and *aahs* put a different spin on it. She put her hands on her belly and looked around the room. She didn't want to share her grief with these women, these strangers, who'd known her husband for more years than Sarah would ever get to have with him. Not her grief, and not her son.

She pasted on a smile and sat up straight. "A boy. Wow. I'm not sure I'll know what to do with a boy."

"Boys are so much better than girls." Peg said this with an authoritative nod and a look around the room to make sure everyone was agreeing with her. She steadied her gaze on Sarah's. "So much easier to deal with. Boys are a blessing."

Sarah shifted. Her back ached, and a change of subject was in order. "Any baby, boy or girl, is a blessing, and I guess we'll just have to wait and see if you all got it right or not. I don't plan to find out until the baby's born. Adam and I always said, of all the surprises in the world, that has to be one of the best."

Agreement and smiles all around. The mood of the room shifted, and Sarah sipped a breath of relief. Candace leaned over and patted Sarah's belly without warning.

"Don't you worry about it, honey," Candace said. "I'll be right here to help you figure it out. I know all about raising boys."

"She does," Peg said. "And you'll love living here in Shelter Grove, Sarah. It's a wonderful place to raise children."

"Well, we won't be living here forever. At some point, we *are* going to get our own place." Sarah let out a stiff chuckle.

Candace's giggle sparkled, effervescent. "We'll just see about that. You're not going to take away our little prince so fast."

Staring around the room at all their bright smiles and shining eyes, Sarah had nothing to say. As the group dispersed into the driveway, she caught Rebecca coming out of the powder room. Sarah touched her elbow so she'd hang back.

"Could I ask you a question? I just wondered if you could tell me what exactly that means . . . all of that stuff about the baby being a prince."

Rebecca looked quickly over Sarah's shoulder, but the rest of the group was still chatting around their cars. She leaned closer to Sarah, her voice lowered. "Well, he was Pastor Peter's bloodline, wasn't he? A prophet, like his daddy. That's what made the Blood of the Lamb church truly special. A direct line from God."

"Couldn't Peter have, I don't know, trained someone else to take over for him?" Sarah was almost afraid to ask.

"Pastor Peter had a real, true calling. You can't train someone into being a prophet; they have to be born with that blessing."

Sarah kept her voice low. "What about the boy they adopted?"

"Did Candace tell you about him?" Rebecca withdrew a step.

"I haven't asked her. Adam told me he had a brother that had some behavioral problems, and they sent him away."

"Such a shame."

"Is that what happened?" Sarah pressed.

Rebecca shook her head with a frown. "Honestly, it was before I knew them. Peg could tell you about him."

Sarah wasn't about to ask Peg about anything. "Do you think maybe they sent him away because they didn't think he had the blessing? Of being a prophet, I mean."

"Well, he wasn't Peter's son, so I don't see how he could have been. Peter was . . . special. And he made *us* all feel so special." Rebecca's eyes gleamed behind her purple frames with a faraway, starry look. There was a sexual undertone to Rebecca's voice, the breathiness of it, the longing. It made the hairs on the back of Sarah's neck rise.

"And Pastor Steve doesn't?"

"Not even close." Rebecca grimaced.

"Why doesn't Candace go to his church? Wouldn't it be better than not belonging to a congregation at all?"

"Candace was married to Peter. She can't possibly go to a church led by another man," Rebecca said in a tone that said Sarah was being deliberately obtuse. "That would be like she was saying she didn't even believe in the prophet's bloodline. That would be a scandal, wouldn't it? She might even make people so mad they'd stop sending her money."

"Who sends her money?"

"Peter's subscribers. He was such a visionary. He really knew how to reach the ones who needed him. He had an entire course set up online so people could learn along with him. *Learning With the Lamb*. You should look it up," Rebecca said.

"So . . . people still send money to a church that no longer exists?"

"Not the way they used to, obviously. But I'll tell you what." Rebecca leaned close enough to murmur in Sarah's ear. "If there was a new prophet from Peter's bloodline, I bet they'd be happy to start sending more."

23

OUR LITTLE PRINCE, Candace had said. *The new prophet*, Rebecca had said. *The bloodline.*

Honestly, it was creepy.

Having grown up in America, there was no way Sarah could be unfamiliar with the basic tenets of Christianity, but she'd never heard of any kind of bloodline. Blood libel, sure, as disgusting and ridiculous an accusation as that was. But blood*line*? Some kind of inherited prophethood passed from father to son? That seemed specific to the Blood of the Lamb church.

She didn't want to ask Candace about it; Candace's stories had a way of . . . shifting, first of all, but also, Sarah wasn't at all interested in being converted and didn't want to even open the door to that conversation. She'd found a few different Bibles on the shelves in the family room, one of which had been filled with handwritten notes, highlights, and other markings for anything referring to King David or his bloodline, which Jesus was supposedly a part of. Had that been where Peter got his teachings? Did they consider Adam a descendent of Jesus?

Did they think her baby was?

The baby shifted, rolling, and Sarah murmured soothingly to it. "Boy or girl, I love you. You don't have to take over any church. I promise. Eight weeks to go, okay? You keep on growing. But maybe ease off on the kicking, just a little."

When she put the marked-up Bible on the nightstand, she knocked it into the book she'd been reading the night before. A note fell out, and she stared at it without bending to get it. The folded piece of paper lay at her feet on the thick, hunter-green carpet. She sat back on the edge of the bed.

Adam had never used a bookmark in his life, or so she'd always teased him. Receipts; envelopes torn in half; once she'd even found a birthday card tucked between the pages of his current read. Sarah had a small collection of tidy cardboard rectangles, some decorated with dangling ribbons, all of them featuring phrases like *Reading is FUN-damental* or *Hold My Place*. If this note had been holding a spot in the book, she hadn't put it there.

Nor would she be able to figure out now if it had been marking a passage meant to be of some significance. She picked it up and opened it, bracing herself for something that would stab her right in the heart. A to-do list greeted her.

Bank Account
Paperwork
Insurance

A few other items, all of them mundane. Without importance. Until she looked at the bottom of the page.

I do love you. Never forget.

The last words had been scrawled over the bottom of the list. Adam's handwriting. She'd have recognized it anywhere with the signature looping *y* and *g*. Sarah closed her eyes and pressed the paper to her heart. This was the book she'd been reading at his bedside in the final weeks before he'd died, and she'd finally allowed herself to pick it up again. She hadn't been able to remember any of the early chapters and had started from page one, or else she might have found this note much sooner.

Grief, that fickle, finicky thing, raked its talons down her back—but the touch was a tickle, not a tearing. A dark humor rose inside her, forcing out huffs of breath that could have been sobs or guffaws, even Sarah couldn't tell. She rocked, clutching the note and trying to stifle her gasping sounds, too aware that her open door meant she could be overheard.

She cried, and she laughed, and she thought of her husband; she loved him, and she hated him, and she began, at last, to forgive him.

Whatever choices Adam had made—to keep his past a secret, to lie to her about his family, to give the Morgans more power over her and Ellie than they deserved—whatever reasons he'd had for doing any of that, Sarah had to trust and believe that he'd done it because he thought it was for the best.

Adam had been the first to say "I love you," and she'd believed him then. From the first night they'd spent together, he'd done nothing but take care of her. Protect her. Support and provide for her. All the rest of what she'd discovered since his death was secondary to that.

I do love you. Never forget.

She would not. She could not. And as the time passed, she would get the pieces of her life back in order. She and Ellie and the baby were going to be okay.

Sarah tucked the note back inside the book and replaced it on the nightstand. The softness of Adam's cardigan weighed too heavily on her today, despite the air conditioning. Carefully, she folded it and hung it over the back of the rocking chair. She pressed her fingertips to her nose but couldn't smell him on her skin. He was fading.

She would not let herself think about that. Today, she decided, she was going to get herself and Ellie into a much better routine. They were going to start doing their puzzles again. Finger painting. She'd start teaching Ellie to read. She'd start doing the lessons in her language app again, the one that had finally stopped sending her vaguely ominous messages about her lack of progress.

But first, lemon bars.

"Because if you can't indulge yourself in lemon bars when you're pregnant, when can you?" she murmured.

The treat had been Adam's favorite from way back in their college days. He'd made them from a recipe scrawled on a piece of lined notebook paper that had been folded so many times it was soft with age. Eventually, they'd made the lemon bars so often, neither one of them needed the recipe.

Sarah had taken a pan of lemon bars to the hospital in those last days, hoping to tempt him into eating. He hadn't been able to. Maybe the nurses had finished them. She'd never bothered to ask or even to get her pan back. It had been white, with mushrooms and other veggies on it. It had been Adam's since she'd first known him, the one in which they'd made thousands of batches of lemon bars over the years they'd been together.

Now she stared at several in the same pattern, stacked in Candace's cupboard. The only one missing from the set was the one she'd last seen the day her husband left her. It was another sign, wasn't it?

"Adam," she whispered. "What are you trying to tell me?"

Probably not to be so silly, she told herself as she searched the kitchen for the right ingredients. She'd never believed in the supernatural before now. If there was a life beyond the one on this earth, Adam was there. Not stuck here.

The bright peal of Ellie's laughter drifted to her from upstairs. Candace had been playing dolls with her for an hour already. "Nanna" had an endless patience that Sarah envied and appreciated.

She'd just finished setting out all the ingredients when Honor came into the kitchen from the sunroom. Sarah smiled. "Morning."

Honor's return smile was cautious. Reserved. She nodded in response and went into the laundry room to switch over the load from the washer to the dryer. Sarah hummed under her breath as she looked for mixing bowls, measuring spoons, a rubber spatula. She started the oven preheating. Aware of Honor in motion behind her, she kept her eyes on the tasks of her recipe. Like trying to tame a fox, she thought. Another memory from Adam. *The Little Prince* had been one of his favorites. For a moment, unease whispered its way around her as she made the connection. Little prince, heir apparent . . . Sarah shook it off.

As Honor put a laundry basket brimming with clean clothes on the kitchen table, Sarah cracked some eggs and added the butter into the KitchenAid mixer bowl. She was used to doing all of this by hand, but hey, when you had the fancy equipment right there on hand, what kind of fool would ignore it?

Not for the first time since waking up like Little Lord Fauntleroy, she wondered what it had been like for Adam growing up here. Every luxury, every amenity, everything top dollar. Sure, the house was showing its age. You wouldn't see hunter-green carpet and brass fixtures in any home decorating magazines these days. But high-end appliances and solid furniture that didn't come from a Scandinavian warehouse store lasted forever, and all of it was finer than anything Sarah had grown up with. Heck, most of it was nicer even than what she and Adam had bought together after the business had started really making money.

And who'd paid for it all? Peter's congregants. Who was paying for the trips to Rodeo Drive, the hair and nail appointments, a live-in housekeeper? Sarah frowned as she concentrated on adding in the ingredients, one at a time. It wasn't her business how people chose to spend their money—unless it was for the promise of a new church, led by her unborn-might-be-a-son.

"I love this," she said aloud now, so Honor could hear her. "This mixer. Look at it go. Growing up, the best we had was a wire whisk. And the handle fell off if you used it too hard."

She kept her tone light and conversational but risked a peek at the housekeeper. Honor had tied on an oversized apron and was unloading the dishwasher. She paused, not looking at Sarah.

"Candace doesn't allow me to use it. She's afraid I might break it, and the pieces are very expensive to replace."

Sarah focused on the soft-yellow goo of eggs and butter mixing slowly. "KitchenAid mixers are really hard to break."

"But did she tell you it was okay to use the mixer?" Honor insisted. Twin pink circles highlighted her pale cheeks.

"No. Not specifically."

Honor bent back to the dishwasher, yanking a plate free and opening the cupboard in front of her so hard the door banged against the one next to it. The plate clattered as she put it in place. To Sarah's alarm, her hands looked as though they were shaking.

"Of course she'd let *you* do whatever you want," Honor said under her breath.

Sarah turned off the mixer. Another rise of laughter from upstairs turned Honor's gaze upward. Her scowl faltered, becoming a pressed-lip grimace. Honor blinked rapidly. Was she holding back tears?

Not for the first time, Sarah sensed a jealous tension between them. Candace favored Sarah and Ellie, and Honor noticed. Sarah understood why it didn't feel good to be treated as less-than, but it wasn't really her place to lecture Candace on how to treat her house-keeper. If Honor didn't like the rules of the house, why did she stay? Anyway, Sarah reminded herself, in a few months Honor could get back to having the run of the house, and her relationship with Candace would continue being none of Sarah's business. Until then, all Sarah could do was try not to aggravate Honor any more than she already seemed to be doing.

Sarah busied herself with finishing the lemon bars. She didn't look at or speak to Honor, whose eyes she could feel boring into her when she had her back turned but whose gaze always miraculously skimmed away when Sarah faced her.

"She gets angry," Honor said finally.

Candace likes to have her own way, Rebecca had said. And when she didn't, was that when she got mad? Sarah slid the pan into the oven, but before she could question Honor, Candace appeared with Ellie on her hip. The kid was covered in pink from top to toe. Bows, frills, a lacy tutu, the works.

"What are you doing?" Candace hitched Ellie up and down.

"She's really too big to be carried like that," Sarah told her. "She's going to hurt your back."

Honor spoke up. "She was using the mixer."

Candace's lips parted, and her arched brows reached for her bangs. "Oh? And what was she doing with it?"

"She," Sarah said lightly, "was making lemon bars."

She held out her arms for Ellie, who reached back. For a moment, Candace didn't let go, and it felt as though there might actually be a bit of a tug-of-war. At the last second, Candace relented and Ellie almost leaped into her mother's arms, knocking Sarah back a step.

"Wow, wow, ketzelah." She laughed.

Ellie pressed her sticky cheek to Sarah's. "Want lemur bars."

Candace stared, mouth now agape. "Lemon . . . bars?"

"It's an old family recipe," Adam had told her. "Very secret. Very hush-hush. You can't ever tell anyone I let you have it."

Sarah had thought he was kidding.

"He taught you how to make lemon bars?"

Uncomfortably, she nodded, and hoped Candace couldn't notice the rise of heat that had to be painting a blush on Sarah's face. "Yes."

Honor burst into tears and ran from the room.

"Oh dear," Candace said.

Oh dear, indeed. Sarah was no fan of managing other people's emotions, but it was clear she couldn't keep ignoring this. She drew in a breath and set Ellie at the table. She faced her mother-in-law. "Candace, Honor's been acting really strange since we got here, and I don't know why. I'd like to let her know that I'm not here to make more work for her; I'm happy to do mine and Ellie's laundry and clean up after ourselves, if that's the trouble."

Candace's eyebrows rose. "Why on earth would that be the trouble, honey?"

"I'm sure she didn't love getting saddled with two extra people to clean up after, without warning. I could at least contribute to her salary, maybe?" Sarah said, thinking of her savings and money going out, not coming in. "And if I'm allowed to use the fancy mixer, maybe she could be allowed too?"

Candace burst into bubbles of laughter that rapidly began to grate on Sarah's nerves. Nobody could sound that much like Glinda the Good Witch without forcing it.

"What's so funny?" Sarah asked bluntly.

Candace shook her head. "Honey, she's not my *housekeeper*."

"She's not?"

"Oh, no, dear."

Sarah waited, but Candace only stared at her with a sweet smile and didn't say anything else. She seemed to be waiting for Sarah to ask. So she did. "Who is she?"

"Well, honey, she's Henry's wife."

24

NOT A HOUSEKEEPER, but a spurned ex. It all made more sense even as it made none at all. "Adam was *married* before me?"

Candace gave a breezy laugh and gesture, like she was brushing away a fly. "He was married in the church. Yes."

A rushing whirr, like the sound of a thousand flies battering a windshield, filled Sarah's ears. The floor rocked. She didn't stagger, not quite, but Ellie's weight was no longer such a comfort. Sarah squeezed, and Ellie squirmed. She put her daughter down.

"I have to sit down." Sarah lurched toward one of the kitchen chairs.

She was here, she was not *here*.

She was *here*, but she was not here.

She didn't want to be here, but she made herself stay anyway. Solid and grounded and centered and present. She pressed her fingertips into her palms, her own touch on her own skin. Hers.

Candace went at once to the sink to draw a glass of cool water, which she put in front of Sarah without a word. Sarah drank it greedily. Candace lifted Ellie with a grunt of effort.

"Let me get her settled," Candace said quietly. Louder, more brightly, she said to Ellie, "Come on, my precious. How would you like to play in your room with your dollies?"

Ellie didn't protest, and although Sarah imagined herself reaching again for her daughter, taking her in her arms, holding her tight, she didn't protest either. She watched Candace take her away. She placed her hands flat on the table in front of her to keep herself from making fists. She concentrated on breathing in. Breathing out.

Staying here, not floating away.

Honor and Adam?

No, she reminded herself. Honor and *Henry*. Henry, who was a stranger to her. Terrified, mousy Honor had been married to Candace's son. But when? For how long?

By the time Candace returned to the kitchen, Sarah had managed to get herself under some semblance of control. She'd even boiled water for tea and poured two cups. The lemon bars cooled on the counter, but she had not yet cut into them.

"Please, sit," she offered.

Candace did. She reached at once across the table to pat Sarah's hand briefly. She folded her hands in front of her with an expectant look.

"When?" Sarah asked bluntly.

"Oh, they were very young."

"Of course he was very young," Sarah snapped. "He was *still* young when he died."

Candace pulled back but rallied and kept her expression from contorting. The words had stung her. Sarah could see it in the older woman's eyes. She would not allow herself to feel guilty about that, though. Truth could hurt, but lies would always hurt worse.

"He was eighteen. A man in the eyes of the church, and his father."

"What about your eyes?"

Candace waved an airy hand, her common response anytime something distressed her. Sarah had learned her tell. "He'll always be my little boy. My baby."

A shudder trembled at the base of Sarah's skull, but she stopped her lip from curling. "So, you approved?"

Candace hesitated. A war fought itself in her expression, but it was impossible for Sarah to tell which emotion had won. She sighed. Shrugged. Gave Sarah a pained smile.

"He was in love," she said finally. "Who was I to stand in the way of love?"

Sarah got up from the table. The chair legs scraped across the floor. She stalked to the sink, rested her hands on the rim, staring into it. Shoulders hunched. She turned around to lean against it, propped herself up.

"He was . . . he said he'd never . . . I was the first." Sarah's voice caught, scraping, raw in her throat. She coughed to clear it.

Again, emotions cavorted over Candace's expression, fighting for control. She blinked rapidly, the corners of her mouth twisting downward. "He *was* married. I was there."

"I meant the first woman he'd ever been with. Had *sex* with," Sarah said deliberately.

Candace flinched. Her fingertips went to the base of her throat. Her brow creased. "But . . . his father joined them in the church. They were absolutely joined in the eyes of God and the Savior."

"He wouldn't have lied to me about it."

"He lied to you about almost everything else," Candace said roughly.

For several intense moments, both women stared at each other, neither looking away. Sarah relented first, closing her eyes. She sagged against the countertop, head hanging.

"When did they get divorced?" She braced herself for a timeline that meant she'd slept with a married man.

Candace huffed. "They didn't."

"Okay, seriously now," Sarah cried, "what the actual fuck?"

"Watch your mouth!"

"I can't. I just can't, Candace. I'm sorry if my coarse language offends you, but you are seriously rocking my entire existence right now."

"I guess I shouldn't expect anything else from you," Candace said. "Considering your upbringing."

"Which means what?"

"You know what I mean, Sarah."

"If you can't even say it out loud, *Candace*, perhaps it's something you realize you ought to be ashamed to say."

Candace set her jaw and met Sarah's gaze head on. "Fine. Because you are not a Christian."

"Thank you for saying what you mean. I appreciate the honesty, finally." Sarah rubbed at the space between her eyes. "Please explain to me how they didn't get divorced."

"We don't believe in it."

"Frankly, I don't care if you believe in it. I want to know why my husband got married at eighteen, met me when he was nineteen, and never mentioned it to me. I want to know how he could have married me while still being married to another woman, without proof of being previously divorced."

Her mother-in-law swiped at tears freely flowing down her reddened cheeks. "I told you. He got married in our church. There is no divorce allowed. He didn't have to do any of that government baloney."

Something horrid occurred to Sarah. "If he was eighteen, how old was Honor?"

"Fourteen."

"Let me guess: a woman in the eyes of the church and your husband?"

Candace took a napkin from the holder and pressed it to her tears. She gave Sarah a hopeful look. "Yes, of course."

"She was a minor."

"Your people say you're a woman at twelve, don't they?" Her expression turned a little sly.

"That's different."

"I don't see how."

Sarah refused to dignify that with a response. "Her parents allowed it?"

Candace made a sour face. "Her parents both died in a car accident when she was thirteen, and we took her."

"And you married her off to your son." Sarah shuddered, pacing slowly as she put the pieces together. "But not legally. Am I right? Because she was underage, so you married them in the church but never had a legal government marriage."

"When she turned sixteen, they were going to deal with the paperwork. But they were already married under—"

"Your church, yes, I get it. But he was already gone by then. And he never had to divorce her because they'd never been legally married, not by the state anyway." Sarah sat at the table again. She sipped her now-cold tea. "And he never told *me* because he was ashamed. Did you tell anyone else? Did your congregation know? Your lunch friends?"

Her mind rocked at the thought of all of them knowing who Honor was, had been, while they smiled at Sarah and tried to determine her child's gender. Of talking about her behind her back, mocking, maybe. Worse, comparing sweet and innocent Honor to Sarah the heathen. Rebecca had said Candace was devastated when Adam married Sarah. Was that how they all felt?

"No," Candace said finally. Deep grooves framed her mouth. Her eyes were red from weeping, her usually immaculate makeup smeared. Even her hair had gone flyaway and messy in its updo. "The Lord spoke to Peter directly and told him they should get married. They needed to bring another prophet into the world. But we didn't tell anyone."

"Was that why he started college a year late?" Sarah demanded.

Candace's chin went up stubbornly, but she didn't answer. She didn't really have to. Sarah already knew Adam had taken a year off between high school and college, although now she doubted it was a gap year so much as it had been meant as the start of his new life as a married man.

"I don't believe they slept together," Sarah said.

"Oh," Candace said with a grim chuckle, "I'm absolutely sure they did."

"What did you do, check the sheets the morning after? Never mind. Don't tell me. I don't really want to hear about it. It sounds barbaric."

"At least we don't mutilate our sons!"

"Adam was circumcised, Candace. I have an intimate knowledge of his penis," Sarah shot back at her.

"But a doctor did that! In the hospital! Not some dirty old man!"

Sarah left that comment alone. Candace's lips trembled. She sipped her tea and blotted her mouth with her fingertips and drew in a shivering, tear-clotted breath.

"They were married. Lived as husband and wife. Right here," Candace said with a jab of her finger in Sarah's direction. "Under this roof. As it was meant to be. Where we could help them, you know?"

"If they were old enough to get married, why weren't they old enough to live on their own?"

Candace scowled. "There's nothing wrong with us helping them. Just because you never had that from your own parents—who knows, maybe your people just don't care enough about their children—"

"You keep saying *your people*. You don't know my people."

"Your *people*," Candace repeated.

Sarah paused. Breathed. She wasn't any calmer, but at least her voice was steady. "Candace, when you say *your people*, it's abrasive."

"I won't apologize for being a good Christian wife and mother!"

Sarah shrugged. "I'm not asking you to. Likewise, I'm not going to apologize for *not* being a good Christian wife and mother."

"You could be, Sarah. You could accept Jesus, you could know his love. I'd teach you. We could go through Peter's lessons together."

"No, thank you. My life and my faith are fine as they are."

"Clearly," Candace said disdainfully, "they aren't."

Carefully, Sarah pushed back from the table. She looked into Candace's eyes without wavering. "Your disrespect is disgusting."

Candace gaped. "I'm just being—"

"And I'm just *being*," Sarah cut her off. "It's very clear to me now why your son didn't want to stay here, and I'm not going to either."

25

"PLEASE!"

The agony in Candace's voice stopped Sarah at the top of the stairs. Sarah turned. Candace had made it halfway up the staircase. She reached out a hand but didn't come closer.

"Please, Sarah. I understand that you don't agree with the choices Peter and I made, but you have to understand that all of it was done because of our faith. And then my son left us, and his father died without ever seeing him again. And then Henry . . . I mean, Adam, since that's what he wanted to be called . . . Adam left this world without me ever getting to see him again. If you can't understand that pain, and I hope, Sarah, I *pray* that you never do, can't you at least imagine it? Only for a second. I won't ask you to think of it longer than that."

"It's terrible," Sarah agreed.

Candace blew out a shivery breath. Her shoulders hitched. She gripped the stair railing and lowered her head for a moment. "I was never able to make amends with my son. But I know without a doubt that he would want me to help you and your sweet babies. I couldn't bear it if you took Ellie away right now. I'd be beside myself worrying about how you were going to manage all on your own."

"I'd manage," Sarah replied stiffly.

Candace nodded, looking defeated. "Oh, I know you're capable of it. You're not like me, Sarah. You're strong. But why *manage* when you can accept help from someone who loves you?"

That was the very question Sarah had asked herself before coming here.

"Mama?" Ellie had come out of her room, half in and half out of one of the gifted princess gowns. "I stuck!"

"Hang on. I'll be right there." Sarah looked at Candace's forlorn face. Her mascara had streaked tracks down her cheeks. She looked worn, defeated, bereft.

Sarah went to Ellie to disengage her from the dress's tangled, fluffy fabric. Candace took the time to finish climbing the stairs. She stood in the hall, wringing her hands. When Ellie skipped back into her room, happily ensconced in layers of tulle, Sarah faced her mother-in-law.

"I will not stay in a place where you don't respect me and my faith. *Without* hidden agenda," Sarah added.

"I just thought maybe it didn't matter so much to you. You haven't done anything Jewish since you've been here."

Sarah drew herself up, stung at the weight of that accusation, which was not entirely untrue. "I don't have to *do* anything to be Jewish. And I don't want to be proselytized to. I thought I made that clear before we came here."

"If you'd just let me show you," Candace began, "if you'd only just open your heart—"

Sarah turned around and headed for Ellie's room.

"Wait! I'm sorry. Please," Candace pleaded from behind her.

Sarah paused, not turning. She didn't want Candace to see the struggle on her face, how much effort she was making to keep herself steady and solid and anchored. She felt the other woman move closer behind her.

"Please let me make it up to you," Candace said.

Sarah gathered herself and turned around. "There can't be any more secrets or surprises. If there's anything I need to know about Adam, how he grew up, anything at all that could affect me or Ellie, you need to come clean with me. Right now."

The older woman slumped. "I guess I should tell you about the money."

The middle of the hallway was not the place to have whatever this conversation was going to be. Sarah sighed. "Let's go in my room and shut the door."

The rush of emotions had made her teeth want to chatter. She looked for Adam's cardigan, but it wasn't where she'd left it. The thought of losing it had her fighting back a gasp, so she focused on digging out an old UCLA sweatshirt from the dresser instead. She struggled into it. The bump of her belly strained the front, but she didn't want to wear any of the clothes Candace had bought for her.

Candace sat on the edge of the bed while Sarah took the rocker. "I had a life insurance policy on Henry. It paid out to Honor when he died."

"How . . ." Sarah had to clear her throat. "How did you manage to take out a life insurance policy on him?"

"I'm his mother. We'd had it since he was a little boy. When Adam left us behind, Peter changed the beneficiary to Honor's name. He said that if his son couldn't bring himself to take care of his obligations in this world, we'd have to be sure that he did it when he left it." Candace's voice shook. "Her and me, you understand, we've only had each other since Peter died. We've worked it out all right. It's not easy, you know. Two women out here in the woods, all alone. When we had the church, it was much better. But people can be so cruel, spreading rumors, speaking evil. Making trouble."

"People do like to do that," Sarah said.

"Honor brings in some money with those little crafts of hers, but it barely covers the utilities. I'm blessed she takes care of that. Since Peter died, it's been . . . hard. The congregation dissolved. They tithe to Steve's church now. Insurance paid out on the church burning down, but that money wasn't going to last forever."

Especially not if you spent it all on Rodeo Drive, Sarah thought. "What about your internet congregation? How much do they send you a week?"

Candace's gaze turned cagey. "What do you mean?"

"Rebecca told me you've got people online who send you money for access to Peter's old sermons."

"Peter was the one who knew how to do all that stuff. I don't know how to keep it updated," Candace said. "There's not very much money from any of that, not anymore."

Sarah studied her. "How much was the policy for? The one on Adam?"

"A hundred thousand dollars. But I used it to help you and Ellie," Candace added quickly, probably at the sight of Sarah's expression.

The *ching-ching-ching* sound of a cash register filled Sarah's head as she mentally tallied up the toys, the clothes, the cost of the plane tickets and the moving truck. The policy she'd expected to pay out had been for a similar amount, and yet it had gone to a trust.

"We had a policy like that. Adam changed the policy to go to a trust under the control of his business partner, who tried to use that as leverage to get me to sign over my baby to him and his wife. We were left with almost nothing."

"Is that why you came here? Not because you wanted to get to know me but because you didn't have enough money? Because they were trying to take your baby from you?"

"That was a big part of it, yes."

"So you have *no* money?"

"Not very much," Sarah said. "Were you hoping I did? Were you going to ask me for it eventually?"

"It would have been nice. I guess I'm not the only one who's kept a few secrets, then, am I?" Candace stood and moved to the rocker to take Sarah's hands. She looked into Sarah's eyes. "But don't you worry about it. They can't have him. He belongs to us."

26

"BELONGS TO ME," Sarah corrected harshly.

Candace cut her gaze from Sarah's, but nodded. "Of course."

"My Jewish child," Sarah added. "I'm Jewish. My children are Jewish, and as much as it apparently hurts you, so was yours. And I'm not sure I can trust you to respect that."

"You can. I promise!" Candace drooped. "If you stay here, I'll give you what's left of the money."

Sarah narrowed her eyes. "It's Honor's money, not yours."

"I'll take care of that." Candace waved a dismissive hand.

"You're really going to bribe me to live here with you until after the baby comes?"

"At least that long. Please. I want us to be a real family. I missed so much of Ellie's life, and I really want to know this baby. He's a part of my baby, you know?"

Sarah pinched the bridge of her nose. "He's not going to be a pastor in your church, Candace. You need to understand that. My child is not taking the place of yours. He's not a prophet, and I won't allow you to use him like a show dog to win prizes for you."

"No. Of course not. Whatever you say, Sarah." Candace looked relieved. "So you're going to stay?"

Sarah had a choice, and she knew it, but the choice to leave felt infinitely harder than staying. Like Candace had said, why simply manage when she could be taken care of? Didn't some small part of her yearn for that still? Wouldn't it make her life so much easier if she could rest here for a bit, until she could put a plan in place? She was in her third trimester of pregnancy. Where on earth could she possibly even go?

"Not forever, but for now." Sarah got up from the rocker, not looking forward to having a discussion with Honor. She had to, though. Married at fourteen? She'd been a victim. None of this was her fault.

Honor's door hung open a few inches, and Sarah peeked inside. At the sight of the younger woman facedown on the bed and the drifting sound of her sobs, Sarah steeled herself to be . . . what, exactly?

To be kind, she told herself. Surely she could manage that.

"Honor? Can I come in?"

Honor sat up, her face contorted and smeared with tears. Her voice cracked with an answer spoken so raggedly that Sarah had to strain to hear it. "You hate me, I know it!"

"Of everyone involved with this mess, why would you think I'd hate *you*?"

Honor choked back another sob and hung her head so the sheaf of blonde hair covered her face. Her body shook. Sarah pulled up the bentwood rocker that matched the one in her room and eased herself onto it with a grateful sigh. She leaned forward to rest her elbows on her knees. She rubbed her eyes, then pressed her fingertips to the closed lids.

There was still time for her to go back on what she'd told Candace. She and Ellie could leave here. They would be fine. She didn't need to be the one to heal this family's mess, not for anyone's sake, and especially not her dead husband's.

Be kind.

"He was being punished," Honor said, "for leaving his true wife and for leaving his faith, and—"

"I don't hate you, Honor, but I'm about to get really, really pissed off with you."

Honor looked at her, chastened. "I'm sorry."

"Adam's gone because he got sick. He had a rare form of leukemia that he was either too old for, or too young, depending on who you asked, and it killed him," Sarah said finally.

A shuffle of feet came from outside the room, but she didn't bother to lower her voice. If Candace wanted to lurk at closed doors, she'd have to deal with whatever she overheard. "I want you to tell me everything. How the two of you met. How you got together. All of it."

Honor looked toward the door with a frown. "My parents belonged to Pastor Peter's church. We always knew each other, ever since we were kids. When they died, Peter and Candace took me in."

"Do other girls in your church get married so young?"

"There is no church," Honor said. "Not anymore."

Sarah tried hard and managed to keep her patience. "Before it burned, then. Before Peter died."

Honor's mouth worked, opening and closing without a sound. Finally, she said, "No. But Henry was the prince. The Lamb. He was special. And that made me special too."

Sarah ran her hands over her face before cupping her palms over her eyes. Without looking at Honor, she said, "You don't need a man to make you special."

That distinctive *beep-boop* sound chimed from Honor's nightstand drawer. They both looked at it. Honor's chin lifted stubbornly.

"Do you want to check your messages?" Sarah asked.

Honor shook her head. "Are you going to tell Candace?"

"I told you I wasn't going to say anything, so I won't, but what *are* you doing exactly?" Sarah paused, hardly able to believe she was having this kind of conversation with a woman who had to be, what . . . twenty-five years old? She ought to be in school, or working, living on her own. Dating. "Are you being . . . safe?"

"I don't know what you mean."

"Honor, I recognize the sound of that app. I used to use it myself, back in the olden times before I met Adam."

Honor looked so scandalized, Sarah was almost sorry she asked. "It's just for talking to people. It doesn't mean anything."

"You're not meeting up with anyone?"

Honor's eyebrows went up. "How would I even do that!"

"I don't know. Maybe at night, after Candace is asleep?"

"She's got bars on the windows and an alarm that goes off when you open the doors," Honor said in a *Don't be stupid* voice.

"Is that because she caught you sneaking out?" Sarah asked matter-of-factly.

Honor looked guilty but shook her head vehemently. "It's because of the vandals. They egg the house. They wrote dirty graffiti on the shed once."

That all sounded unpleasant, but still like kids playing pranks, nothing dangerous. "Did they really break in and take stuff?"

"Oh yes," Honor said.

"But why? I don't understand."

"They hate us. Christians are the most persecuted people," Honor said.

Sarah burst into astounded laughter, shaking her head. "I can assure you, Honor, you're not. Anyone whose religious holidays are also federal holidays is definitely not being persecuted."

Honor was quiet for a moment. "Doesn't it bother you that you're going to hell?"

"I don't believe in hell."

"What if you're wrong?" Honor asked, sounding genuinely concerned.

Sarah shrugged. "What if you are?"

"But I'm not."

"Well, then," Sarah said with another shrug, "I guess I'm going to hell."

Beep-boop.

Honor took the phone out of the nightstand and turned the sound off. She held it in her hand for a moment, looking at the screen with an expression Sarah couldn't interpret. Shame, but also pride and defiance, overlaid with a faint shadow of self-loathing. Sarah had every reason to hate Honor, but all she could find was pity.

"Have you ever thought about moving out of here?" Sarah asked.

"Where would I go?" Honor looked confused. "To do what?"

Sarah rocked in the chair, rubbing her belly in small, slow circles. The baby somersaulted inside her. "Anywhere and anything you want to."

"I couldn't. Candace has always been so good to me. After Peter died and the church burned down, it didn't feel right to leave her here alone. She needs me."

Something occurred to Sarah. "And you were waiting for him to come back?"

Honor looked embarrassed. "We always thought he would, once he'd had his fill of worldly things and was ready to come back and fulfill his responsibilities. But once his father died, I knew he wasn't going to."

"Did you know he'd gotten married? Had a child?"

"Yes . . ." Honor hesitated, looking down at her hands. "He told me all about you and Ellie."

Sarah coughed abruptly and sat up straight. "What? When did he tell you that?"

"Three years ago."

"On the phone? He called you?"

Honor shook her head. A fist clenched Sarah's heart. Her hands curled over the chair's bentwood arms, but her feet went flat to the floor to stop her from rocking. She needed solid ground.

"No, when he came back here," Honor said. "When he came to ask me if I'd forgive him."

CHAPTER

27

THREE YEARS AGO, right after Ellie was born, Adam had gone on an unplanned business trip, allegedly to salvage a deal about to fall through. "Flash" usually handled those things, but Graham had been out of the country securing a different deal. At least that was what Adam had told her when he apologized for having to leave her alone with a newborn. A week after his return, his routine doctor visit had led to the first of many, then to the diagnosis of the illness that would take his life.

The hits just didn't stop coming.

"What were you supposed to forgive him for?"

"Leaving. Leaving me behind," Honor amended. "He said he wanted to help me leave Shelter Grove, but . . . how could I? When he was already married to someone else? With a baby?"

Sarah closed her eyes, trying to imagine what it would have been like if Adam had shown up with his ex-child-bride in tow. Would she have been gracious? Probably not.

"He asked you to go away with him?" Sarah asked carefully.

"He . . . just offered to help me. That's all he said. Then he told me he was never coming back, and he never did. He chose you. You should be happy about that," Honor said.

"I would be, except I never knew I was a choice he even had to make." Sarah got up, leaving the chair rocking wildly. "I'm going to bed. I can't really think about any of this right now."

She needed some quiet, some darkness, a pillow to press her face against. In her room, she undressed and got into bed, turning on her side with a pillow between her knees and another clutched to her chest. She didn't cry; at this point, what use were tears?

Her body ached, worse even than her heart. At some point, she'd have to go numb. Hours passed while she tried, and failed, to sleep. At last, she sat up on the edge of the bed with a heavy sigh and flipped the cap on her tube of lotion. She squeezed out the last of it and rubbed it into her swollen belly with smooth, steady strokes and tried not to dwell on the memory of Adam doing this for her when she was pregnant with Ellie. She wrapped her arms around the bump and rocked herself and the baby inside her.

Who would ever touch her this way again?

Who would ever take care of her the way Adam had?

Who would ever love her?

No, no, no. Sarah forced herself to sit upright, to breathe in and out, separating herself from this pain that would, if left unchecked, tear her into pieces so small she could never be put back together again.

I am a cloud. A bird. A faraway star.

Distant from her body, she was able to finish rubbing the lotion into her skin. She could take note that she needed more. She was aware of her tear-scalded eyes and the heat of her cheeks, but she didn't *feel* them. She stared at her hand, curling the fingers in and out, turning her palm upward and doing it again. She might have been watching a movie. She could have been dreaming.

Finally, she closed her eyes and counted the seconds of each breath in, each one out, and the steady, relentless, dual thump of each heartbeat. When she opened her eyes, everything in the room looked a little fuzzy. Tilted.

She had tried to explain to Adam what it was like, this floating sense that her body did not belong to her, that she was watching someone else go through the motions of her life. How it happened to her sometimes when she didn't want it to, but other times she could find that weird distance on purpose and sink into it, like a luxury.

"I know why you did it as a kid, but why do you do it now?" he'd asked her.

She'd shrugged. "I guess it's a way of avoiding stress. Disappointment, grief. Anger."

"Does it feel good?"

She'd been able to answer truthfully. "Yes. Sometimes, it's better to go away than to feel the anxiety. I know it's not okay."

He'd kissed her then and wrapped her in his arms. "No matter how far away you go, you will always have me here to bring you back."

Consciously, Sarah sharpened her gaze. She brought herself back. She could not afford to make herself an untethered balloon, floating off into the sky where she only had to see everything from far away. She had to be here, in this body, in this life. For Ellie. For the baby.

He doesn't belong to them. He belongs to us.

Candace's words rang in Sarah's mind, leaving her unsettled. If Candace gave Sarah the money, she could afford to get a new place, but the money came along with the promise that she'd stay. Could she stand it for the next eight weeks and then beyond, another six months, maybe? Give herself time to have the baby, figure out where she wanted to go, all of that? Arching, Sarah rubbed the small of her back. She could barely get up from bed all by herself. There was no way she could manage another move, not this pregnant, not while also caring for Ellie. She was stuck. Anyway, how much worse could anything possibly get than finding out the housekeeper was actually her sisterwife?

Sarah stifled a yawn and considered a late-night shower to help ease her back into sleep. Before she could turn on the nightstand lamp, a flash of light ran across her window. Then another.

She peeked out the window and saw the same flashing lights bobbing along the lawn as she had before. The same shadowed figures. She tried but failed to see a fall of auburn hair.

She stepped back from the glass with a hand pressed to her chest. There was no way Ava and Graham would be running through Candace's yard at night. To believe that was to dip into the territory her mother had defended with stacks of magazines and aluminum foil shields over the electrical outlets. Someone *was* trespassing, but it wasn't anyone looking for Sarah. She had to believe that.

She watched the darkness for a minute longer and saw only a few faint flashes through the trees. She looked at the clock radio's warm orange glow. Three thirty. A warm shower was definitely in order. Maybe she'd even sneak downstairs and have a lemon bar and some milk.

Ellie's wail had Sarah lumbering down the hall.

"I'm coming!"

The little girl was still sobbing when Sarah got to her. She burrowed against her mother's neck, crawling into her lap despite the lack of room. Sarah kissed Ellie's temple, feeling for the heat of fever, but found none.

"What happened, ketzeleh?"

"Daddy," Ellie whispered.

Sarah's arms tightened around her. "You miss Daddy?"

"Daddy was here."

A chill tickled the back of Sarah's neck, like the gust of a breeze through an open window. "You must have been having a dream."

"No. Daddy was here," Ellie insisted. She struggled out of Sarah's embrace, squirming to turn toward the closet. "He stood there."

Only a few months ago, Ellie wouldn't have been able to string a sentence together like that, and for a moment Sarah allowed herself to admire again how fast she was growing up. She shifted the girl so she could look at her tear-streaked face. Sarah smoothed the tangled hair off her forehead, feeling again in case there was any hint of fever, but Ellie's skin was cool.

"Daddy can't be here, Ellie. I know it's hard to understand, but he can't. You must have been . . . pretending, in your brain."

"I'm not pretending!" Ellie grumped, looking so very much like her father that it stung Sarah straight to her core.

"Did he say anything to you?"

"He said, 'Be quiet, Ellie.'"

Sarah pressed her lips together for a second. "Why did he want you to be quiet?"

"Keep a secret."

"Ellie," Sarah said quietly, "is Daddy in here right now?"

Her heart pounded fiercely as she drew in and held a breath. Why? Out of hope that somehow Adam was here in some incorporeal form? Not a dream but a ghost, haunting their daughter and therefore, somehow, accessible to his wife? She was being ridiculous.

Ellie's small, dark brows arched upward into her bangs. She burst into laughter. "No, Mama! Silly Mama."

"You're right. Mama's silly." The breath she'd been holding sifted out on the words.

"Mama." Ellie pressed her hands to Sarah's cheeks, squeezing to purse Sarah's lips. She moved her hands to turn her mother's head until Sarah looked into her eyes. "Daddy said you want him to go away."

"Daddy was being silly, then. Because I love him. Just like I love you."

Ellie didn't look convinced. She strained to look over her shoulder. A sound in the doorway caught Sarah's attention, but it wasn't the ghost of her dead husband, just the figure of her once-believed-to-be-dead mother-in-law.

"Everything okay in here?" Candace hesitated, one hand on the doorframe. "I heard her scream."

"Let me tuck you in. You go back to sleep, okay?" Sarah almost wished Ellie would protest and demand to sleep in her bed tonight, which would end up in Sarah losing sleep but would also somehow be gratifying, letting her know that Ellie wanted her more.

Her vocabulary and speech patterns weren't the only thing that had advanced, though. To Sarah's chagrin, the little girl simply crawled off her lap and slid under the blankets, already turning onto her side and closing her eyes. Sarah tucked the covers around her and kissed her forehead.

"I love you, Ellie."

Ellie murmured something that sounded like "Love you." Sarah retreated. Candace waited in the hall. She wore a flowered housecoat, her hair in large curlers.

"What happened, a bad dream?"

"Yes. Something like that." Sarah moved past her, toward her own room.

Candace huffed a sigh. "I thought maybe she'd been seeing her daddy again."

"Again?" Sarah turned, frowning. "What do you mean?"

"She hasn't told you? She's been seeing Henry in her room at night. She told me about it a few days ago." Candace shrugged. Without lipstick, her mouth was small and pinched, the lines over her upper lip and parentheses in the corners more clearly defined. In this light, her hair looked more white than blonde. "Although if that's what happened, she wouldn't have been scared. Not of an angel."

Everything inside Sarah felt drained, empty, her limbs leaden. She wanted her bed and a good eight hours of unconsciousness, but she'd settle for five and be grateful for that. She most definitely did not want to be debating the existence of angels.

"Adam is not an angel," Sarah said firmly anyway. This was a battle she had to keep fighting, one word at a time, no matter how weary it made her.

Candace straightened her shoulders, but if there was going to be a face-off, she'd clearly decided to back down from it. "A dream, then. Of course, it's only natural she'd be dreaming about seeing her daddy. She misses him so. As we all do, of course. She's so young, she can hardly understand that he's . . . gone."

Watching the older woman's expression crack, her shoulders slump, Sarah felt her throat close on a lump of emotion. Once again, she could not escape the fact that this mother had loved her son, and she missed him, and she mourned. It might not seem fair, but Sarah had no right to take that from Candace, and she didn't get to decide that her own grief was greater or more important.

Reluctantly, she crossed the few steps between them to give Candace a hug. The older woman clung to Sarah, hitching with sobs. Unlike Ellie, Candace's skin felt warm. Moist. Her breath smelled of mouthwash, but beneath it was the bite of liquor. When Sarah tried to release her, Candace gripped harder for a second or so before stepping away.

"We should get to bed," Sarah told her.

Candace swiped at her eyes and nodded. "Good night."

Passing Honor's door, Sarah paused to listen. No light shone from underneath, but from inside, she heard rustling. Maybe the murmur of a voice? A conversation? She knocked lightly, just once. Honor didn't answer. Sarah didn't knock again.

Back in her own room, Sarah pulled back the blankets to get into bed. Her fingers encountered something soft that was not a pillow. She pulled it gently from the tangle of sheets.

It was Adam's missing sweater.

28

ANOTHER TRIP TO town for a doctor visit. Time was flying. For-tunately, everything looked good, according to Dr. Maple. She gave Sarah the information on making an appointment to tour the hospital where she'd give birth, and also on how to contact the prac-tice she coordinated coverage with in case she wasn't immediately available.

"But don't you worry. I'm not planning on being out of town around your due date. Once you tour the hospital, you're going to feel much better about it all," Dr. Maple said. "I'm measuring you at six weeks to go, but you should be ready anytime after thirty-seven weeks. Are you ready?"

"Is anyone ever?" Sarah tried to keep her voice light.

"In my experience, the ones who say they are usually are the ones who aren't. You're in good shape, Sarah. The baby's doing great. You've got a good support system in place . . ." She trailed off with a quizzical look. "Is there anything else we need to talk about today?"

"I don't really like Shelter Grove. I don't want to stay here. But I feel stuck." Sarah gestured at the mountain of her belly. "So close to the end. I feel like I can't do anything to change my life until this baby is born, but at the same time, I think about how much harder it'll be to move with a newborn and a three-year-old. I'm feeling overwhelmed."

Dr. Maple nodded thoughtfully and scooted her rolling stool a little closer to where Sarah sat on the exam table. "It's pretty common to start having some anxiety closer to the end, especially after a loss like yours. Death of a spouse, pregnancy, a change in residence, selling a house . . . all of those are huge stressors that are considered leading contributors to illness. Now, you can't do anything about what's happened, but I do believe that acknowledging all of that and being kind to yourself can help how you react to all of it. Instead of thinking of yourself as stuck, what about looking at this time as an impermanent situation that will be resolved as soon as you're capable?"

"What if I'm never capable?" There. She'd said it aloud. Sarah wanted to clap both hands over her mouth but forced herself to keep them folded on top of her stomach.

"You're capable."

"You don't really know me," Sarah said.

Dr. Maple shrugged and smiled. "What would help you feel more in control?"

"Not being dependent on Candace. Finding a new place to live that I can afford. Making a plan to get out of this town."

"And how can you do that?"

"Well, I need access to the internet at home, for one thing."

The doctor didn't even seem surprised that there was no service at Candace's house. "Can you work on that?"

"Yes. I'm going to the coffee shop after this appointment to get some things done, but I can definitely try to do more research into either a new cell phone plan or run the internet out to Candace's house. Or," Sarah said, thinking even more broadly, "I can have her run me into town more often. Or I could look into buying a car for myself."

"It could be good for you to get out of the house. I know you're feeling ungainly, but being more active could help too. Nothing too strenuous, obviously, but it doesn't do anyone any good to sit around doing nothing." Dr. Maple paused. "If you really find that you can't deal with the stress, we can talk about options for treatment."

"Drugs?"

"It's not my first choice or even second. I recommend some lavender essential oil on your pillow to help you sleep. Chamomile tea. I know you love your coffee treat, but switch to decaf for now. I'll see you back in two weeks, and if things still aren't better, we'll discuss the next steps for a prescription. Okay?" Dr. Maple stood and gave Sarah's shoulder a reassuring pat.

At the coffee shop across the street, Sarah ordered a decaf coffee with cream and took a seat at the table in the window. The moment she got on the laptop she still didn't think of as her own, her email notifications began multiplying. She sipped her coffee, savoring it to make it last, and opened a browser window. She had an hour before Candace was due to show up with Ellie, and she wanted to make the most of it. She typed quickly.

Out here in Shelter Grove, only one company provided internet. When she typed in Candace's address, she got the frustrating message *New service not available at that location*. All the more reason *not* to live out the rest of her days here in quiet, friendly Shelter Cove.

She did a quick search on used cars she could get locally. A car meant insurance, maintenance, gas, a monthly payment. She didn't want to deplete her savings. She'd need money for an apartment deposit, first and last months' rents. She did another quick search of places in the Columbus area and almost slammed the laptop lid shut. Every place she checked cost nearly as much as her former mortgage payment. She looked up Cincinnati. Philadelphia. Rents in Brigantine were totally out of reach.

Undaunted, she searched *best place for single moms to live in the United States*. A list of towns came up. Shelter Grove was not on it—not a shocker.

Back to the used-car listings. She needed something practical. Reliable. Her search took her to the site of a local newspaper story about a dealership. Her typing fingers slowed. She hadn't thought about looking up the local news—but what else might she learn if she did?

Her initial search didn't turn up much, so she expanded the date range. A few more hits turned up. The church fire had been almost two years ago. The story had been big enough to get picked up by the Columbus and Cincinnati papers, but the reporting was brief in each. She had better luck with a new search on Adam's father's full name. His obituary didn't tell her anything she didn't know . . . other than the date of his death.

Three years ago?

For some reason, she'd assumed he'd died much longer ago than that. Sarah studied the photo. Adam favored Candace, but she could see him in his father's face too. Something about the expression, the press of lips that was meant to be a smile but looked more smug. It wasn't a flattering comparison to the man she'd married. She scanned the block of text and sat back in her chair hard enough to slosh drops of coffee onto her keyboard. She wiped them quickly with a paper napkin, sending the cursor up and down, losing her place on the web page and setting off a pop-up ad. She tapped the trackpad to return to where she'd been.

"*Survived by,*" she murmured, "*son Henry, daughter-in-law Sarah, and granddaughter Eleanor Granatt.*"

She stared at the words. Her own name, right there, honoring a man she'd never met. All these years, Candace had known about her and Ellie while she'd been kept a secret. Sarah could tell herself to just get over this a million times, but she wasn't sure she would ever be able to.

She went back to the search results. *Pastor Investigated for Tax Fraud.* That one was beyond a paywall, but she could read the first few paragraphs. Pastor Peter had apparently been less than honest with the IRS about his income. She checked the date—five years ago. More search results pulled up a blog post from a name she recognized—Rebecca of the purple-framed glasses. She'd written about a retreat, Pastor Peter at the helm. The photo she'd included showed Adam's father surrounded by a group of women, some of them the familiar faces of the other women who'd come to lunch.

Clicking through to Rebecca's social media accounts, Sarah scrolled back to find other photos of Peter and Rebecca. The posts changed in tone right before his death. Lots of song lyrics.

"Oof," she said under her breath. She knew what *that* meant.

Next, she searched on *Learning With the Lamb.* The website was out of date and featured blog-style articles written by Peter, along with typical calls to action about paying for the subscription. She watched a minute or so of a sample video but clicked away within the first minute. She didn't like seeing the face of her beloved on his father, spouting some kind of nonsense.

The laptop pinged with new emails to Adam's account. He was still getting copied on some client messages, most of which she ignored. She opened one that had been marked urgent, but it was an automatic request from the accounting department for him to fill in his monthly expense sheet. Curious, she clicked the link, which took her to the company's cloud system, which she was unable to access without a password. On a whim, she tried *!!ILoveSarah!!.* It let her into a world where Adam Granatt was still filling in his expense sheets, still replying to clients.

A world where he was still alive.

Sarah bent her head as the laptop screen blurred. She pressed her fingertips to her eyes, holding back the stream of tears. Of course nobody at FlashDrive had forgotten about Adam's death. They were simply careless and hadn't taken him out of the system. Or maybe for them too, leaving him "alive" there was some kind of comfort. Eventually, they would remember to delete his user account. Eventually, he'd be gone everywhere except the memories of those who loved him.

The coffee shop had been empty when she came in, but now a cluster of moms entered. Some had strollers. A few had toddlers, whom they settled into high chairs they pulled from the stack near the sugar-and-creamer station. The moms looked bright and happy, with wind-flushed cheeks, sparkling eyes. They bought coffees and teas and pastries while Sarah watched surreptitiously . . . and with a longing that surprised her.

If she packed up her things and went over there, her bulging belly the price of entrance, would she be allowed to join their club? She'd caught snippets of conversations about preschools and Bible study and a few good-natured digs about husbands who didn't pull their weight with the housework. She wasn't going to fit in with them.

A rush of heat flooded up her chest and throat into her face, and she packed up her things quickly, before she could make a scene. She went to the outside patio seating and gulped the humid midsummer air. Living in Southern California, she'd always missed the change of seasons, but not the brutality of them. Sweat trickled down her spine and accumulated in her armpits.

What would make her feel as though she had control? Making a plan. A car. An apartment. A job. She could be out of here by September if she tried. She had ten minutes left before Candace picked her up. She'd do another job search, if only to remind herself that she was capable. She was resourceful. She did have control.

Her phone was still getting one bar of the coffee shop Wi-Fi, but it wasn't showing up as a choice on her laptop. It popped up when she went back inside, but she didn't want to stay in there. A quick search on *ways to find a WiFi network* showed a list of apps, and she downloaded one quickly. Back on the patio, she used the app to scan for networks. The coffee shop Wi-Fi still didn't show up, but now she could also see a list of other networks that hadn't been there. They were all password protected, without names, and when she clicked on one, it prompted her to enter both the network name and the password to connect. She closed the app. The network list disappeared again.

Peter used the internet. It was all bundled in with the cable TV and the phone and my cell phone.

No new service available.

No *new* service.

But there was still cable TV, there was a wall phone, and even if Candace proclaimed to hate it and never use it, she did have a cell phone. What was the likelihood that she'd somehow managed to cancel only one piece of the overall package? It made far more sense that it was still active, whether or not she ever used it.

So why didn't it show up at the house? The router could be disconnected. Sarah hadn't seen one anywhere. She opened the network finder app again quickly, reading the *About* information. The network at the house could be completely online, just hidden the way these other networks were hidden.

When she got back to Candace's house—she wasn't going to let herself think of it as *home* anymore—she'd see what she could find. If there was still no internet out there, she'd make Candace take her into town sooner than her next doctor appointment. She'd keep working on solutions to getting her life in order. By the time the baby came, she could have a solid plan in place. She could do this, Sarah thought with determination.

She had six weeks.

She spent the rest of the afternoon with Ellie, making more lemon bars, doing puzzles, playing tea party. Honor offered, unexpectedly, to teach Sarah to crochet, and they spent an hour or so doing that while Candace entertained Ellie. Then it was dinner, and bedtime for Ellie, and Honor excused herself to go to bed too.

"You've been awfully quiet all night. Was everything all right with your visit?" Candace made herself at home on the couch next to Sarah.

Sarah forced a smile and closed the book she'd been reading without bothering even to use a finger to hold her place. She hadn't been retaining any of it anyway. She'd been fighting with her emotions and making mental lists about everything she needed to research and put in place. "Fine. Did she give you any fuss?"

"She never gives her Nanna any fuss. She's such a good girl." Candace patted the couch cushions, then paused. "Are you sure you're all right?"

"Tired. Cranky. The usual pregnancy things." Sarah's smile stretched thinner, hurting the corners of her mouth.

Candace frowned. "Why don't you let me make you a nice cup of tea and get you a snack? We can put on a rom-com. I do love a good rom-com, don't you? How about that one with that cute Sandra Bullock?"

"Sure. That sounds really nice." And it did sound really nice, Sarah couldn't deny that. Since she'd threatened to leave, Candace had made good on her promise to be more respectful. She'd ramped up the maternal gestures too.

She needed to relax, Sarah told herself fiercely as she watched Candace go into the kitchen to bustle around. It wasn't good for her, or the baby, to be so fretful about what was going to happen months and months from now. Back and forth, up and down. One second she was close to disintegrating with sobs, the next she was floating, floating up to the ceiling, or stifling hysterical laughter, or imagining a carefree life of being coddled and fussed over, or picturing herself at Ellie's wedding, standing under the chuppah with her and a faceless bridegroom, nobody at her side to watch with pride as their daughter got married.

"I feel like I'm losing my mind." She said it softly. Then louder. Candace didn't seem to hear her, but relief filtered through her at saying the words aloud. She twisted in her seat to look up as Candace brought in a steaming mug. "I think I'll make another appointment with Dr. Maple before two weeks. To talk about what I can do for some . . . anxiety. She said I could get a prescription for something."

Candace's thin-plucked brows arched. "Oh."

"I'm feeling incredibly unsettled." Sarah rubbed her cheeks with both hands. "Anxious."

"What on earth do you have to be unsettled or anxious about, honey?"

"Life. Everything. Money. About getting a job. A car. A place to live. About how I'm going to raise Ellie and the baby on my own." A sob tickled the back of her throat, worse than a gag.

Candace murmured voicelessly and sat next to her. She took Sarah in her arms and rocked her without a word as Sarah wept. Her hands patted up and down Sarah's spine, and Sarah clung to her, hating the helplessness. Powerless to stop.

"Shh, shh. You've just got baby brain right now, honey. It's all going to be fine. You're here with me, and I'm going to take care of you and Ellie and our sweet little prince, and you don't have to worry about anything. Okay? It'll all work out."

Those were the words Sarah had often longed for her own mother to say, but her mom had so often been swept up in her own struggles that she'd been the one to lean on Sarah. Thinking of her mother made Sarah sit back. She wrestled her emotions back under control. She'd always done her best to understand where her mother had been coming from with her fears and the methods she used to regulate them, but she hadn't always understood how her mother must have *felt*. She'd been too busy convincing herself she wasn't following her mother's path for that.

Sarah was not her mother. She was herself, with her feelings. Her own fears and ways of managing them.

"I know it will," she said. She would make it work out.

"I think I'm going to turn in. Are you going up?"

"No, I'm going to read a bit longer."

"All right. I'll just set the alarm and head up, then. Good night."

"Night."

Sarah waited for the sound of Candace's footsteps to reach the top of the stairs before she got out the laptop she'd last opened at the coffee shop. She logged into the app and waited while it searched. And then . . .

One network found.

CHAPTER

29

"ARE YOU SURE you don't want to come along?" Candace asked.
Sarah pressed her fingertips to her forehead. "I'm going to
take it easy today. You all go on and have a great time."

Candace gave her a worried look. "Are you feeling all right?"

"I'm feeling like I'm in my third trimester."

Candace had offered to take Ellie to a downtown festival. Live
music, fried food, a petting zoo, that sort of thing. Honor was
going along, which would give Sarah an unexpected few hours
alone in the house. It had been two weeks since she'd found out
about the hidden network, and she needed that time to look for the
router. She'd already searched the entire downstairs as well as all
the bedrooms. Last night, she'd tried the door to Peter's home
office. It was locked, but Sarah was hoping Candace would leave
the keys behind.

The app didn't list the hidden network's name, only its existence.
Without a network name, she couldn't connect, but their router in
California had listed the information on a sticker, and she hoped the
same would be true here. Candace and Honor had lied about having
internet, or else they'd been paying for a bundled service they didn't
know how to access. Either way, she wasn't going to bother asking
them about it. She was just going to find the damn router herself and
figure it out. They'd never even have to know.

"You sure you'll be all right by yourself?" Candace fretted.

"Totally," Sarah replied cheerfully. "I've got a set of booties to finish, and I plan to take a nap."

Oh, how easily the lies came, once they got started.

As soon as the crunching of the tires faded into the distance, Sarah pulled the keys from the hook by the garage door. They jangled, loud as a clatter of pots and pans, and Sarah clutched them tightly into her palm to quiet the sound. Was it a little paranoid to imagine her mother-in-law driving away, parking the car, and sneaking through the trees into the backyard to get back into the house without warning? Maybe.

Maybe not.

Her upper lip tasted like sweat. Her pits were damp with it too, and so was the small of her back, which ached from standing in this position for too long. The bigger her belly got, the worse it felt. She could abandon this stupid game and spend the afternoon in the recliner, enjoying the peace and quiet before they all came back. She could simply give in to life here, let Candace take care of them both the way she'd promised to do, the way she insisted her son would have wanted.

But no. Sarah was stubborn, Sarah was determined, Sarah needed to get online so she could get the hell out of Shelter Grove.

Setting Adam's laptop carefully on the thick, hunter-green carpet of the hallway, she tried four keys before one slipped into the lock, sweet as the prince putting the glass slipper on Cinderella's tiny foot. The knob turned easily, and the door opened without a squeak. Sarah grabbed the laptop, ducked inside, and quietly closed the door behind her. She took another deep breath, expecting the room to smell of dust and stagnant air, but the scent of lemon furniture polish and men's cologne wafted to her in the breeze she'd caused by shutting the door.

Peter's office looked as it must have the day he'd last left it. A heavy wooden desk with a matching throne-like leather chair sat in front of the bank of windows overlooking the side yard, the one away from the driveway. Louvered blinds, closed, let in diffuse sunlight that would be blinding without a barrier. Bookcases lined the room's other three walls, and an open door gave her a glimpse of a bathroom with a shower—this room would've been a nice one for her to have so she wouldn't need to share the one in the hallway. Too bad there'd be no way for her to suggest it without revealing that she'd snooped. Then again, she thought, what difference did it make? As soon as she could, she was getting out of here.

On the desk, a leather blotter matched a cup holding pens and a pair of scissors. Next to it, a heavy black stapler and tape holder rounded out the standard desk accessories. The router, green lights blinking, sat on the corner of the desk. It was the only piece of equipment. No computer, which seemed strange only because everything else in the room looked untouched. Maybe he'd used a laptop.

She went to the windows and peeked out. From this angle, she could catch the barest glimpse of where the driveway disappeared into the trees. The rest of the yard on this side featured scrubby grass and boulders. In the moment before she turned away, a glint of something caught her eye. Squinting, she looked harder. Something shone through the leaves, something bright and brief. She moved from side to side, up and down, trying to see if it happened again, but there must've been a breeze or something. She couldn't see much beyond the green.

Wait . . . there. An opening in the trees, half obscured by the tangles of overgrown raspberry bushes. It looked like it might be the head of a trail.

Time was ticking, Sarah told herself; no time to mess around in here. She could explore the yard another time. Right now, Wi-Fi.

The router lights all shone green, one with a slow, steady blink, so that meant everything was working correctly. She looked on the back of it for a network name and password. No sticker. Small smudges of glue gave a clue that there might've been one. Maybe in the direct sunlight from open blinds, the sticker had dried up and fallen off. Bending, one hand on the desk, Sarah did her best to look on the floor without actually getting on her knees. Still nothing.

She pulled open the closest desk drawer to look for the information possibly scribbled on a piece of paper. She found the missing laptop, along with its power cord and a mouse. Sarah pulled it out carefully and opened the lid. The lock screen showed a generic picture of a field along with the username *BOTL*. It required a passcode but also showed a Wi-Fi icon with full signal, which meant that it was connected.

BOTL. Of course. On Adam's laptop—when would she stop thinking of it that way? Sarah typed the letters into the hidden network's name field.

"Boom," she murmured.

The Network BOTL requires a password

This time, she said an expletive.

Quickly, she pulled open the other drawers. One had hanging files, all of them empty. The drawer below it, the same. The one in the middle yielded her a trove of miscellaneous items—rubber bands, envelopes, extra boxes of staples. The desk's other top drawer was heavier than the others, and it stuck a little before she could tug it free. Stacks and piles of papers filled this one. Yellowed newspaper clippings, small photo albums, a stack of CDs in slim, colored plastic cases. She used a fingertip to sift through the top layers, gently moving them but not trying to rearrange anything. No convenient list of passwords, but she did see a few loose photos. The visible corner of one stopped her.

She knew that sleeve. That hand. She knew this photo.

Her hand trembling, Sarah pulled out the picture. The five-by-seven print showed a young man in a graduation cap and gown, grinning and pumping his fist in the air. Adam on his UCLA graduation day. She knew this picture, because she'd been the one to take it. This picture had hung in Adam's office at home for years.

Had he sent a copy of it to his parents? Or, ugh, to Honor? Sarah ran her fingertips over the photo's edges, which were rough with the tape. The picture in Adam's office had been in an eight-by-ten frame using a five-by-seven mat, and she'd taped the edges to secure it, but anyone could have done the same thing. She flipped it over.

"This guy is going to run the world!"

Her handwriting.

This picture had come from her house.

T HE STORAGE SHED was on the other side of the house, which meant she couldn't see it from these windows, but she went to look out to the trees beyond the yard anyway. *Think, Sarah,* she scolded herself. *Think.*

Had she packed up that picture? Taken it from the frame for some reason and tucked it in one of the boxes she'd had sent here to Ohio? She couldn't remember doing it, but she also couldn't remember throwing it away. She couldn't recall seeing the picture when she was cleaning out Adam's office of anything too personal for the estate sale. She might have; it was the sort of thing she'd have tossed into a box without looking at too carefully, but considering her state of mind when she was clearing out the house in California, wouldn't she have paid attention to a picture of her husband, taken moments before he'd proposed to her?

If she *had* packed that picture, finding it in this room meant Candace or Honor had gone digging through her private artifacts. The back of Sarah's neck prickled into gooseflesh. She crossed her arms over her chest. It was huge now, breasts straining the front of her T-shirt, belly stretching it below. She cupped her belly with both hands, looking down. A tiny foot pressed against her palm, and she cooed, wordless and soothing as she rubbed the bump.

"I'll take care of you," she whispered. "Mama will always take care of you."

She dug through the rest of the drawers. Glamour shots of Candace. A wedding photo of her and Peter. Candace wore a mermaid-tail dress festooned with ruffles, huge puffed sleeves, and a matching headpiece. Sarah wanted to stop before she was forced to look at a photo of Honor and Adam on *their* wedding day, but as she shoved all the pictures back into the drawer, she found a snapshot of two young boys. One she knew at once was Adam by the shock of blond hair. The other boy, dark haired, much smaller, grinned at the camera with two thumbs up. Adam's arms slung around his shoulders.

This must've been the boy they'd adopted. The one they'd returned after six months because he'd had behavioral problems. Looking at the photo, Sarah couldn't see anything but a happy, bright-eyed boy. Adam had said he'd had night terrors, wet the bed, that sort of thing.

"And she sent him back, like a dog to the pound," Sarah murmured aloud.

She returned the photo to its place, along with everything else except the picture of Adam from their house. That she folded in half and shoved into the pocket of her skirt.

The rest of the office didn't turn up anything more of interest.

She went back to the window. Honor must be using the laptop for her online shop. Why else would it still be charged? The question was, would Honor keep a list of her passwords somewhere? If not, could Sarah somehow figure it out? Get on the laptop and somehow copy the internet password? It sounded complicated but not impossible.

From the yard below, shadows moved, and she caught sight of that glint again. From this angle, the trailhead was clear. It must be where the "hooligans" ran at night, she thought. But where were they running to?

She wasn't going to bother trying to guess the password while she was still in here, but she wasn't going to give up. Closing Adam's laptop, she pressed her ear to the door, listening for any signs that someone might be lurking in the hallway. Carefully, Sarah opened the door and peeked out. Spotting no signs of anyone there, she ducked out and pulled the door shut behind her. She made sure to lock it again.

She went out the French doors to the yard beyond.

In the sunshine, Sarah stretched. She breathed in the fresh air. In California, she'd have been way more active than she'd been here—walking Ellie to the park and back every day, for instance. She'd let herself get too sluggish here. Dr. Maple had said it would be good for her to keep her body moving, within reason. She had a lot to think about, and getting some exercise would help her mentally chew through what was going on. The sun beating through the open spaces in the trees was brutal, but that mystery path through the trees looked nice and cool. Why not find out exactly what was so appealing about it that it drew local kids to risk a shotgun blast?

Briar bushes sprouted along the tree line, half hiding the path entrance. Once past that, Sarah found a lovely little path covered with pine needles but otherwise clear. It meandered for a short way before turning. She looked over her shoulder, making sure she could still see the house through the trees. Getting lost in the woods didn't seem likely, but she was far from an outdoorsy adventure girl, and she wasn't going to take any chances.

Birds chirped and squirrels chased each other through the branches overhead. She kept a wary eye out for bears but honestly didn't believe she'd run into any. Here in the shade, the temperature felt a good few degrees cooler. Breathing felt good too. Fresh. Soothing.

Free.

Which meant she'd been feeling like a captive, and the realization of that struck a somber note in Sarah's heart. She'd come *to* Shelter Grove as an escape, but would she need to escape *from* it? How serious was Candace about her ownership of Sarah's child?

"Why can't anyone just leave us alone," Sarah said aloud, startling a squirrel into scampering through the trees. Soon, she promised herself. She'd get through the baby's birth and be out of here by the end of the year, and she could choose how much presence Candace had in their lives.

Pondering all of this, Sarah moved a few feet along the path and stopped at the sight of a small clearing surrounded by a waist-high wrought-iron fence. A concrete angel wept, wings spread, head bent. At its feet and around it, someone had placed a festoon of fake flowers. Solar lights ringed it, and several garden hooks swung with wind chimes and metal spinners that twirled in the breeze.

A cemetery.

31

A PRIVATE CEMETERY WASN'T the weirdest thing she could have imagined finding in the woods, but it still seemed pretty strange. Didn't they usually belong to much older houses, ones that had been built not at the turn of this century but of the last? It wasn't anywhere near the spot where the church had been either. From a distance, she could still clearly see that the big headstone was smoothly polished, not worn from the elements or covered in moss. She took a few steps closer, but she already guessed what name she'd read on it.

"*Peter Granatt*," she said aloud, along with the dates beneath. "*Beloved husband, father, pastor. The Lord hath given him rest from all his enemies.*"

If Candace didn't want people tramping back and forth through her private property, wouldn't such a "beloved" pastor have been better laid to rest in a public place where his congregation could visit his grave? Closer to the church itself?

The site wasn't neglected, which meant someone visited it often enough to replace the faded fake flowers with fresh ones, to stand up the fallen solar lights that had tipped over. When a small breeze sifted through the trees and spun one of the wind catchers, Sarah shivered and looked around. There wasn't anything to fear from a small plot of land designed to honor the dead; her chill didn't come from that.

There was more than one gravestone.

Behind the huge, ornately carved granite headstone and hidden from view until she moved closer, Sarah found two other stones, side by side, each half the size of Peter's. She went around to stand in front of them. One bore the chiseled name *Bethany* and the inscription *Blessed are the pure in heart, for they shall see God.* It had no dates on it, but Candace had said that after Adam, she hadn't been able to have any more children. Of course, she'd also said that Adam had been conceived on their honeymoon, and that story didn't sound like the full truth.

Sarah read the other stone. *Henry Adam Granatt. Adored and cherished by his family. Left this world too soon. No one lights a lamp and hides it; instead, he puts it on a stand so that those who come may see the light.* There were no dates on that one either, but at least Candace had been telling the truth about his name.

Sarah sank onto her knees in the soft mound of grass in front of the twin headstones and tried to work her brain around what was in front of her. Hot sun beat on the back of her neck as she bowed her head. About a year before they learned Adam was terminal, he'd introduced her to a series of short videos online called *The Backrooms.* The clips always featured a variation on the same theme—a first-person point of view from someone lost in a maze of hotel hallways lit with flickering fluorescent lights, empty spaces, endless rooms, and sometimes, a glimpse of something horrifying.

Adam had been big into liminal spaces and also the uncanny valley. Sarah had never understood his fascination with feeling separate from oneself. For her, depersonalization and dissociation were something she had to manage, not use as entertainment.

There was nothing like those back rooms in this forest clearing, but nevertheless, the sheer incongruity of it, the off-ness of it, had Sarah feeling tilted upside down. Adam was dead. His body was in a cemetery back in California, no headstone adorning it, because she'd planned to follow the custom of waiting almost a year for the unveiling. The location of this stone felt wrong. The lack of dates on it, wrong. Her finding it this way instead of Candace simply sharing it with her—all of it was wrong.

For a moment, she imagined herself looking down at her own body, kneeling in front of the dual gravestones, her head bent, her hands folded in her lap. She pictured herself flying up, up into the sky, casting a shadow. She closed her eyes before she could see the darkness curling out from under her, an echo of herself fixed onto the ground.

"Breathe," she reminded herself. "One breath in. One breath out."

She did not lose herself. The heat didn't help, nor did her thirst, but she concentrated on the grass under her knees and the sound of the birds chirping. The breeze lifting the wispy ends of her hair.

Touch one thing.

See one thing.

Smell one thing.

Hear one thing.

When she opened her eyes, she focused on the stone next to Adam's. He'd never mentioned a sister, much less one who'd died. Sarah sat back on her heels. She was centered in herself. Here, present, real. It took some doing to get herself to her feet again, but she managed by putting one hand on the stone bearing her husband's name.

"No," she said aloud.

That stone had been carved with the name of someone her husband had refused to be. She'd never know why he'd kept so many secrets from her, but she'd loved him enough to believe he had his reasons. She had to.

If she couldn't do that, then everything in their life together would become a lie.

She searched the ground for a rock and placed it gently on top of his headstone. He wasn't in the ground there, but it was the only memorial she could get close to right now. After a moment, she found another rock for the sister-in-law she'd never know.

By the time she got back through the woods and into the yard, she'd begun fantasizing about a tall, cold glass of Honor's lemonade and the biggest tuna sandwich she could stuff into her mouth. Gross, sure, but if you couldn't indulge in weird food combinations when you were pregnant, when could you?

The glass of lemonade was sweating in her palm when the door from the garage opened and Candace entered, Ellie on her hip. Honor ducked in behind them and gave Sarah a glance before heading off to the sun-room without a word. Candace didn't quite stagger, but it was clear the toddler's weight was a lot for her, even though she tried to hide the huff and puff of her breath.

"She really should walk on her own, Candace."

Candace rubbed her cheek to Ellie's and pressed smacking kisses on it. "One day I'll put this sweet angel down and never pick her up again, and I think about that every time I pick her up."

"That's depressing," Sarah said.

Candace fixed her with a hard look. "Maybe you should think about it too. Time passes so fast. Before you know it, this little one will be all grown up and off on her own, and you can only pray for her and remember these days."

That was no less depressing, but it was also not untrue.

Ellie squirmed, and Candace finally put her down with a long, hard sigh.

"Mamaaaa!" Ellie cried and ran into Sarah's arms.

"Hold on, ketzeleh." Sarah held the lemonade out of the way and encircled the little girl with her other arm. Yes, it was wrong to feel that spark of triumph at the sight of Candace's expression, but if the woman insisted on believing Ellie preferred her to Sarah, it was her own fault when she was proven otherwise. "Let me put this down, or else you're going to be wearing my lemonade."

She must've already spilled some, because Ellie's hair was damp, and so was the back of her top. Sarah put the glass on the counter and hugged her daughter with both arms. She ran her hands over Ellie's back and frowned. She might've splashed a little bit, but not that much. She gave Candace a curious look, but her mother-in-law busied herself with hanging up her purse and touching up her hair in the wall mirror.

"I thought you were taking her to the festival today."

Candace didn't turn around. "I did. We saw the baby pigs and goats, didn't we, Ellie? And a clown."

"Why is her clothing damp? And her hair?"

"Well, it's hot outside, isn't it, Sarah?"

Sarah pressed her palm to Ellie's forehead, then her cheeks. She scanned the little girl's face, not expecting fever or anything, but something seemed . . . off. "Yes, but . . ."

She cut herself off and gathered Ellie close. Ellie babbled in a singsong voice about baby cows and a ride on a "horsie that went round around."

"You went on the merry-go-round?"

"Oh, they had a whole bunch of rides for the little ones, didn't they, precious princess? And a bounce house, and a big inflatable slide. She went down that, oh, it must've been a dozen times. Nanna bought Ellie-belly a whole book of tickets, didn't I?"

Sarah frowned at Candace's baby voice but didn't correct her. "You spoil her."

"That's a nanna's job, isn't it?" Candace beamed and gave a single, firm clap. She fixed her gaze on Ellie. "Now. What did Nanna say we had to do when we got home?"

"Don't wanna take a nap." Ellie shook her head so hard her entire body rocked in Sarah's arms.

Sarah glanced at the clock. It was later than she'd thought. While nap time had always been sacred, Ellie had been going to bed without such a fuss and sleeping through the entire night. If Sarah missed the hour or so of time in the afternoon, she also liked having a full night of uninterrupted sleep . . . at least uninterrupted by anything other than her own body. Sarah tipped Ellie's chin to look her in the face. Tired eyes, yes, but also a familiar stubborn pout that meant Ellie would fight the nap until she gave in to exhaustion, and that could take an hour's worth of tantrumming to happen. Not only did Sarah not want to listen to the screaming, she didn't want to put the kid through that either.

"How about we work on one of your puzzles, and you can tell me all about what you and Nanna did today. Okay?"

"You told me she had to be home in time for her nap," Candace said. "We could have stayed longer."

This time, Sarah didn't glance at the clock but gave it a pointed, hard stare before looking back at Candace. Two hours past nap time, but she didn't say that aloud. "If she naps now, she won't go to bed on time. I'd rather she get a good night's sleep so I can have one too."

The change in Candace's demeanor was subtle. A tightening of her lips. Small straightening of her shoulders. She gave Sarah a nod but didn't contradict her, although Sarah could see a ripple of emotions crossing the woman's expression. None of them pleasant. Still, did it matter if Candace's felt stepped on, so long as she didn't argue about it? Sarah would take that as a win.

Without saying anything else, Sarah took Ellie's hand and went with her into the den. She let Ellie pick out a puzzle from one of the dozens on the shelf, and they scattered out the pieces on the coffee table. Candace hovered in the archway for a moment or so before going away again. From the kitchen, Sarah heard the bang of pots and pans, a slamming of cupboards.

"What funny, Mama?"

"Oh, nothing. Here. Look." Sarah held up two of the puzzle pieces. "See how this piece has a part that goes in, and this piece has a part that goes out? And when you match them up, they make the picture. Do that."

The tip of Ellie's tongue crept out as she concentrated. Sarah couldn't stop herself from leaning to hug her daughter. Ellie's damp curls clung to Sarah's cheek when she pulled away.

"So, what else did you and Nanna do at the festival today?"

Ellie pressed a piece down, but it didn't fit, so she took it away and turned it around to see if the other side would. Sarah watched, moved and proud, and they both clapped when Ellie was able to press the piece into its correct place.

The little girl picked up another piece. "Swimmin'."

"Hmm?" Sarah paused in looking over her own puzzle piece.

"Swimmin'," Ellie said again, and added a frustrated grunt at the puzzle piece in her hand that wasn't going into place.

"Ellie. Look at me." Sarah waited until she did. "Did you say Nanna took you swimming?"

Ellie nodded.

Swimming.

Sarah's mind spun. What could that mean? Candace hadn't mentioned anything about taking Ellie to a swimming pool or a lake. She didn't have a bathing suit. Ellie couldn't even swim. Sarah had planned to start her on swimming lessons when she turned three, but the idea had fallen by the wayside.

"Stay here."

Sarah found Candace in the kitchen, beating cake batter by hand. For someone who was so proud and protective of her freaking stand mixer, Sarah thought, she sure didn't use it very much. Candace didn't turn around when Sarah came in, and that's when she knew something had happened. Something Candace didn't want Sarah to know about.

"Candace, Ellie says you took her swimming."

"I did not." Candace remained with her back to Sarah, but the hand gripping the spoon slowed.

"Why would she make something like that up? Why were her clothes and hair damp? Candace, if you took her swimming without my permission—"

"I did not take her swimming, Sarah." Candace whirled. Twin spots of bright color highlighted her cheeks. Her eyes glittered. "But fine. Fine. If you must know, I had her baptized."

32

"BAPTIZED." SARAH REPEATED the word, certain she'd misheard it. Candace put the bowl down on the countertop so hard that batter splashed out. She waved the spoon, then tossed it into the sink so she could put her hands on her hips. Her chin jutted up and out. Moments ago Sarah had been noticing how much Ellie looked like her father; in this moment, she noticed how much Adam had looked like his mother.

"Yes. Baptized," Candace said defiantly.

Sarah recoiled both physically and mentally. Her body took a step back. Her mind simply . . . blanked.

For a moment, she looked down at herself, shoulder blades and the back of her head bumping the ceiling, her arms outspread, staring down at the top of Candace's head and Sarah's own. The only thing stopping her from flying up, up, and away into the sky, into the black vastness of outer space, was the kitchen ceiling.

She forced herself to blink, hold her eyes closed, then open them. Sarah anchored herself. Feet on the floor. Inside her body. The baby squirmed in her belly, agitated, and she cupped the heavy weight there to soothe it, and herself.

"You promised you'd stop," she finally said.

Candace dashed away bright tears before they had the chance to slide down her pink cheeks. Her lips wobbled, and so did her voice, but she kept her gaze strong and fierce on Sarah's. "I had to!"

"You didn't have to. You chose to."

"I had to," Candace repeated in a lower voice gone gravelly with emotion.

There wasn't much else to say about this; they were never going to agree. And in this, too, she could draw a line of comparison between her husband and his mother—there'd been only a handful of times in her life when Sarah had felt incandescent with rage, and all of them had been sparked by Adam or Candace.

Without a word, she turned on her heel and left the kitchen. She peeked in on Ellie, who was still working on the puzzle. She went upstairs and yanked out a bag from her closet and tossed her clothes into it—not all of them, not the ones Candace had insisted on buying her. She wasn't going to take anything from this house that she hadn't brought into it.

In the hall, Honor saw her and drew up short. "What are you—"

"Did you know about it?"

"What?"

Honor's quivering voice and cringing demeanor could've meant she knew nothing or had been in on it the whole time. Sarah didn't care. She set the suitcase outside her doorway and gestured at Honor.

"Get out of my way."

When Honor didn't move fast enough, Sarah pushed past her. Their shoulders knocked together hard enough to spin Honor away. She let out a cry louder than seemed necessary, and Sarah didn't look back.

In Ellie's room, she pulled another suitcase from the closet and began filling it the same way she'd filled her own. It was harder to leave behind everything Candace had gifted, because Ellie'd grown so much in the past few months that hardly anything they'd brought with them still fit her. Sarah struggled for only a few seconds to justify filling the suitcase. Her kid still needed clothes.

She scanned the room for any of Ellie's old toys. Her original stuffed bear went into the bag, and after a moment's hesitation, her favorite of the dozen princess dresses out of the toy box.

The floor squeaked behind her, and she tensed. Sarah turned toward the doorway.

"You can't leave," Candace said in a flat, calm voice.

Sarah ignored her and kept stuffing things into the suitcase.

"Did you hear me?" Candace demanded.

"Did you *ever* hear *me*? Ellie is my daughter. Mine. I decide how to raise her. I decide what to teach her about God. Not you." Sarah took a slow, deep breath. "I've never, not once, asked or expected you to not practice your own faith, Candace. All I've ever asked is that you respect our right to practice ours."

Her mother-in-law frowned. "It was a little water and a few words. If you really don't believe, then what harm did it do?"

"If you don't understand, then I can't explain it to you. Let me finish packing our bags, and we'll be out of here. I'll arrange for someone to pick up the stuff in the shed."

"You can't leave," Candace said again.

"Yes, I can. I should have already, months ago. Maybe I should never have come here at all."

Candace's head swayed back and forth. "Don't say that. Don't go. I won't let you."

"You can't really stop me," Sarah began, but Candace's short bark of laughter cut her off from saying anything else. The older woman didn't say anything else. She didn't really have to.

Bars on the windows to keep "a house of single women safe." The security system that locked the house up tight as a safe from dusk to dawn—it would be easy for Candace to simply keep all the doors locked the rest of the time too, and without the code, there was no way Sarah would be able to get out without alerting her, at least not from the ground floor. And how would she get out from the second floor, dangle herself from a window? Drop to the ground, risk hurting the baby? And what about Ellie? Even if she could get both of them out of the house, if Candace wouldn't drive them the eight or so miles into town, how else could Sarah get them there?

Everything that had kept Sarah feeling so safe was now going to keep her a prisoner.

Candace's expression morphed into wide-eyed, innocent affront when Sarah said so aloud. "You're being ridiculous. Keep you prisoner? That's quite an accusation. Why don't you let me make you a cup of tea, and we can work this all out."

"I don't want any tea. I want you to stop trying to convert my child."

"If you don't want to accept Jesus into your heart, well, that's your own business. But to deny it for your child? What kind of horrible mother would do such a thing?"

"Your own child denied it for himself, so maybe you ought to ask yourself a similar question," Sarah said.

"You don't understand!" Candace's voice shook, cracked, broke. Her hands curled into fists. She took a step into the room. "I had to, for the sake of that sweet little angel. What if something happened to her and she was denied her eternal place in heaven because she wasn't baptized? How could I live with myself, knowing I had the chance to make sure she would be welcomed into the arms of the Lamb, and I didn't do it? If something happened to her—"

"Nothing's going to happen to her! Stop talking like that. Stop manifesting harm coming to my child!"

Candace went very still. Her lips parted, exposing her teeth. "Manifesting? I honored your silly superstitions about the baby clothes, but your ridiculous myths shouldn't be allowed to stop me from saving Ellie. That's all I wanted. To keep her safe. If she dies without being baptized, her precious soul will go straight to hell!"

Sarah shouted back. "She's not going to die!"

"Any child could die!" Candace's voice splintered, rough and rasping. "You think you've done everything you can to keep them safe, you do your best, and the Lord can still decide to call them home at any time. You haven't lost a child. You have no idea. None."

Weariness overtook her. Sarah sank onto Ellie's bed. Her hands trembled, so she clasped them in her lap. "Adam never told me about his sister."

"Sister?" Candace shook her head. Fine blonde strands came free from her French twist and waved softly around her face, which had gone pink with emotion. "He didn't have a sister."

"I saw the graves. I thought . . ."

"Oh, you mean Bethany? She wasn't Adam's sister. She was Honor's daughter."

33

SILENCE RANG LIKE a bell in Sarah's ears. "You never said anything about Honor having a child."

"Of course not," Candace said. "It broke the poor girl's brain. How cruel do you think I am, to talk about her dead child?"

"You talk about yours all the time," Sarah said.

Candace ground a noise out of her throat.

Cogs turned in Sarah's brain. *Don't think about it, Sarah. Don't dwell. Remember what Honor said: He chose you. Don't drive yourself over the edge making assumptions that might not even be true.*

"What happened to the baby?"

Candace looked uncomfortable. "Crib death."

"I just . . . never knew."

"You weren't supposed to, were you? Didn't I tell you to stay out of the woods? But you wouldn't listen. You don't know anything, Sarah, and how could you? It's not like you ever really asked. You had this picture in your head of me before you got here, didn't you? Because of things my son told you about me, about his father, about this life. Well, let me ask you this: What makes you think anything Henry ever told you about me, about his father, was true?" Candace looked angry, but she sounded defeated. Worn down.

Sarah could relate.

"He never actually told me anything about you. You can't stand that, can you? You're so hung up on being special. It must drive you insane to know he made you nothing," Sarah said. Inside her, the baby kicked and squirmed, one small foot digging deep into a kidney. She had to pee.

"If he made me nothing," Candace spat, "what do you think he made *you*?"

Candace sniffled and then took a tissue from the box on the desk Ellie was still too small to use. The desk she'd set up in advance of them coming to live here, Sarah thought, watching her. Everything she'd prepared in this house spoke to how long she'd expected them to stay—long enough for Ellie to start school, to need a desk where she could do her homework. It had seemed sweet when they got here, if a little bit overkill. Now, it seemed more menacing.

Candace had never intended for Sarah to move out when the baby was born.

Adam's mother kept talking, seemingly unaware that Sarah hadn't so much as made a murmur to indicate she was listening. "You've never lost a baby, so how could you possibly understand what it's like? You think your grief entitles you to know mine? Or Honor's? I'm sure she would have talked to you about Bethany if you'd ever asked, but you never did."

Don't ask, Sarah.

But she had to. "When did the baby die?"

Candace didn't even flinch. "Right before Henry ran away."

"Is that why he left?"

"You'd have to ask him." Candace curled one frosted pink lip. "Oh, that's right. You can't ask him anything anymore."

Icy fingers curled around the nape of Sarah's neck. She half expected to see her breath puff out of her. "I don't believe Adam fathered a child with someone before we met and he never told me. I won't believe it."

"Why should it matter if he did? It was a girl."

"What's that supposed to mean?"

Candace's gaze fell at once to Sarah's belly. Cooing incoherently, she reached to touch it. Sarah, trapped on the bed, warded off Candace's desperate embrace by putting out a hand. "My son was special, like his father. And his son will be special too."

"I need you to stop," Sarah said as firmly as she could while trying to keep her voice from shaking. "Stop all of this. It's not right."

"It's not right to be excited?" Candace fell back with a frown, but her fingers still curled with yearning, straining toward Sarah's belly.

No. She wasn't reaching for Sarah at all but the child inside her. Sarah kept her hands out, pushing forward as she took a step sideways. Her mind raced, thoughts tangling. She needed to get herself settled, she thought, her eyes fixed solidly on Candace to be sure the other woman didn't suddenly lunge toward her. She needed to be calm. To pay attention. She could not dissociate. She could not drift. She needed to figure out how to get herself and Ellie out of this house.

"Hasn't your life been easier since you got here? No worries about anything? We've cooked for you, cleaned up after you, we've watched over Ellie so you could do whatever you wanted. When you got here, that child was a beast at bedtime, but I took care of that, didn't I? She goes right to sleep, right like that." Candace snapped. "Nanna's little pink drink works every time, and then we all can get a good night's rest."

"Little pink . . . what?" Sarah's throat constricted as her mind raced. All the nights Ellie had gone to sleep without crying, how she'd slept through the alarm going off, how she'd gone back to sleep after being woken. "What did you give her?"

"A little allergy liquid—it puts them right to sleep. At least it wasn't a sip of whiskey, which is what my mother's mother used to use!" Candace cried, indignant.

Sarah choked on a reply, struggling to form a rational sentence after the horror of discovering Candace had been drugging her daughter. "You could have made her very sick. Or worse—"

"Don't be stupid. It's rated for children."

Honor appeared in Ellie's bedroom doorway, where she lingered silently. Candace turned and snapped at her. "Did you bring it?"

"Yes." Honor moved forward with a small zipper pouch and handed it to her.

"Sarah," Candace said in a singsong, pulling something from the pouch. One hand went out as she approached Sarah. The other held not a bottle of allergy medicine but a prescription bottle. "Let's get you calmed down."

"What is that? No!"

Candace and Honor both moved to flank her, cutting off access to an easy exit. Sarah froze in place, thinking desperately. She kept her eyes on the bottle. Tried to keep her voice calm but failed.

"You don't have to do this," she said.

Candace clucked her tongue against the roof of her mouth. "Come on, now, Sarah. It's all going to be okay."

"Don't hurt my baby!"

"You said yourself you wanted Dr. Maple to get you something to help you calm down. This is just a little something to help you get some sleep. Perfectly safe," Candace said.

"I don't want it. I don't need it." Sarah held up her hands, and Candace stopped coming toward her, and for a moment, she had a flash of hope that this wasn't going to go as badly as she was thinking.

"You're not thinking straight," Candace told her.

Sarah looked past her. "Honor. Call the police."

"The police aren't going to come all the way out here just because you're having hysterics," Candace said.

Sarah gritted her teeth. "What are you going to do, drug me up so I can't try to leave? Are you going to keep me sedated for the next *month*? Is that the plan?"

Candace laughed, but Honor didn't. Sarah slid one foot to the side, followed by the other, and inched toward the doorway. It didn't help her. Both women moved at the same time to block her path. She cast Honor a desperate look, but the younger woman wore a blank expression.

"Come on, now. Be a good girl and take this pill," Candace said in an infuriatingly calm voice. With a lunge, she grabbed Sarah's arm and pulled her forward.

"Fuck. You," Sarah bit out, and braced her feet on the floor as she used her entire force to bring her hammer fist down, hitting Candace's forearm and breaking her grip. Possibly breaking Candace's arm too.

Candace went sprawling, knocking Honor off-balance as she tried to catch her with one arm. Sarah ran, lumbering past Honor, who made a halfhearted attempt to grab her. Sarah ducked her and headed for the stairs.

She had to get to Ellie.

And then what? *Think*, Sarah commanded herself as she headed for the stairs. Raised voices followed her, but she didn't dare take the time to look over her shoulder. They caught up to her, of course, at the top of the stairs. Candace, Honor on her heels.

Candace reached for Sarah, mumbling a string of words she couldn't interpret over the buzzing of panic in her ears. Candace's voice was calm, but her face was annoyed. She had both hands out.

"It's just to help you sleep, Sarah!"

Sarah put her hand on the railing, gripping it hard as she took the first step.

"Honor, grab her!"

Hands raked down Sarah's back, yanking her shirt, pulling her backward. Sarah jerked herself away. Candace hollered incoherently. The bottom of the stairs went wavy and distant, like Sarah was looking at the them through a rain-covered window. She tried to step back onto the top landing, but with Honor and Candace behind her, she had no space. They grabbed her, pulled her, and she pulled free.

Then there was open space beneath her feet, and she was flying.

CHAPTER

34

SARAH'S GRIP ON the railing tore free, and her hands slapped each post, *thunka-thunka-thunk* as her feet skidded out from under her. Her butt hit each riser, sending pain shooting up her spine. At the bottom of the stairs, she sprawled on the cold, hard tiles and looked up to see Candace and Honor both staring with wide eyes and exaggerated open mouths.

She hadn't tumbled head over heels, and she hadn't bumped or landed on her belly, baruch Hashem, but her body hurt and her head spun. She pushed herself as upright as she could, ungainly as a turtle on its back. Her palms pressed the cool floor as she tried to get onto her hands and knees, at least, and then from there to her feet.

Candace hurried down the stairs to kneel next to her. "You just calm yourself. Don't you move. What on earth were you thinking? Stupid, stupid girl."

"I was thinking," Sarah gritted out, "about getting away from you."

She shrugged off the arm Candace slipped behind her shoulders, but the other woman persisted. Honor had also come down the stairs, more slowly, and stood on the bottom step to stare at them both. Sarah groaned as she rocked her bulk, but it was useless. Even if she got herself up, what was she going to do. Run?

"Mama?" Ellie came out of the den to stare at them. "You 'kay?"

"She's fine, sweetheart. Mama tripped, that's all. Why don't you go with Honor, and she'll make you a snack? Honor," Candace snapped when the younger woman didn't move immediately. "Take the child."

"Leave her alone," Sarah said.

Honor clearly wavered, but when Candace stood up and flapped her hands at her, she took Ellie by the hand to go into the kitchen. Candace bent again to pull Sarah upright. Sarah wanted to protest, but she wanted to get up off the hard floor even more.

"Come on. Let's get you up. You skidded down those stairs like you were in a Three Stooges movie, my word."

Together, with a struggle, they got Sarah to her feet. Breathing hard, she gripped the railing and closed her eyes, concentrating on her body to catalog her aches and pains. Her butt ached, and so did the small of her back where her shirt had ridden up and the carpet had burned her. Her jaw ached, probably from her teeth rattling. No cramping, though, no pain in her belly.

"You should go on up to bed and take a rest," Candace said.

"I should go to the doctor. I'm pregnant, and I just fell down the stairs." Sarah hissed out a pained breath, hand on her back, as she concentrated on measuring her injuries.

"That's your own fault. You ought to have simply taken the medicine and had a nap."

"I need to call Dr. Maple." Sarah limped over to yank the handset off the wall. It took her a minute to figure out how to use the dial—she'd seen old phones like this, of course, but hadn't ever used one. She stuck her finger in the 9 hole, moved the dial. Then 1. Then another 1.

Candace gave Sarah a triumphant look. "It's not connected."

Sarah pulled the handset from her ear and looked at it.

"You need a dial tone. Isn't it funny how you kids are so tied up with your gadgets, you have no idea what it's like to use a telephone? So caught up in your internet and your smartphones. It's like you can't live without them." Candace laughed airily.

"You said you used this one."

"Guess what. I don't." Candace laughed again.

"Honor's phone gets a signal." Sarah ran her hands over her belly, around and around. The baby shifted, pushing a tiny foot against her palm, and she said a silent prayer that it was moving. Now that her heart had stopped pounding, aside from the scrapes and some bruises she could feel forming on her elbow, she didn't feel terrible. She was lucky.

"Honor's—?"

Candace spun on her heel and stalked into the kitchen, hollering for Honor. Sarah followed. She helped Ellie out of her chair and whispered for her to go upstairs and play with her toys. Ellie gave Candace the side-eye and ran off at once, while Sarah stood up to face her. She was fighting with Honor over something from the younger woman's pocket.

Her phone.

"You went behind my back? How dare you?" Candace tore the phone from Honor's hand and swiped at the screen before shoving it back at her. "What's the password?"

"You don't have to tell her, Honor," Sarah interjected. "Let me have the phone. I won't let her see it. I'll make the call and give it right back."

Candace turned on her. "You. Shut your whore mouth. This is none of your business."

Tears leaked down Honor's cheeks. "Mother Candace, I'm sorry—"

"You shut your mouth too. What have you been doing on this? Password!" At Honor's mumbled answer, Candace slapped in some numbers. She swiped furiously at the screen.

Sarah's bowels burbled. She pressed her thighs together, a hand on the back of the kitchen chair, as cramps rolled through her. She needed the toilet, and urgently.

"Please call Dr. Maple, Candace."

"Fine." Candace held up the phone. "I'll call her right now."

"I need to use the bathroom." Sarah moved as fast as she could to the powder room, where she managed to get her leggings down and her butt onto the seat before her body betrayed her. She groaned as more cramps rippled through her guts and heat rushed out of her. It was better than throwing up—but not by much.

It took her a few more minutes to finish up and wash her hands. She gave Jedi Jesus a long, hard stare, hoping he was ashamed of what was being done in his name. She heard her own name when she opened the bathroom door.

"Oh no, Doctor, it was nothing you did. Sarah decided that she wanted to move back to California before the baby came. Yes, she was just feeling too anxious and unsettled here. Apparently, she had some friends out there she felt more comfortable staying with. I'm sure she'll have her records sent out there. Yes, it was rather sudden, but it's not like I could keep her here against her will, right?"

Candace's voice rose in a light lilt, not quite laughter but nothing in it that would raise any suspicion. "You take care too. Bye now."

She disconnected before Sarah had the wherewithal to shout out in protest, and the hope she'd been harboring faded and died. Like a flower pressed between the pages of a book, it crumbled to dust. Dr. Maple would have no reason not to believe Candace's lie. She wouldn't try to get in touch with Sarah. She wouldn't have any idea that Sarah was, in fact, being held against her will.

"Who's going to take care of me when the baby comes?" Sarah demanded when she made it back to the kitchen. She looked to the hook by the garage. The keys were gone. Her fists clenched, and she wanted to give up . . . but she couldn't.

Candace tutted. "Don't be so dense. You know perfectly well I'll take care of you. I've lost count of how many babies I've delivered over the years. You're in good hands. My hands."

"*You* told the doctor I wanted a home birth. Did you plan this from the start? To have me deliver here?"

"Women have been having babies at home since Eve gave birth to Cain."

"Yeah, and a lot of them died," Sarah snapped. "What if something goes wrong?"

"You're such a worrywart, Sarah, my goodness. Trust in God."

"I almost died when I had Ellie. I bled out, almost hemorrhaged to death," Sarah said desperately.

Candace snorted her derision. "You're lying. I saw on Henry's internet picture account that everything went fine with Ellie's birth. He said you were a real champ. You labored at home for a few hours, then went in to the hospital, got checked in, you were ready to push, and boom, out she came. *Our beautiful Ellie*, that's what it said. It really should've been Eleanor."

Sarah closed her eyes. That was exactly what had happened. "But you didn't hear it from him. You saw it on his social media. He kept everything public, so you didn't even have to let him know you were looking. You could just creep around, pretending to yourself you knew all about his life, all about us. Did he ever really tell you I didn't want you around? Did he ever really talk to you at all, or did you just stalk him online?"

"If he told the world about it, he certainly would have told me."

"But he didn't." Sarah pushed the words out around the grin that wouldn't stop spreading across her face. "He never told you I was fragile. He never said anything to you at all. You've been lying to me this whole time."

Beep-boop.

Candace lifted the phone in her hand. She looked at Honor, who visibly cringed. The phone chimed again. Candace swiped. She stared.

"*Can't wait to see you again, sexy*," she read aloud.

She swiped.

She stared.

She thrust the phone screen toward Honor.

Sarah could see a popular photo-sharing app. Pictures of Honor making kissy faces, her face heavily made up. Honor sobbed, hands over her face, while Candace made a low, disgusted noise from deep in her throat and put the phone on the table with a slow, deliberate *thunk*, as though she were daring Honor to grab it. Honor didn't move. Candace's lips twisted into a thin, smug grin.

"Honor. You go on upstairs and check on the child. Miss Sarah here and I are going to have a little chat."

Honor scuttled away.

Candace waited until she'd left the kitchen, then moved on Sarah. Sarah had never moved so smoothly in her life, with such purpose and intent, with such force. She backhanded Candace across the face, sending the other woman reeling, arms flailing, feet slipping on the tiles. Candace collided with the counter hard enough to shake the dishes in the cupboard.

The women faced each other. Sarah's fists were in front of her. Candace had a hand on the cheek Sarah had hit. Her expression went stormy and dark. Both of them looked at the phone still on the table. Sarah went for it, but Candace got there first.

Candace slammed the phone facedown on the table, cracking the screen. Then again. Again. The phone broke apart, and Candace threw the pieces of the phone into the trash. Breathing hard, she faced Sarah.

"You're lucky I don't put you out on the street, right now. What would you do then?"

"I want you to put me out on the street. I want you to let me out of this house. I want you out of my life!"

The other woman's gaze dropped to Sarah's belly. Her face worked. Her hands made fists. She looked again at Sarah's face with a grimace.

"After the baby comes, I don't really care what you do," Candace said. "But until then, you're staying right here."

Another surge of discomfort rose inside Sarah's gut, and she concentrated on breathing through it. It felt like food poisoning but faded without her having to run to the bathroom again. Sarah shambled to the front door and tugged at it, but it was locked, and even when she turned the bolt, it wouldn't open. With a low growl, she went to the security system and flipped open the cover to hit the panic button. The alarm blared.

"We'll see what the police have to say," she said.

Candace came out of the kitchen. "The police aren't going to come."

The horrendous *wah-wah* drilled into Sarah's ears, so she made no protest when Candace pushed past her to stab in the code. Silence fell, but Sarah's ears still rang. She could hear Ellie crying from upstairs and Honor soothing her.

"What good is a security system that doesn't call the police for you?" Sarah put both her hands on her lower back and rubbed at the ache there.

"It's to scare people off from trying to break in—I told you that. The people in town have hated us ever since Peter built his church on our land and they couldn't tax us anymore. The system has to be connected to the internet if you want it to call the police automatically, and I told you, I don't have it out here," Candace said. "Now come on and have some tea—"

Sarah slapped her hand away. "You're delusional. Also, I know you're lying about the internet. I found the hidden network and the router up in Peter's office, and I found the photo you stole from my house. So stop your lies. All of them."

Candace froze, eyes going wide. "What router? What are you talking about? I didn't take any photos from your house."

"I found it all in the desk drawer upstairs. Peter's office."

Candace pushed past Sarah and headed for the stairs. Sarah followed but had to pause for another wave of cramping to wash over her. She was sweating but clammy. Her butt ached, and so did the small of her back. She held onto the railing and looked to the top of the stairs, where Honor stood.

"She's going for the router," Honor said.

35

"STOP HER, HONOR!"

But Honor looked too scared to move. She only shook her head and backed away. Sarah had no choice but to rush to the bathroom and evacuate her bowels again. More sweat collected on her forehead and upper lip, and the room spun a little bit as she managed to get through the worst of it. She splashed her face at the sink and waited to see if another rush would run her over. She felt okay for the moment.

By the time Sarah got up the stairs, Candace had destroyed the router in the same way she'd demolished Honor's phone. She'd left the pieces scattered on the desk and was berating her. Honor took the insults without looking up from the floor.

"You went behind my back, all this time. All these years? I gave you a roof over your head, I fed you, I clothed you, I treated you like my own daughter!" Candace's voice shattered into sobs. She beat her breast hard enough that the thuds sounded as though they'd leave bruises. "For what? So you could keep sneaking off in the night to have your nasty sex hookups? So you could mock and betray every blessing you've ever been granted?"

Candace spun around to Sarah. "Now you see why I had to lock everything up? It was to keep her safe. To keep us all safe. Well, you can forget about helping yourself to whatever you want from my refrigerator, letting yourself in and out of my house, taking advantage of my generosity. I've got the keys, and don't you think you'll get them away from me. The two of you can sit and stew in your own godlessness. The sight of you makes me sick to my stomach."

Candace left the office. Sarah closed her eyes, getting in tune with her body. All the years of separating herself from it, and right now she didn't think she'd ever been more focused and aware of each part of her. Every sensation, breath, the thump of her heart, the push and pull and tension of her muscles as she moved.

"Are you okay? Is it the baby?"

"I'm trying not to poop my pants," Sarah said matter-of-factly and let out an abrasive chuckle. She opened her eyes. Each word tasted like metal. Like blood. "I think I'm okay for now. How are you getting out of the house at night?"

"I go out the attic window. I use a fire ladder to climb down." Honor's voice shook, but her gaze flickered with fury as she stared hard into Sarah's eyes. "You shouldn't have told her about my phone or the internet. You've ruined it all."

Honor was mad. Good. Angry people could be pushed to make rash decisions.

"She shouldn't have tried to hold me hostage," Sarah said.

"She wants what's best for you."

"Do you think my baby is destined to take over Peter's church and rebuild it?"

Honor didn't answer at first. She went to the window and looked out through the blinds, then crossed her arms. She turned, shrugging.

"Only if it's a boy," she said. "Girls don't matter."

"My daughter matters. I matter. You matter," Sarah said fiercely. "Just like your daughter mattered too."

Honor sagged and wove unsteadily to the chair behind Peter's desk, where she sat with a thump. Sarah took the chance to sit in the leather chair near the bookcase. She really wanted to get into bed and pull the blankets over her head.

"How did you find out about her?" Honor asked.

"I saw the cemetery. And Candace told me. I'm so sorry."

Honor nudged several of the broken router pieces. "I thought if I had a boy . . . but I didn't."

"How did she die?" Sarah fortified herself to find out something horrible.

"She was too small. She died in her sleep."

"But you had her here. At home. With Candace?"

"Yes," Honor said.

"Do you think Adam was a prophet?"

"Yes," Honor answered at once, not a moment's hesitation. "But he gave it up when he left us."

"What will happen if this baby is not a boy? Will Candace let us go then?"

Honor shook her head. "I don't know. I don't think so."

Sarah cleared her throat, choosing her words carefully. "Do you think she'll hurt the baby if it's a girl? Do you think she might have hurt your baby?"

"No! Never!"

The question poised on the tip of Sarah's tongue. Was Adam Bethany's father? Was there any chance at all?

It doesn't matter. Don't ask. Knowing won't help you.

Never knowing might be worse.

He chose you, she reminded herself, and forced herself to remember the man who'd loved her, not the one who'd betrayed her.

"How do you get up to the attic?" Sarah asked.

Honor hesitated. "There's an access through the ceiling in Ellie's closet."

Sarah caressed her belly. There was no way she was fitting through a panel in the ceiling of a closet. A thought occurred to her. "You can get her keys, get the car. You can go into town and bring back help."

"I don't know how to drive."

"You could *run* there," Sarah lashed out. "Honor, please. You have to know how wrong this all is."

Honor ducked her head. Her fingers laced and unlaced, a church with a steeple, wriggling people dancing inside it. "I don't want to hate you, Sarah."

"I don't want to hate you either. And I don't. We can work together, okay? We have to."

At last, Honor met Sarah's gaze. "Candace has always been so good to me."

"Has she? Really?"

"She'll be good to your baby. Look how good she is to Ellie!"

Sarah snorted out her derision. "I came here to get away from people who thought they could take my children away from me, and

I'm not going to let Candace do the same thing. This is not the life I want for my children. Or for myself. And, Honor . . . It's not the life you want either."

"Maybe it is," Honor retorted defensively.

"If it is, why do you keep sneaking out at night to run around with local boys? Why would you have a stash of those worldly clothes in the back of your closet, and lipstick and eyeshadow and social media accounts where you post sexy pictures of yourself?"

"Because I'm . . . Because . . ." Honor's voice stuttered into silence. She made fists with both hands. She looked away from Sarah's face. "Because at least they want me. And *he* never did. He only married me because of the baby. And then she died, and he went away, and he left me here!"

Sarah closed her eyes for a few seconds. Adam hadn't only been married before her, he'd had a baby with someone else . . . She couldn't think about that now. Couldn't dwell on the past.

"You could stay with me until you get yourself settled. We could help each other out. What about going to college?"

Honor frowned. "For what?"

"Anything you want. How about business, or marketing? Look how successful you've already been with your MadeIt shop," Sarah said, although she had no idea if that was true or even if Honor had even graduated from high school.

"Henry always told me I was smart enough to go to college." Honor looked hopeful, then downcast again. "But it's so expensive."

Sarah bit her tongue for a moment, just a second, to keep herself from feeling angry that Honor had once been married to her husband. She was probably never going to get past it. Jealousy that he'd been married to someone else; fury that Honor had been so betrayed.

"You have whatever money's left from the life insurance policy," Sarah pointed out.

Honor stood and paced a few steps in one direction, then the other, before standing still, as though she couldn't decide which way to turn. "Oh, the money, the money. It's always about the money. You want that money? You think it should be yours?"

"It doesn't matter what I think about it. It was done. That money is yours, and you should have control of it. Not Candace. Not me. And I do think Adam would've been glad to know you were being taken care of with it."

"He should have made sure you were being taken care of too." Honor sniffled. "I can give you half of it. You should have half of what's left, anyway."

Sarah closed her eyes for a second. "Yeah. He should have. But I'll be okay. I've got *some* money, and I can work. I've lived on my own already. I can support myself and my kids. You can support yourself too."

The younger woman twisted to look at her. "You think so? I really could go to school, couldn't I? Do you really believe I could?"

"I really do."

"If we leave Candace, she'll be all alone."

Sarah did her best to keep her expression neutral, her voice calm. "You don't have to abandon her. You can still have her in your life, even when you live on your own. But I do need you to help me and Ellie get out of here, Honor. Can you understand that?"

"Once the baby's born—"

"No. It'll be even harder then. We have to go soon, before he's born."

A half smile tilted Honor's lips. "You said *he*."

Sarah rubbed her hands over the mound of her belly. "He or she."

It wasn't going to work, Sarah thought, watching Honor's brow wrinkle. Honor was too tangled up with Candace. Too scared. She wasn't going to be able to pull herself out of this, and she wasn't going to help Sarah do it either.

Honor straightened, squaring her shoulders. "All right. Tell me what we have to do."

36

"SEE WHAT A good night's sleep can do for a sour heart? See how nice this can all be? I'm so glad you had a change of heart, Sarah, I really am. We're going to all be just fine." Candace set the platter of burgers and hot dogs on the deck's glass-topped table and gestured toward Honor. "Run inside and get that plate of fixings. Oh, and the macaroni salad."

Sarah put her hands on the arms of the chair. She and Honor had spoken long into the night, plotting the best ways to get the three of them away from the house. Having Honor walk into town in the dark to bring back help was the fastest solution, but Sarah had an uneasy feeling about what Candace might do if she checked Honor's room and discovered her gone. Bed checks weren't out of the question now that she knew Honor had found a way to bypass the security system and barred windows. Sarah hadn't wanted to be alone here with Ellie in case Candace really went over the edge.

They'd decided Sarah would distract her while Honor searched for the car keys, and then they'd drive away together, leaving nobody behind. Sarah watched Honor head into the house through the French doors. She didn't fully trust her, but what other choice did she have? Honor had said she wanted to help, but when it came right down to it, Sarah didn't think Honor would be able to hurt Candace—and wasn't that what it would come to? They'd have to find a way to incapacitate her.

"How are you feeling today, honey? Is your stomach all right? No more doodle troubles?"

Sarah cringed inwardly at the euphemism. "Much better, Candace, thank you."

"It's the first sign, you know. Your body flushing everything out. Are you sure you're not in labor? If you are, you shouldn't be eating such a big meal."

"I'm not in labor," Sarah said tightly. "I'm only thirty-six weeks."

Candace clucked her tongue. "Babies are born at thirty-seven weeks all the time. Ellie, tell Nanna what you want. A burger or a dog?"

"She'll have a burger. No cheese."

Candace scoffed. "Of course she can have cheese on it. She needs it for those growing little bones, doesn't she?"

A ripple of discomfort passed through Sarah's abdomen. Her lower back twinged even worse, and she leaned forward to put her hands on the table as she tried to ease the rising pain. She sipped in a breath. Held it. Let it out. She hadn't had to rush to the bathroom since last night, but the cramping pains were definitely turning into full-blown contractions.

"What's going on?" Candace stood too close and bent to look suspiciously into Sarah's face.

"I'm just hungry. I'm dying for some of your amazing macaroni salad." Sarah forced herself upright and gave Candace a smile as bland as she could make it.

"Maybe you should go inside," Candace said. "We don't want you to get overheated."

"It feels so nice. It's gorgeous weather. And it's perfect here in the shade." Sarah forced that smile bigger, wider, brighter. Pushed the pain down and far away.

If they went back inside, there would be no getting out. Her baby was coming, and Candace would take it from her. What would happen to Sarah after that, when Candace didn't need her anymore? She didn't want to find out.

"I'm starving," she said now, and reached to stab her fork into the stack of burgers. She speared two and put them on her plate. She took another and put it on Ellie's plate.

Honor appeared with the platter piled with sliced tomato, onion, and pickle. She put it on the table and gave Sarah a harried look. "Is there anything else I can *serve* you?"

"You forgot the cheese," Sarah managed to say without so much as a dip or a waver in her voice.

Candace clucked her tongue again, shaking her head. "You'd forget your own head if it wasn't sewn on. You didn't bring out the macaroni salad either! I guess I'll have to go in and get it myself."

"No," Honor said quickly. "It was my mistake. I'll go get it. I . . . need to use the private room anyway."

With her back to Candace, blocking the older woman's view of her expression, Honor went wide-eyed and apologetic. She opened her hands slightly to show they were empty and patted the pockets on her dress. No keys.

"Hurry up, then, the food's getting cold. And this little one can't have any dessert until she eats her dinner, isn't that right?" Candace bent to snuggle her cheek against Ellie's.

"Here, Ellie." Sarah dropped a burger patty on a bun and added a dab of ketchup before putting it on Ellie's plate. "You don't have to wait for Honor. You can go ahead and eat."

Deftly, she cut the burger in half and added some more ketchup to the plate so Ellie could dip. She waited for Candace to complain about there being no cheese, but the older woman appeared too irritated with Honor to notice as she took her own seat at the table and began assembling her burger. Sarah risked a glance into the house. She couldn't see Honor moving around in the kitchen. Hopefully, that meant she'd run upstairs to search Candace's bedroom.

"What could be taking her so long? I'll go get it." Candace left the deck.

Less than a minute later, car tires crunched on the gravel of the driveway. A car horn booped as someone locked it. Sarah pushed backward from the table, ungainly and awkward and slow.

Graham came around the corner of the house.

"Sarah. Thank God." He moved close to her, too fast for her to get away.

His hands were on her before she could stop him, but his touch was gentle. His eyes searched hers. When he noticed the way she shrank away from him, he let go. Stepped back.

"Atlantic City," she croaked. "You thought I went back to Brigantine? You were looking for me this whole time?"

Graham frowned. "No. I was checking the company's cloud server yesterday, and I noticed that Adam's laptop had logged in to the service a couple of weeks ago. All of our company equipment has tracking on it. As soon as I saw you were in Shelter Grove, I booked a flight."

Before she could ask him how he'd figured out she was *here*, he looked past her. His expression went stony, but there was also an odd light in his eyes. Sarah turned to see what he was looking at. Candace had come out of the kitchen carrying a bowl of macaroni salad.

"Hello, Candace."

Candace gave him a curious look. "Hello?"

"You know Adam's mother?" Sarah asked.

"Of course I know her," Graham said. "She was my mother too."

37

CANDACE DROPPED THE plate. It shattered, and she swayed backward, arms pinwheeling. Her heel caught the edge of the loose throw rug and sent her tumbling back through the French doors and onto the kitchen floor. The crack of her skull hitting the floor was loud enough to send a shudder of sympathy through Sarah, but Candace barely cried out.

She struggled to sit, a hand to the back of her head, and brought her fingers around to show off the crimson tips. Her legs bicycled in the air without doing anything to get her back on her feet. Sarah pushed upward on the table with both hands, but her bulk pinned her in place. Graham went to Candace and slipped an arm beneath her shoulders. Candace writhed, pushing at him, but he didn't give up until he'd managed to help her stand.

"Let's get some ice on that bump," he said.

It was the right thing to say, in the right tone, with the right amount of concern. Candace let him take her into the kitchen. Sarah watched in stunned silence, half convinced she had imagined the entire event. But no, she could see Graham standing in the kitchen, guiding Candace toward the table. She watched him go to the freezer and pull out some ice to wrap in a kitchen towel he took from the drawer. He opened the cupboard and took out a mug and set the kettle on the stove. He took out the box of tea bags.

He knew where everything was. She noticed that immediately.

She was my mother too.

You know he was family to me.

Tension rippled slowly over her belly. The baby squirmed, pressing hands and feet against her insides. A weight shifted, dropping, centered between her legs. The baby's head, pressing her cervix. The contraction eased, gone almost before she understood it had been there at all.

"Nanna okay?" Ellie asked in a watery voice, tears brimming.

"She bumped her head. She'll be okay. Just a little boo-boo. Stay here and eat your burger. I'll be right back."

At last, Sarah was able to get out of her seat. She waddled into the kitchen just as the kettle whistled. Graham looked at her over his shoulder as he poured boiling water into a mug and dunked a tea bag in it. He set it in front of Candace, but she didn't take it. She got up from the table and tossed the towel and the ice into the sink with a rattle.

"You did this? You brought him here?" Candace wheeled around on Sarah.

Sarah drew in a breath and put both hands to the small of her back. She kept her expression neutral to hide the pains coursing through her. Deeper now. Lasting longer. "I didn't."

"But you know him. He knows you," Candace accused in a wavering voice.

"Graham was Adam's business partner. They've been friends since college."

Candace stabbed her finger in Sarah's direction. "He's the one who tried to take your children? Why would you ask him to come here? Why wouldn't you tell me you knew him?"

"I didn't know he was Adam's adopted brother, Candace," Sarah snapped. "He tracked my computer to find me."

Graham groaned. "We weren't *trying* to track you down. Once you left, I told Ava it was over and she had to drop it. I would never have guessed you'd end up here, but once I saw that you were, I had to come right away. Adam told me he never wanted you to know his mother was still alive. Not after what she'd done."

"Done! What I had done!" Candace flapped her hands at him, her voice squeaking. "All I ever did was love him and want the best for him! I was a good mother!"

"Oh, the best." Graham's voice was thick with sarcasm. "Not that I would know, seeing as how you rejected me."

Candace's fingers curled into claws. "Reject you! *Reject* you?"

"What else would you call it?" Graham challenged her.

Sarah groaned under her breath as another wave of pain began its slow spiral through her back and belly. Her inner thighs hurt too. The baby had gone still, but she could feel the lump of its rump. She cupped it. Rubbed.

"Returning a child you adopted is definitely a rejection," Sarah said.

Candace turned to him. "Since when did you start calling yourself Graham?"

Graham took a step in her direction. "I was eventually adopted by an older couple, Graham and Virginia. Graham died when I was sixteen. I changed my name when I turned eighteen. I didn't want to have any ties to anything you'd ever given me. When Adam left Shelter Grove, he managed to find me. I was going to UCLA, and he decided to go there too. Which is where he met Sarah."

"You don't understand, Sarah. You could never"—Candace's voice broke, hitching, gasping and raw—"understand what it was like! He was horrible!"

"I was a *child*!" Graham shouted and advanced on her. His voice broke too, a slow and staggered rasp of gears grinding into silence.

Candace turned to Sarah with a desperate, searching expression. "You can't understand what it was like."

"No." Sarah shook her head. "I don't suppose I can."

"Oh, go right ahead. Tell me how the view is from up there, Miss High and Mighty. You think it was so easy, don't you? Did Henry ever tell you how bad it was? Did he tell you how we had to put locks on all the cupboards and the refrigerator, because he"—Candace pointed at Graham—"would get up in the night to ravage anything he could get his hands on?"

"I was hungry," Graham said.

"I can tell by the look on your face you think I'm being cruel, keeping a child from food." Candace drew in a shuddering breath, and Sarah didn't bother to deny it. "He didn't just eat it, Sarah. He destroyed it all. He'd gorge himself until he made himself sick, and then he'd go back and eat more. He's put his fingers in everything. Take a bite here, take a bite there. And when he'd stuffed himself until he threw up, he'd dump out the containers. And why? Maybe you can tell her that!"

Graham closed his eyes and shook his head. "I don't know. I was *hungry*."

"Oh, they'd told us he had problems. Peter said it was our Christian duty to take in a child who hadn't known the love of Jesus, of a home, and I wanted to give Henry a brother so bad, so bad . . . Peter wanted more children, and he was going to have them, whether or not I was able to carry them. But even he had to admit we couldn't handle *that*." Again, she pointed at Graham, who recoiled as though she'd slapped him.

"Adopting a child isn't like picking out a puppy who gets too big!" Sarah said.

Candace's lips twisted. "People return dogs that piss and shit all over the floor."

Graham ground out a rough noise.

"A child," Sarah said in a low voice, "is not a dog, Candace. Piss and shit can be cleaned up. You don't betray a child because of something you can wipe away with a rag."

"And what about a dog that bites?" Candace's eyes gleamed as she moved closer to Graham. She slapped at the air in his direction. "A nasty, dirty, biting dog that hurts your own child, the one you carried in your own body?"

He flinched again, shoulders drooping. Body shrinking. A shred of pity unwound itself from the tight coil of tension tangled in Sarah's rib cage. Graham had played his part in ruining her life and forcing the path that had led her to this place . . . but he had also come to help her.

He'd been a *child*, subjected to betrayal, abandonment, denial, and cruelty. Sarah didn't have to excuse his adult behavior, but she could begin to understand it. To empathize.

"I never hurt him!" Graham shouted.

This time, Candace stepped close enough to slap him across the face. That he towered over her by half a foot and outweighed her by probably close to a hundred pounds seemed to make no difference. The blow sent him staggering back, hand to his face. A muted noise leaked from deep in the back of Graham's throat, a mangled moan that tightened Sarah's own throat.

"Stop it, Candace," she said.

Candace spun to face her. "What if you'd gone into your baby's room, your sweet and innocent baby's room, and found *that*—" She slapped again at Graham, hitting him this time on the shoulder. He made no attempt to get away. "That one there, on top of him. Doing . . . evil things. What would you do then, Sarah? Tell me that!"

Sarah's shoulders straightened. Her lower back ached, throbbing and deep. Her entire belly rippled, side to side, or at least that's how it felt. "What are you talking about?"

"Him. It." She punctuated each word with another slap. "This disgusting piece of trash molested my son!"

Graham shook his head, daring to look Sarah in the eyes. "I never did. She just said that because she wanted a reason to get rid of me—"

"Shut up! Shut up, you filth!" Candace rained a flurry of slaps every place on Graham she could reach. "I found you! I saw you!"

"We were just kids, fooling around! And Henry was the one who started it!" Graham's voice rose. He stood up straight. When Candace tried to strike him again, he caught her fist and curled his fingers around it, holding her back. "I didn't know any better. Jesus, Candace, we were nine years old! He said he had a favorite game he could teach me, but we couldn't tell anyone else about it."

"Liar! Where would he have learned a 'game' like that, unless from you?" Candace screeched.

EDOPHI, Sarah thought. The stuffed toy and splashes of red paint had been a prank, but the graffiti had been serious. What had the rest of the word been? What accusation had someone scrawled on the church sign? Had it been *pedophile*?

Graham tossed Candace's hand aside, and it was her turn to take a few unsteady steps backward. He turned to Sarah, his expression pleading. "The stuff about the food . . . yes. I was a fucked-up kid with behavioral issues. Believe me, I've been through decades of therapy to unravel everything that happened to me when I was a child, both before and after the Granatts adopted me. And I know I'm still a mess, I know I'm made some bad choices, but I never meant to hurt you, or Ellie."

"Did Peter do things to him? To you?"

Graham shook his head. "Never to me. Adam told me he saw his daddy playing a game with some other kids from the church. We never talked about it after that. Candace sent me away, and when he and I reconnected years later, we just pretended it had never happened. He blamed himself for his mother's actions. No matter what happened when we were kids, Adam truly was my brother. He really did ask if Ava and I would be Ellie's guardians if something happened to you. When I changed the insurance paperwork to make the trust the beneficiary, I was trying to honor his wishes."

"*You* changed it?" Sarah charged.

He looked ashamed, eyes bright, color high on his cheeks. "It was easy enough. We signed things for each other all the time."

"Did you know about him and Honor? About the baby?"

Graham nodded solemnly. "Yeah, but Sarah, that baby wasn't—"

When the pointed end of the knitting needle appeared at the base of Graham's throat, he let out a gurgle that cut off his words. He clutched at it. Sarah blinked, confused about what she was seeing. When the first crimson drop of blood slid down Graham's skin, she yelled out in shock, just as his body jerked. He clapped both hands to his neck and went to one knee, revealing Honor standing behind him.

She had a knitting needle in one hand.

And then Sarah's water broke.

38

"HONOR, WHAT DID you do? Oh, you stupid girl!" Candace wailed.

On the floor between them, Graham writhed and choked. Sarah pressed both hands to her belly, which had gone taut, hard as a rock while the contraction worked through her. All she could do was wait for it to pass. This baby was coming, and soon.

"Sarah made a mess," Honor said.

"No, *you* made a mess," Candace snapped as she whipped open a kitchen drawer and tossed a handful of dish towels onto the floor at Sarah's feet. "What were you thinking? Were you trying to kill him?"

"Yes, I guess—"

"Well, you did a piss-poor job of it!" Candace took another handful of dish towels and dropped to her knees next to Graham. She pressed a towel to his neck. It bloomed red.

Sarah placed most of her weight on her hands as she bent over the kitchen table to wait out the contraction, which was finally fading. "We need to call an ambulance."

"He'll be fine," Candace snapped. "I'll just keep the pressure on until the bleeding stops."

"Not just for him, for me! The baby's coming." Sarah's words trailed off into a strangled moan as another contraction rose.

"Honor. Get down here and hold this on like that." Candace got to her feet and yanked Honor forward by the sleeve, forcing her to her knees. Graham had gone unconscious, but as far as Sarah could tell, he wasn't bleeding out. Candace used one foot to push the other dish towels around, mopping up the puddle of amniotic fluid. "We're not calling an ambulance, Sarah. You're not going to the hospital. You're having this baby right here. I told you that already."

"No."

"Yes," Candace said, calm and cool and smooth. "If you have him in the hospital, nothing bad will happen to you. You'll be just fine."

"And . . . if I have him . . . here? Won't I be fine here too?" Terror shredded Sarah's throat, but she didn't have the capacity for fury. She gripped the back of a kitchen chair to keep her knees from folding. The urge to squat hit her hard, but she fought it. If she got down, she wasn't sure she'd be able to get back up.

"Honor, quit standing around with your mouth open like you're a goddamned fish. Go into the garage and get that bucket of zip ties."

Honor had goggled at Candace's curse. Sarah, on the other hand, laughed. "I knew it. I knew you weren't as godly as you pretended to be."

"Honor, so help me, you go get me those zip ties, or I'm going to stab you myself!"

Honor fled. Sarah groaned. Her fingers gripped the chair so hard they went numb.

"That baby's coming too fast for an ambulance anyway. Let's get you upstairs."

"I'm not . . . I can't climb the fucking stairs. You're out of your mind!"

Candace *tsk*ed as Honor came back in with a fistful of zip ties. "Don't be such a Wendy Whiner. Women in labor can most certainly climb stairs. You're having a baby, not getting all four limbs amputated."

Graham stirred. Candace nudged him with her toe. She grabbed the zip ties from Honor and quickly trussed up the man on the floor—wrists behind his back, ankles pinned together by linking the ties. She lifted the bloody towel to check his neck.

"Get me the duct tape from that drawer," she ordered, and Honor obeyed much faster this time.

Candace worked quickly to secure the towel around Graham's throat with the duct tape. Breathing hard, she got to her feet. When she pushed the flyaway hairs off her face, her fingers left streaks of blood. She gestured at Sarah.

"Come on. Upstairs to my room. We can run the bath for you. You can have a water birth."

Sarah's head moved back and forth. "No, no . . ."

"Fine. You want to have the baby right here? It's coming, no matter what you do, so you might as well take the chance to decide," Candace said.

"Is Graham going to live?" Sarah said through gritted teeth.

Candace looked down at Graham on the floor. "I think so. But honestly, what do you care? Isn't he the one who was trying to take your baby away?"

"It doesn't mean I want him . . . dead . . . fffffuck."

Sarah huffed out a breath, her body moving into a half squat without her conscious effort. Candace braced her, and although the woman's touch made her skin crawl, Sarah took the support. When the contraction had passed, she shook off Candace's help. Her fingers gripped the back of the chair hard enough to start going numb.

She had to get Candace out of here, so she could . . . what? What could she do? Sarah strained to keep herself focused.

Think.

What can you do?

Graham's keys had to be in his pocket, right? Honor could get them. And then . . . and then . . . Sarah tried to work out a plan in her head, but it was so hard to focus on anything but the deepening pain inside her again as her cervix eased open with every contraction. Honor could get the keys, and Sarah could drive them all away, once the baby was born, she could drive them away . . .

She let out another long, muttered curse that became a garbled growl. Candace laughed and patted her arm. "C'mon, honey, let's get you upstairs."

But there was no way Sarah was going to make it. The urge to push overtook her, immobilizing and unaltering. She reached blindly for the back of a kitchen chair and gripped it as she spread her feet apart and let the contraction ride her. Behind her, Candace tugged at the waistband of her leggings, pulling them down and urging instructions Sarah heard but could barely comprehend.

"You need to hold on, Sarah. Breathe through this. I've got you, but you need to hold on. Honor, get the clean towels and the instruments I put aside in that bin in the laundry room. Get the kettle going. Sarah, I need you to listen to me. I'm going to guide you through this."

Candace had turned from flighty and giggly to competence and firm guidance. Sarah was helpless to do anything other than bear this child, but Candace was there to catch it when it slid out of her in a slippery, heated rush. Sarah had been squatting, and when the baby left her body, she fell forward onto her hands and knees with a low, grateful cry. In the next moment, she heard her baby wailing. She rolled onto her back, boneless and limp.

"It's a boy," Candace said.

The world went gray.

"You're bleeding too much, Sarah. I need to stitch you up. Stay with me, okay? I need you to recite the alphabet. Come on now." Candace's voice didn't lose its steady cadence.

Something stung Sarah inside her, and she yelped but began reciting the letters she'd known since she was Ellie's age. She was aware of a warm weight on her chest, the smell of blood, the press of cold tiles against her bare skin. When she turned her head, she could see Graham on the floor not far from her. His eyes were closed. Blood had seeped into the towel wrapped around his throat.

Her baby was in her arms.

"Honor, you need to pack all this between her legs."

Sarah looked down beyond the infant on her chest and saw Candace and Honor kneeling between her feet. Honor had a folded towel she pushed on top of another one blooming with crimson.

Darkness

The baby wailed. Sarah tried to hold on to it, but it slipped from her arms. The buzz of voices hummed in her ears. Arms went around her. She was lifted or dragged . . . she didn't know what was happening.

Darkness

Ellie was crying

Darkness

"You have to make it look like we at least *tried* to help her, Honor. Oh, get out of the way."

And then there was only the dark.

CHAPTER

39

S ARAH CAME TO on the couch in the den. Layers of towels and some plastic garbage bags covered the cushions, crinkling beneath her when she tried to move. Pain stabbed her internally as she shifted, so she went still and moved only her head and eyes.

A bassinet was a few feet away, but if her baby was in it, she couldn't tell. She drew in a breath for strength and pushed herself up. A long, slow gush eased out of her, and faintness encroached.

"You're bleeding out," Honor said from the kitchen doorway.

Sarah's voice croaked out of her, dry as matzah. "Can I have some water?"

"You're probably going to die."

Sarah swallowed hard. She didn't feel like she was going to die, but how would she know what that felt like? "Please, a drink."

Honor turned on her heel and disappeared. Sarah rallied. She sat up. She could reach the bassinet with one hand. It was on wheels, and she pulled it toward her. The wicker creaked. She held her breath as it got close enough for her to look inside it.

Her baby slept, expertly wrapped in a flannel blanket. He shifted and pursed his small lips, sucking on nothing. Sarah's breasts ached—it would be a while before her milk came in . . . wouldn't it? How long had she been unconscious? She rested her head on the edge of the bassinet and allowed herself to weep in relief. Of the oceans of tears she'd cried over the past few months, these were welcome.

"Here." Honor handed her a glass of water. "You should be careful. You're—"

"Thank you." Sarah sipped the water, almost choking on it before she slowed herself. "Where's Ellie? I need to see her."

"Candace is upstairs with her."

"Where's Graham?"

"Still tied up in the kitchen. He woke up, but we gagged him. He's not going anywhere."

"Someone will come looking for him, Honor. You need to get his phone and call for help."

Honor looked into the bassinet. "He looks like you."

"Babies don't look like anyone when they're first born."

"Mine did. She looked like her father." Honor stroked a finger over the baby's soft cheek and looked at Sarah. "She was supposed to be a boy. If I'd had a boy, he'd still be alive today."

Sarah sipped more water and put the glass on the coffee table. If she moved slowly, unconsciousness remained on the edge of the playground, taunting her but not knocking her down. "I'm sorry about your baby. We have to get out of here, though, okay?"

"She's not going to let you leave. She's going to let you bleed to death and then call for help, like it was something that couldn't be avoided. An accident," Honor said.

"We aren't going to let her do that. You're going to find Graham's phone, or better yet, his keys. You're going to get Ellie for me. And we're going to take his car and get out of here. Okay? The four of us. You, me, Ellie, the baby."

"What are you going to name him?"

"I don't know. Honor, please . . ." Sarah swayed. "I need. You. To. Focus."

"What about Candace?"

"If she gets in the way or tries to stop you, I need you to hurt her enough that she can't," Sarah whispered.

Honor's eyebrows lifted. "You want me to kill her?"

"You don't have to kill her. If you can just knock her out or incapacitate her . . ."

In the bassinet, the baby snuffled. Honor looked into it. Her lip curled. When she turned her face toward Sarah, her expression was contemptuous.

"Why did you do this to yourself? Tie yourself to something so greedy. All it does is eat, cry, sleep, and make a mess." Honor shook her head. "Why would anyone ever want to become a mother? All you do is lose yourself."

"Not everyone loses herself," Sarah said. "I never did."

"Because of them, you lost everything else," Honor replied with an edge in her voice.

Sarah drew into herself, taking stock of the pains, her weakness, where she might still be able to find some strength. She had to get up, off the couch. Once she was on her feet, she'd have to stay standing. Once she was standing, she'd have to find a way to get to Ellie. Take the baby, get out of the house. Get to Graham's car.

The world blurred around the edges. Sarah's head drooped. Her eyes wouldn't stay open. Every part of her ached. Heat swelled between her thighs, sticky when she shifted.

"You're ruining the couch. Candace is going to kill you."

Sarah's mouth opened, and she couldn't quite close it again. Words slipped out, mushy and jumbled. "... we ... work together ..."

"It wasn't supposed to be like this! She was supposed to take your baby and have her precious little prince back, and she'd be done with me," Honor said. "She'd give me the money, and I could get away from here, from her, from this town. I was going to get away!"

"You can still . . ." Sarah's head bobbed, and she jerked it up. She could not allow herself to pass out. "Honor. You can still get away from here. I can help you."

Another hot, slow gush of blood surged out of her. Again the world around her faded into darkness. When the colors returned, Honor's face was so close that Sarah could count each freckle sprayed across her nose.

"You stole my life, Sarah!"

Pain in her upper arms, a pinching, twisting sharpness. Sarah was aware of her body being shaken, of how her head lolled, how she was sliding limply off the cushions. She'd hit the floor soon. There would be more pain. These thoughts were distant and soft edged.

"I was married to Henry. My baby was meant to be Candace and Peter's next precious little prince." Honor's voice grated in Sarah's ear. Only Honor's pinching grip kept her upright. "I was supposed to have a place of pride in the congregation, and be taken care of, and have comfort and joy. When he came back here, I thought it was so he could take me away with him. Peter found us talking. He wanted to keep Henry here, but Henry talked him into eating all those lemon bars, all that sweet sugar, and his sugars went up, and then

Henry gave him too much insulin, and he died, and Henry went back to you! He said if I wanted to leave too, I'd have to be alone, because he was with *you*. You. Stole. My. Life."

From someplace deep inside, Sarah pulled some strength. Her back straightened. Honor let go of her and stepped back.

"You were taken advantage of by people who were meant to protect you." The words sounded sticky and oozing, drops of honey from a spoon. "You deserved more than this. You still do."

"Why do you want to help me? Why?" Honor's steam-engine whistle pierced Sarah's ears.

"Because," Sarah gasped out around the pain in her belly, the pressure in her lungs strangling her. The ringing in her ears blocked out the sound of her own voice. "You. Deserve. More."

"I did it." Honor spoke in a flat voice, void of affect. "I was with Candace in California. I went with her to your house. You didn't notice, there were so many people there. You didn't know me, so it was easy. I took the extra key from under the pot on the porch. I stayed behind. I clogged the toilet and made sure there was a leak. It was supposed to make you need her. Candace, I mean. So she could have access to the baby. We didn't know about the baby until we got there. We were just supposed to see the woman he'd abandoned us for. You weren't supposed to come back here with us!"

"Honor."

Sarah could make out Candace's bleary form in the kitchen doorway. How long had she been there? Had she heard everything? Adam's mother moved toward her. She bent over the bassinet to look at the baby and then stood to face Honor.

"What do you mean, when Henry came back here?" Candace asked in a shaking voice.

"I never told you," Honor said. "Henry was gone again, for good, so why did it matter? He left me, and he left you, and he went to *her*. He broke the bloodline, and guess what, Candace? There is no such thing. I see that now. How stupid I was to believe him. How stupid you all were! That was all something Peter made up to get money out of people who really should have known better."

"Oh ye of little faith—" Candace began, but Honor cut her off.

"You wanted to be special, and you wanted people to think you made something special, but you didn't! You wanted this baby so you could be special again, so they'd start tithing again, so you could spend their money, but it didn't work! Nobody wants to be part of your church anymore, not without Peter to flatter them. All your friends were fucking your husband, Candace, because he made them feel special, but without Peter, none of those whores care!"

Honor's tone rose and became shrill, but that was a relief. It meant she wasn't an emotionless robot. She was *feeling* something, and Sarah could work with that.

Honor lifted the baby from the bassinet. Sarah lunged off the couch but lost her balance. The baby snuffled, then wailed. Honor rocked it, shushing. Her expression softened.

"Please don't hurt my baby," Sarah said.

Honor looked surprised. She settled the baby back into the bassinet. "I'm not going to hurt him."

The world wavered as Sarah struggled to sit up. She could smell the blood, thick and rich, like the smell of earth and metal. "Get Graham's keys. Then get Ellie. You're going to have to drive us to the hospital."

Candace had been silently sobbing this entire time. Now she raked at her face, scoring it with her fingernails. Her hair tumbled down, sticking to the blood on her cheeks. Her lips skinned back over her teeth as she turned to Sarah.

"Yes. You need the hospital. Those stitches I made weren't very good, I'm sorry to say. It's been a few years since I practiced on anyone. They're probably all pulled free because you insisted on getting up even when I told you to rest," she said. "What a terrible tragedy."

"Honor. Go get Ellie from upstairs. Then get the keys," Sarah repeated.

"Don't you do it," Candace cried. "Don't you betray me!"

Honor's fists shook in front of her. "You're the one who betrayed me! All your promises, all your lies! I hate you!"

"You're like a daughter to me," Candace began, but Honor's shriek cut her off.

"You made me your servant. That's all I've ever been, someone to use to get what you want! You kept me here so you didn't have to be *alone*!"

"I kept you here to protect you," Candace said. "You'd never make it out there in the world. It'll eat you up alive."

"If you wanted to protect me, you should have kept your husband out of my room at night. The only reason Henry agreed to marry me was so nobody would know what Peter did. He was willing to be a father to my baby. And then she died, and he left me! He.

Left. Me!" Honor's voice rose to a teakettle pitch, then dropped to a feverish whisper. "You said I could go once Sarah got here, and you lied about that too."

Candace let out a soft, wounded moan and covered her face with both hands.

Honor headed for the stairs. Candace launched herself after her, snagging the back of her dress and ripping it as Honor fell to her knees. Candace was hitting her wherever she could reach. Honor jammed an elbow into Candace's belly, bending her over, and started crawling up the stairs on her hands and knees. She kicked backward, sending Candace falling back.

Sarah couldn't tell one minute from the next, only that time was passing, and she was bleeding, and she had not yet gone unconscious again. Her skin was clammy, and nausea surged up her throat. She pushed on the coffee table to get herself standing upright.

Honor came back. She jingled keys in her hand. How long had she been gone?

Candace and Honor were fighting. Pulling hair, slapping, shrieking like predatory birds. Candace was screaming, laughing, words Sarah couldn't understand.

Sarah took a step toward the coat closet. She'd never used a shotgun, but she could figure it out. How many steps to get there? She lost count after the first but kept her feet moving. She zombie-lurched toward it. She put her hand on the door handle.

The closet wouldn't open.

Behind her, the caterwauling continued. Sarah picked up the brass umbrella vase. More blood gushed. She didn't have the strength to slam the vase down, but it was heavy enough that when she let the weight fall, it snapped off the handle, which went flying onto the tile floor.

She stared at it, not quite believing she'd done it.

She took out the shotgun.

She pointed it at the two fighting women.

"Get me those keys and get me my children, or you're going to see Jesus a lot sooner than you'd planned," she said.

40

ADAM'S MOTHER TURNED. Breathing hard, her fists clenched, she took a step toward Sarah. "You don't look good. You'd better let me help you."

"You don't want to help me." Sarah swayed.

Candace inched forward. Sarah brought the gun up again. It was too heavy for her. The barrel dipped toward the floor.

"You're not going to shoot me. Have you ever seen what a shotgun will do to a person? It blows them to pieces," Candace said. "You don't want to do that."

"Are you really going to let me die?"

Candace shrugged.

"Were you always going to make sure I died?"

Another shrug.

Sarah swung the gun up again. She pulled the trigger. The only thing that happened was a dry click. Candace doubled over in a fit of giggles.

"Not loaded," she chortled. "Doesn't even work. You can't even load it. It's just for show. You really think I'd leave a loaded gun around where a child could get to it? I know you think I'm a terrible mother, Sarah, but that just hurts."

Candace had moved within a foot of her when Sarah mustered the last of her strength. She twisted the gun in her grip to grab it by the barrel. Both hands. She swung it like a baseball bat and clocked Candace right under the chin.

Candace went down, first to her knees, then onto her face. Sarah sagged against the front door. Red and gray haze swam in her vision. She could hear Ellie crying, the baby crying, Honor shouting, but she couldn't really make out what was going on.

Honor's face swam into view. ". . . in the car . . ."

Sarah found a way, some way, to focus. She looked through the sidelight window. Graham's car was directly in front of the house. She could see Ellie through the back window. Honor put an arm around her. Lifted her.

"I . . . didn't . . . steal . . ." Sarah couldn't finish, the words thick like syrup in her mouth.

"I don't need your life anymore," Honor said. "I want to have my own."

The alarm bleated, over and over. Broken glass scattered the kitchen floor. Honor had busted the French doors. She helped Sarah through the broken frame. They made it around the corner of the house and into the driveway. Motion through the sidelights caught Sarah's bleary attention. Honor helped her into the front seat. Ellie and the baby screamed, and Sarah twisted enough to see Ellie buckled into her car seat. The baby was on the floor behind the driver's seat, wrapped in blankets.

Honor got into the driver's seat just as the front door flew open. Candace, blood soaking the entire front of her, stumbled onto the front porch. She screamed at them, but Honor shut the door and shoved the key into the ignition. She yanked the car into gear. Too much gas. No control. The car spun out, leaping like a rabbit, and Honor drove way too fast down the narrow driveway.

Dying, Sarah thought as she let her head fall back. No seat belt. Covered in blood. She was dying, but Honor was getting them far away from Candace and that house.

Honor took the corner too quickly. The car fishtailed. She revved it again. They were close to the state route now, nearing the edge of the woods. She hit the gas again. The car roared and shot out of the gravel road and onto the asphalt.

It kept going, right into the ditch on the other side of the road.

*   *   *

"Wake up, Sarah," Adam said.

Sarah stirred. The seat belt chime was dinging repeatedly. She roused herself with a forced effort, not sure where she was or what was happening, only that she had to wake up.

Adam wasn't there.

A scream tried to rip from her throat but was choked back as she threw her hands in front of her face. A second later, she realized the weeds were not rushing toward them—the car wasn't moving. She looked to the driver's side door, which was hanging open. Honor was gone.

The children were screaming. Sarah twisted in her seat to look behind her. Ellie strained toward her. Sarah couldn't move enough to get to her. She opened the passenger door and eased out of the car. Her thighs, bare under the hem of her long shirt, stuck together from the blood and stuck, too, to the thickness of the folded towels between them. She fought her way out of the car and to the back passenger door. She got it open. She put her arms around Ellie.

"Mama's here. It's okay. Ellie, I need you to stop crying, okay? So I can help you."

Ellie's sobs died off. The baby still wailed. Ellie writhed in the car seat.

"Baby cryin', Mama."

"I'll get him in a minute. Let me look at you." Sarah looked her over. No blood, just tears. She unbuckled the seat. "You have to crawl out, Ellie. Mama can't lift you right now. I'm going to the other side to the get the baby, okay? Can you get out?"

"Yes, Mama."

Holding on to the car, Sarah got herself around the back of it and to the other passenger door. She yanked that one open and grabbed the bundled infant. Pain flared inside her and between her legs when she lifted it, but she managed to get herself and the baby onto the road without falling. The baby's tears snuffled off into hitching sobs as she cradled him close.

She looked in one direction, then the other. The road stretched out for miles with nothing but fields and forests on either side. They were never going to be able to walk it. But she was still upright, she thought fiercely. She wasn't dead.

A voice began speaking from inside the car. Soothing, modulated, almost robotic. It said something like "Crash detected. Emergency first responders have been alerted to your location."

Faintly, the sound of a siren began bleating. It got louder. Sarah gathered Ellie close to her, moving them off the side of the road. The baby snuffled and squirmed. Over the crest of the hill, an ambulance appeared.

It stopped a few feet away from them. Two EMTs jumped out of the back. Then there were questions, and a soft bed and kind hands and nobody was crying but Sarah could no longer keep her eyes open and she let them close.

"Sarah, you have to stay awake," Adam said.

She reached for him, and he took her hand. He leaned close, and she smelled him, that familiar mix of coffee and soap and a hint of sweat, the particular odor of her husband. He kissed her, the press of his lips on hers soft and sweet and far too brief.

"Got a woman here, looks like she . . . shit, there's a baby and a kid. Looks like she just gave birth. Ma'am, did you just have a baby? How long ago?"

Stay with us, Sarah whispered, or maybe she only thought she did. Adam smiled and took a step away. Then another. One more.

She cried his name, but he was gone.

41

T HE UNVEILING SERVICE had been brief but lovely, and although there was a luncheon starting soon, Sarah had stayed behind after everyone else left. Ellie scampered between the graves, plucking dandelions. Seven-month-old Asher slept in his car seat. Sarah had already placed a pebble on the headstone, but she sifted her fingers through the grass now, looking for another. She wanted to sit here in the sunshine for a few more moments, in the quiet.

"My belly's hungry," Ellie said.

"We're going to have lunch soon." Ellie clapped her hands and jumped on Sarah in joy, earning a grunt of surprise from her mother that stirred Asher in his seat. Sarah hugged her little girl close to her. "Just give Mama another couple of minutes, okay?"

She hadn't invited the Morgans to the unveiling, nor the luncheon. Graham had come through with the salary agreement for her, though, which had allowed her to buy a condo not far from their old neighborhood and a sturdy SUV crossover. He'd also had the trust release the funds that should have gone to her first. Guilt or shame? Sarah didn't care about his reasons, only that he'd fulfilled the promises he'd made to the man he'd called his brother. She had friends and support from Temple Beth Or. Although she didn't have to work to pay the bills, she'd picked up a remote job tutoring students learning English. It wasn't the quirky bed-and-breakfast overlooking the sea that she'd always yearned for, but it helped people and paid well enough to make it worth her time. That would have to be enough until the kids were both in school.

She hadn't heard from Honor since waking up in the ditch. She'd had the police search the roadside, in case she'd wandered away from the accident and collapsed somewhere, but they'd never found her. Sarah didn't care if they ever did, but she did think of her now and then, usually when a noise woke her in the night and she opened her eyes expecting to see a form in a dark hoodie standing over her. She'd installed her own alarm system and kept her doors locked, and she didn't miss the irony of that.

Asher let out a complaint, rubbing his eyes. Sarah got up to lift the car seat and took Ellie's hand. They'd be back to the car in a few minutes, the restaurant a few more after that, and she hoped she could hold the baby off without having to nurse him until then.

The sight of an oversized envelope stuck under the windshield wiper stopped her short. Ellie tugged her hand, looking up in confusion. Sarah ordered her to stay put. She looked around, over her shoulder, around the car. Theirs was the only one parked here, and aside from a groundskeeper in the distance, they were the only people. She plucked the envelope free. It was bulky but flexible.

Inside was a stack of ten money orders for a thousand dollars each.

No note, but there was a copy of a news article that had been printed out from the *Shelter Grove Daily*. Two months after they'd fled Candace's house, it had burned with Candace inside it. She'd been trapped by the bars on the windows, the locked doors. There was no mention of arson. The fire had been determined to have started in the forest, sparked by sunlight through a prism hung on a wind chime near the private cemetery, and spread so quickly that emergency services had been unable to get there in time. Another small clipping was for Candace's obituary, several paragraphs long, that listed her survivors as Honor Granatt, Sarah Granatt, Ellison Granatt, and Asher Granatt.

Sarah looked around again. They were still alone. She put the money orders and printed clippings back into the envelope.

"Look." Ellie held out the small bouquet of flowers she'd picked.

"Very nice. Don't pick anymore, though."

"Why not?" Ellie stood on one foot, a skill she'd recently learned and which she took every opportunity to show off.

"Because flowers are better when they're alive."

Ellie held up the flowers, which were already wilting. "Like people."

Not all people, Sarah thought. Some, at least, did more good to others once they were in the ground.

"Come on," she said to both of her children, her dear ones, as she opened the car door and began to settle them inside. The envelope went carefully onto the front seat. "Let's go home."

ACKNOWLEDGMENTS

I HAVE TO GIVE my husband, Rob, a sincere shout of gratitude. Thanks for helping me work through all the details of my twisted, terrible tales. I cherish our daily walks and the "What would you do if . . . ?" conversations we share. I'm working hard toward that gap year in Chicago.

To the team at Crooked Lane: My editor, Melissa Rechter, helped me make this book the best it could be. If you like it, she helped. If you don't, that's all my fault. Thai Pérez, Madeline Rathle, Dulce Botello, and Mikaela Bender keep me in the loop about anything or everything I need to know. I appreciate the care you all take!

Thank you also to Nicole Lecht for the cover. If a book is a writer's baby, well . . . a mother will always love her baby's face, even if it's ugly, but it's so much nicer when there's a beautiful face to love!

Finally, to anyone who's reading this—thanks for spending some time with me. You could have picked up any book, and I appreciate your choosing one of mine.